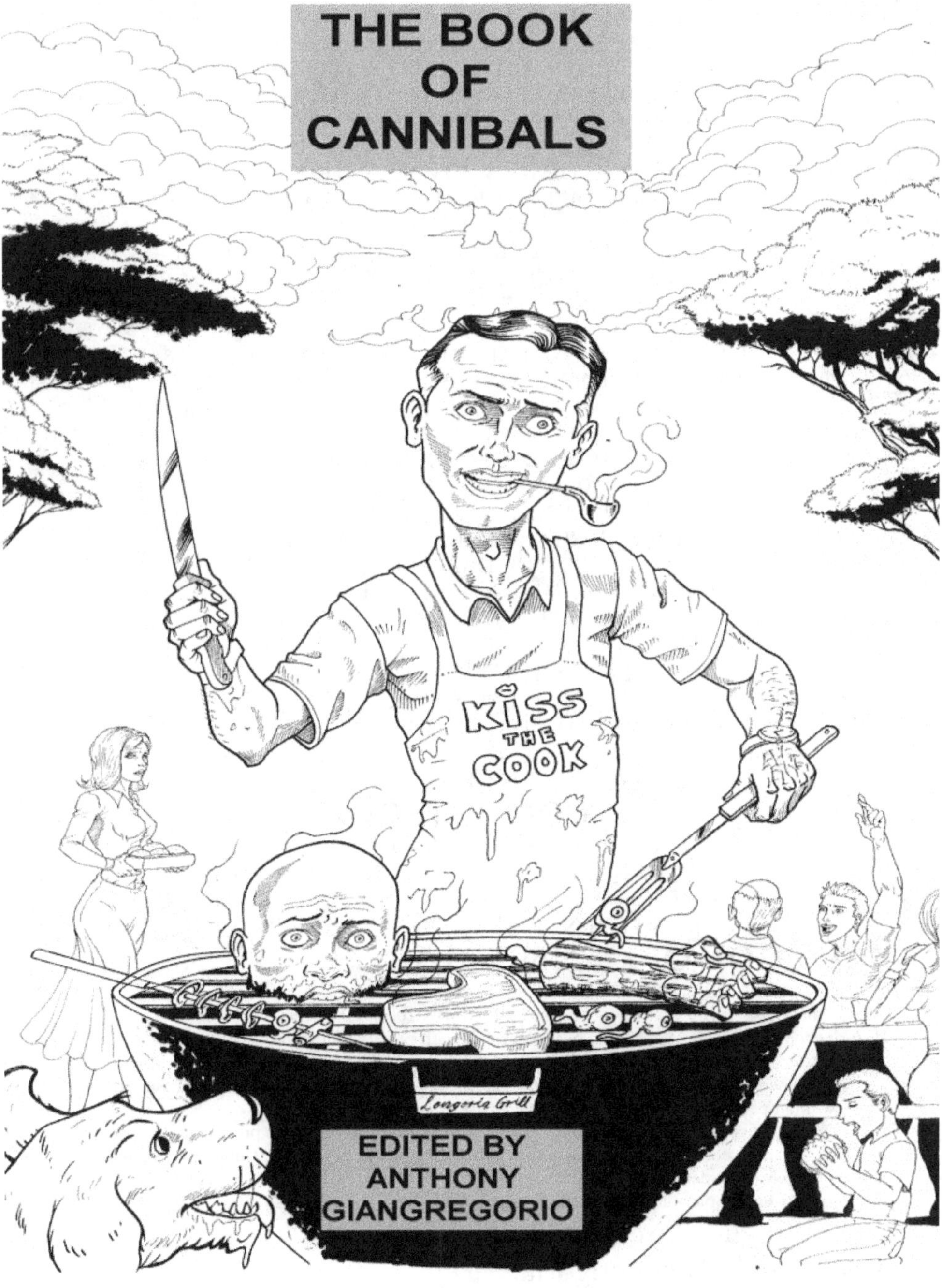

THE BOOK OF CANNIBALS

EDITED BY ANTHONY GIANGREGORIO

OTHER LIVING DEAD PRESS BOOKS

THE BOOK OF CANNIBALS

www.livingdeadpress.com

Cover Art by Ozzy Longoria.
Colored by Jordan Schwager

Table of Contents

THE CLUB BY KELLY M. HUDSON 1

YOU ARE WHAT YOU EAT BY ANTHONY GIANGREGORIO 16

EATING FEAR BY DAVID BERNSTEIN 30

STEW MEAT BY JOHN GROVER 42

CANNIBAL CAMPING TRIP BYANTHONY GIANGREGORIO52

CLEANING UP FOR DINNER BY MATT NORD 74

THE FIRST KILL BY MARK M. JOHNSON 81

COOKING WITH GRACE BY WILLIAM TODD ROSE 100

SAVING MONEY BY MICHAEL D. GRIFFITHS 111

BEST MEAT EVER BY ANTHONY GIANGREGORIO 124

SOCIAL STIGMA BY DANIEL FABIANI 139

OF PRIAPSIM AND BREASTS BY KELLY M. HUDSON 152

CANNIBAL CABAL BY KEITH LUETHKE 162

THE NEXT BIG THING BY ROB ROSEN 178

DRESSED IN BLACK BY NICK MEDINA 188

DAYS IN A BARREL BY SPENCER WENDLETON 200

ABOUT THE WRITERS 217

Longoria Grill

THE CLUB

KELLY M. HUDSON

Tom was the newest initiate in the Club, and with much pride and not one hint of arrogance, he was sure he was the finest candidate they'd ever seen. First, he had impeccable credentials.

He came from a poor family, a fatherless childhood raised on the bad side of town, and had worked his way up, putting himself through college, getting good grades, and winning a couple of student elections. He'd since become president of the biggest bank in the area, the youngest to ever ascend to such a highly regarded place. Some questioned that rise to power, given that his wife, the adorable but nagging Anna, was the daughter of the major shareholder. Some considered that nepotism, but Tom knew the hours he put in, the late nights and the hard work. Maybe he didn't deserve the job any more than anyone else, but he certainly didn't deserve it any less. So, he had money, he had power, and he had a wife that was even more powerful than he was. Add to that an inheritance that was his once Anna passed away, and his status was further improved. Her father had died shortly after Tom was named bank president and his fortune and title passed on to her. And she, in short order, made up a will making Tom her sole beneficiary. Not that he was having any untoward thoughts about her life expectancy, but it was still good to know that if anything bad happened, he would be set forever.

Second, he had a great track record in the community.

He did many philanthropic works around the city and his name was in the papers quite a bit. And for the good things, not the bad, from charity work with the poor to volunteering at a local children's hospital.

And finally, he had cultivated a taste for human flesh that rivaled those of the longest-standing members of the Club.

The Club was full of the most important dignitaries of the Tri-State area, from former and current senators, governors, mayors, to business leaders. The Club was exclusive; the most elite of any organization save for the Skull and Bones.

And this Club, it was devoted to fine dining, and that feasting was solely devoted to consuming human flesh.

How had he been brought to their attention? Why, through Anna, of course, although she was ignorant to what their true purpose was. When he became bank president, she threw a cocktail party to celebrate, and many members of the Club were in attendance, primary of which was the chairman, Chuck Shultz.

Chuck was a former governor and had his fingers in many business ventures, all of which conspired to make him filthy rich. And powerful, and eventually, the leader of the most clandestine and influential group of men in the entire country—The Club.

They met every other Thursday of every month. The meetings consisted of business talk, where each member shared with the others potential ways that all of them could profit from moves that the others were making or about to make. Yes, it was illegal, and yes, it was immoral, but then again, that was the point, wasn't it? The rich and powerful had every right to remain on top and guide and control those beneath them. The Club was one of many conduits to do so.

After the official business was through, the feasting would begin. Each time, a different member was responsible with providing the main course. The meal was made of human flesh, human meat, and whatever various organs the preparer brought to the meal. It was all served fresh and piping hot. They gorged themselves, slobbering up the meat, enjoying the nuances of the various dishes. Each member had their specialties; Mayor Robinson made marvelous beef goulash, Councilman Payne cooked an excellent soufflé, CEO Spivey grilled succulent thighs and shoulder meat, and so on and so forth. Each meal was different and delicious in its own way.

Tom remembered the first meal he ate as a prospective member: it was steak and potatoes. The meat had been provided by the newest initiate, Devon Wright, and it had come from his very fat mother-in-law. Tom didn't know this for sure, of course, because no member was ever allowed to fully divulge where their meat came from, except to give little hints. A common one was the 'trip'.

Asked about where the meat had come from for this meal, Devon Wright mentioned that his mother-in-law had taken a 'trip' to see relatives in Canada. When Bob Horn, another new initiate, served his spaghetti and meatballs, heavy on the meatballs, he mentioned how his oldest teenage step-son, a malcontent if ever there was one, had been 'sent to boarding school.' And so it went. The rich were never questioned, never put to the test. They were too powerful to be scrutinized, and the one time a reporter had gotten too close to the story, he'd been sent on a 'trip' of his own: a special assignment to Alaska, by his boss, the publisher of the paper and fellow member of the Club, who that same night as the reporter was 'sent' off to the top of the world, served a fabulous meat loaf.

In any event, Tom's first meal had been quite the moment in his life. When he was approached by Chuck to join, he thought it was just another one of those secretive groups, like the Masons, but when actual human meat was put before him on the table, steaming and bloody, grill marks making tiny X's across the top and bottom, he wasn't sure he could go through with it. Oh, he'd found it amusing at first, thinking this was just some joke, some type of hazing that the members gave to their prospects. They asked him how he liked his steak and he jokingly said rare and laughed. The others giggled with him, many saluting him on his good taste, but Tom's own mirth had turned sour when the actual piece of meat was placed before him and he knew, down to the core of his being, that it was truly a chunk from a formerly living human being.

Of course, Tom did what any other ambitious young man, always on the outside looking in, would do; he took his knife and fork, carved a bloody piece out, dipped it in ketchup, and gulped it down.

Surprisingly, it was the finest tasting meat he'd ever eaten.

He dug in then, finding the flavor of human flesh not only delicious, but intoxicating. He ate his steak and asked for seconds; this drew riotous laughter from Chuck and his compatriots. Tom had never felt prouder than when Chuck put his arm around his shoulders and declared, "This man, he's one of us!" And the others, beating their silverware-filled fists against the table, chanted, "One of us! One of us!" over and over again.

They discussed the business of the Club after the meal. New members were only accepted when old ones passed on or were too feeble to continue. That's how Tom was elected—Anna's father's passing was his ticket to the inside. The Club was exclusively male, and white, although the meeting on that first night Tom was there included talks of adding some color and femininity to the group.

He could hardly remember any of it. He was so full, his head was swimming. He'd never eaten so much in his life and, if he'd had a bigger belly, he was sure he would have eaten more.

The rest of that evening was a haze, with folks chatting, smoking and sucking down dessert—Blood Pudding; he didn't have any so he wasn't sure if it was really made of blood or not, he was too damned full. Chuck stayed at his side the entire time, asking him questions about Anna and her old man, the recently deceased father.

"He was always so secretive," Chuck confided. "That man, he was a member in good standing, never missed a meal, but always kind of kept himself to the side, if you know what I mean."

"To be honest," Tom said. "I never liked the bastard. He was cold and calculating and I knew he didn't approve of me marrying his daughter."

"That's right," Chuck said. "I remember. You graduated from that community college, didn't you? What was its name?"

"Carter Community College," Tom said. "It always burned the old man up that I didn't go to some posh university. No offense."

Chuck roared with laughter and slapped Tom's back. "None taken! By God, I like your style, son. I like your honesty and your appetite. I took the liberty of having my chef set some aside for you to take home. What is it the little people call it?"

"A doggy bag?" Tom said.

"That's it!" Chuck chuckled. "Exactly. The chef will give it to you on your way out tonight. Just make sure your dear wife doesn't get hold of it."

"I won't," Tom said. "No way she's touching that meat!"

The night wore down, and as Tom ventured to the door to take his limo back home, Chuck pulled him aside.

"Don't forget your doggy bag," he smiled. He guided Tom to the kitchen where he met, for the first time, the chef.

Every meeting was held in Chuck's mansion and he had a personal chef prepare the meals when he was in charge of the dinner. The chef was a large man, tall and gaunt, with spindly arms and legs, and pale skin with a mop of black hair on top of his head. He reminded Tom of a Daddy Long Legs spider. The chef shook Tom's hand and handed over the bag. He took it with relish and bid both of them a good night.

He was home half an hour later, his stomach settled finally from being so full, but his adrenaline still pumping nearly out of control.

He'd eaten human flesh! He'd actually consumed the meat from a person who, up until recently, was living and breathing! It was both thrilling and sickening, the breaking of such a large taboo, and it filled him alternately with disgust and delight. But the longer into the night he went, his distaste was gradually replaced by happiness. For the first time in his life, he'd been truly accepted as an equal, and this amongst men of supreme power.

Before going to bed, he stopped in the bathroom, relieved himself, and looked in the mirror. The eyes staring back at him were the same ones he'd had all his life, but they were different now. He'd become something different in the last few hours, even if his physical appearance didn't reflect that reality. He was still the same old Tom, with healthy skin and a full head of hair and a slight paunch growing around his waist like some kind of flabby tumor. He made a mental note to start a workout regimen soon. He flexed his arms, pleased there was still some muscle mass there. He'd worked out quite a bit when he was younger, but in recent years, because of his marriage and the demanding hours at the bank, he'd slowed down.

Feeling horny, he left the bathroom and slid into bed next to Anna. She was dead asleep, her eye mask pulled down tight. He lifted it and rubbed her breasts until she woke.

"What is it?"

"I'm horny as hell," he said.

She looked up at him, her deep blue eyes the perfect companion to her bleached blonde hair. Her lips, permanently tattooed a deep red, glistened as she wet them with her tongue.

"Now?" she said.

"Oh, God, yes!" he said. He slid his pants down and she groaned.

"You must have had quite the dinner," she said.

"It was wonderful."

He pulled the lace that bound the top of her nightgown until it opened and her large breasts spilled out. They shone in the moonlight, spilling in past the sides of the closed shades. They whispered promises of pleasure and he took them full in his hands, caressing them intently.

"Go ahead," she said, pulling the mask back down over her eyes.

He mounted her and rode her like a champion cowboy. Anna fell asleep halfway through, and when he finished, he rolled off her, gasping for air and smiling so hard he thought his face would split.

As he lay there, exhausted but still thrilled, he thought of the doggy bag he'd brought back from the party and where it sat, hidden behind his bottle of cheap beer that Anna stayed far away from in the refrigerator. His stomach rumbled. Tomorrow, he'd slice up what was in there and make himself a sandwich.

The sweet tang of human flesh tingled the tip of his tongue as he drifted off to sleep.

He ate the meat the next day, packing it away as a lunch, and when he was alone in his office, he locked the door, sat down, and savored every last drop. He couldn't believe he was not only eating human flesh, but enjoying it so much.

Tom couldn't wait for the next meeting.

In the meantime, he made do with what he had to, which was regular old, boring cow meat. He ventured out, trying different meats, from buffalo to ostrich, but none of it ever came close to comparing. Still, he tried, upping his carnivorous appetite to heights he'd never reached before. Tom had always enjoyed meat, but he ate it in moderation, keeping away from the red and sticking with the white. Now, though, with this new awakening, he threw caution to the wind. He ate and ate, and in the process, his stomach grew.

Over the course of the month, he kept promising himself he would hit the gym, but he never did. He was too caught up in the changes going on in his life.

First off, all the business tips he got at the meeting had paid off, and handsomely. He was richer than ever.

Between their meetings, Chuck scheduled a lunch for the two of them, booking a table at Ricco's, one of the most expensive places in town. When Tom arrived, the host quickly rushed him to a table in an exclusive room in the back of the restaurant. Chuck greeted Tom with a broad smile and a warm clap on the back.

They made small talk, ordered steaks, and then ate silently for a while, until Chuck finally spoke up.

"Not as good as our little meals, is it?" Chuck asked.

Tom shook his head. "Not even close."

"Isn't that amazing? Ricco's has the finest steaks in the country, and yet it pales in comparison to the meal we just had a week ago," Chuck said. "We're both lucky and spoiled men, Tom."

"You're right."

Chuck's eyes narrowed and he set his utensils down. He studied Tom for a moment and for the second time in his life—the first being his initial meeting of Anna's father—he felt like a bug on a slide in a microscope.

"The boys like you," Chuck said.

"I like them, too," Tom said. He felt his throat constrict. There was a 'but' in there somewhere, he was sure of it.

"But," Chuck said. And Tom thought, *Aha!* before settling back down. "You know there's a price to pay for admission."

Tom nodded.

"I told you before, but I want to make sure, absolutely sure, that you understand what that price is," Chuck said.

"Go on."

"You must prepare a meal. This meal must consist, as do all of our meals, of human flesh," Chuck said.

"I understand," Tom said.

"But it's not enough to provide a fine dinner," Chuck added. "You must also sacrifice. Just like all of us have, you must prove your loyalty to the Club before anything else. That's why it's re-quired that a member of your family serve as your first meal."

Tom nodded slowly. He didn't say anything because he had nothing to say. This lecture was the same he'd been given after enjoying his first wonderful meal with the men. He waited for Chuck to go on.

"You understand this, don't you?"

"Yes," Tom replied.

"Do you have a candidate in mind?" Chuck inquired.

Tom thought of Anna. He thought of all the money that would be his once she was gone. He smiled and nodded. It wasn't an evil thought; in fact, it was quite the opposite. He truly loved Anna, but her attentions, like the sex the other night, had been waning. He wanted to be with her, in her, but things were changing now. She was growing more distant, increasingly colder. Truth to tell, he couldn't think of a finer way to honor his love for her than to consume her, from head to toe, so she would forever be a part of him.

"Good," Chuck said. He seemed to relax as he exhaled slow and even. He lifted his glass of wine and took a sip. "If you want, you may use my chef to prepare your meal. Some of the others are good cooks, but I'm not, and you have the option, if you wish."

Tom laughed. "I have two left hands in the kitchen, so yes, thank you for the offer."

"You don't have to provide for a few more months yet. You still have to pass your probationary period," Chuck said. "Although I don't see any problem with that happening. So relax and enjoy your time, my boy. These are the salad days."

"More like the all you can eat buffet," Tom laughed.

Chuck chuckled with him, offering a wink and a sly tip of his wine glass.

At the next meeting, they were served with a fully dressed hu-man body, glazed and laid out just like a pig, down to the last detail, with an apple in its mouth. It was a man, or had been, as testified by the burnt and crisp penis, sitting atop the man's groin. Tom noticed that the first person to dig into that particular body part was none other than Chuck the Chairman, and it made him wonder. He shrugged, however, because he didn't really care.

He accepted a thick chunk of calf, brittle on the outside, warm and soft and bloody on the inside. He let the pink meat slide between his lips and rolled it around on his tongue, tasting every last drop of the red juice. The cook had soaked the body in lemons, he could tell, and peppered the outside with just a hint of garlic. It was delicious.

He had his helping and then another, this time of the body's right cheek. He found this portion a bit tougher. It almost had a beef jerky consistency and some of it got stuck between his teeth. He didn't mind, though. He could suck on it and enjoy the sensation longer.

Tom watched as Chuck spooned one of the eyeballs out and then paused, catching his gaze.

"Would you like the other one?" Chuck asked casually, as if he was offering him the last slice of pie. Tom must have given him a funny look because Chuck smiled and nodded his head like a parent dealing with a dumb child. "Yes, it's an acquired taste. But you may enjoy it."

Tom decided he had nothing to lose, so he took his spoon, dug out the left eye, and watched for a moment as it sat there, quivering, the orb seeing nothing at all but still looking so very alive.

"It's best if you slurp it," Chuck said. "Roll it on your tongue, bite it in half, and then swallow. If you let it linger, you may find that it has a bitter taste at its core."

Tom watched as Chuck ate and then did as he did. He sucked the blue eye from the spoon and let it ride over his tongue. He gagged for a moment as the thick, viscous fluid choked him, then he relaxed and enjoyed it, swallowing the excess fluids, which had no real taste of their own, and then, in one swift motion, bit the eyeball in half and quickly swallowed it.

Indeed, a bitter taste did flood his mouth, making it water, but it was only for a moment and then it was gone. The aftertaste was delightful. It was rather like eating an oyster.

Chuck laughed as he watched Tom and soon they were both giggling like schoolgirls.

Later that same night, a black man, a prominent businessman, was inducted into the Club on probationary status. Everyone stood and applauded.

"This is a big moment for us," Chuck said. "After all, we have to keep up with the times."

Tom thought that was odd, since the Civil Rights Act had been passed over three decades ago. But he shrugged it off. He didn't care how backwards or reticent they were; the Club was his new home, and he loved everything about it.

"Can I ask you a question?" Tom asked. Chuck, putting away a good-sized piece of steak, nodded and wiped his mouth.

"Where does all the food come from? What I mean is: not every meal is a serving from a family member. They can't be. We eat twice a month, so the meat must come from somewhere else."

Chuck took a long drink of wine, letting the liquid dribble from the corners of his mouth for just a fraction of a second before sucking it back up and smacking his lips together. He reminded Tom of a fish.

"Excellent question," Chuck said. He arched his eyebrows and a slight smirk filled the bottom half of his face. "Would you be surprised if I told you we had our own farming system? That the people elected for this honor were unaware of what they were ultimately volunteering for?"

"Not at all," Tom said. His stomach rumbled and he felt a healthy belch coming on. He seemed to have grown two pant sizes since the first meeting and he was showing it, the way his cheeks were bloated and his belly was becoming a round basketball sitting over his crotch. "In fact, it seems the most intelligent way of doing such a thing."

"Indeed," Chuck said. "What we do is, we have a contact in the social worker community, and for a minor fee, this man weeds through potential candidates, selecting only those that are truly healthy and devoid of any diseases or substance abuse problems. He then sends a dossier to me and I peruse it, selecting those I think best. We then pose as a new company and offer our selection a job, through our social worker contact, and then we have our private doctors check them out thoroughly. If they make it past this stage, we stamp them 'Grade A' and then send them out of the city to the countryside, where we fatten them up with easy living, wine, and lots of comic entertainment." Chuck sighed and rubbed his eyes. "You'd be surprised how laughter and mirth lends to a more tender meat. In any case, when the time is right, we harvest our subject and they end up on our serving table, with any leftovers frozen to use the next time."

Tom smiled. It was a wonderful machination. You could pluck from the poor and indigent populations for several life times and no one would be the wiser.

"Do you really stamp them with a 'Grade A' symbol?" Tom inquired.

Chuck laughed and waved him off. "Of course not!" His face turned purple from glee and Tom, caught up in the humor, doubled over and giggled. In this moment, he realized he was happier than he'd ever been in his entire life.

Later that night, he wasn't so happy anymore. Anna was having none of his advances, and although he was horny as a teenager that snuck into an adult film convention, she acted bored and even a bit put out.

"No!" she said flatly. She slapped his face when he tried to slide his hand inside of her nightgown.

"Please," he said. "I need it."

"Go to sleep," she said, turning over so her back was facing him. For the briefest of moments, he considered raping her. Thoughts of ripping off her nightgown and taking what he wanted filled his mind. He would treat her like the piece of meat she was; unworthy of anything but satiating his appetites.

Then he thought of the meal soon to come, and an idea grew in his mind, insidious and evil. He rolled back over, not interested in sex anymore.

He slept that night like a baby, the remembered taste of human flesh dancing on the tip of his tongue, the memory more than enough to appease him that night.

"Have you thought how you're going to do it yet?" Chuck asked him. They were having another one of their lunches, two months later, and the date of Tom's initiation drew nigh. In actuality, they were enjoying dessert, a fat piece of chocolate cake for the both of them.

"Yes," Tom said, licking his fork clean. He'd gained another ten pounds these last few weeks. He'd gone to the gym a few times, but it was for naught. He actually didn't mind the extra weight and thought it looked good on him. He'd always been a little skinny and now he was filled out full and proper.

"I was meaning to speak to you about that," Tom said.

"Go on."

"Well," Tom continued, "I have something special in mind, something I don't think that you or the Club has ever tried before."

"You do have me intrigued," Chuck mused. He dropped his fork and let it rattle on the empty cake plate and lifted his coffee to take a sip.

"I have an idea but I'll need your help in pulling it off, if that's okay with you," Tom said.

"Tell me what you need."

And so Tom shared with him the name of the paralyzing drug he wanted but couldn't obtain on his own, and the work his chef would have to do, and how exactly he wanted to pull this feat off.

When he finished, Chuck was silent for a moment, absorbing the information. Then, after a few more seconds, a slow and sly smile spread across his face and he nodded.

"Absolutely," he said.

The night was here.

Tom was a bundle of nerves. He'd set the whole deal up, telling Anna they were to attend a dinner party at Chuck's and to wear her finest dress. She was all excited, chattering with him anxiously, happy to be in his presence for the first time in months. In fact, she was so cordial and sweet that for a moment he regretted what he was about to do to this lovely woman. Then he remembered all the times she'd held out on him, and the other times, the worse ones, when she'd lorded her inheritance over him. Those were the times he most hated her, when she reminded him where he came from and how he was born to a nothing family. He let those thoughts linger in his mind whenever he felt his sentimentality growing.

They arrived at Chuck's mansion an hour later, and as fretful as he'd been on the ride over, Tom was now perfectly calm. He mingled amongst all the friendly faces of his colleagues, pleased to know that, in a few hours time, he would be an equal among them. No longer would he be the man from the poor family, who worked three jobs to get through college and who then rode the coattails of his wife to his current status in life. Now he would officially be one of them, one of the elite, and he could hardly wait for the coronation.

The time came, and his calm now firmly in place, he invited Anna to stand in the midst of the group of men, all white but for the one black member, with no other females in sight. A funny thought occurred to him then, flitting through his mind for just the briefest of moments: How come Anna hadn't noticed? She'd moved through the party, friendly with everyone. But why wouldn't she be? These were people she'd know her entire life. Still, the oddity of being the only woman should have made some kind of impact on her. Then he realized how vapid she was, how she'd soaked all the attention in, and how she'd enjoyed being the only female in attendance. She'd noticed, and loved every moment of it.

Chuck slid up behind Tom and placed a hand on his shoulder. Tom met his eyes and Chuck nodded, producing the syringe with the paralyzing agent.

Tom smiled and cleared his throat. "Anna, my dear," he said. "Come join me."

She glided over to him and turned her back to him, her neck long and inviting in her low-cut evening dress.

"I want to show you, gentlemen, the love of my life," Tom said. He nodded for Chuck to move closer and immediately felt Chuck's warmth next to him.

"She means more to me than anything in the world," Tom said. "Anything except for you, gentlemen. For you see, my dear wife is to be my sacrifice."

Anna giggled and Tom felt the bite of the needle in his own neck and panic hit him. What was going on? Was Chuck confused? He'd gotten the wrong person! Had he become so excited that he made the simple mistake of jabbing the wrong neck with the syringe?

Then the liquid in the needle hit his nervous system, he felt his legs go out from under him, and he tumbled to the plush carpet amidst a cacophony of applause and cheers. He couldn't move now; the only parts of his body that seemed to respond were his eyelids and his inner organs, keeping up their functions. The rest of him was unresponsive.

He lay still and watched, his mind sharp as ever, as Anna took several bows and Chuck moved to her side, putting an arm around her waist and nodding approvingly.

"Gentlemen, I give you our newest member and first female to join the Club, Mrs. Annabelle Gilchrist."

The room exploded with more applause and cheering. It was so thunderous Tom feared he would go deaf. But as he lay on the floor, pondering just what had happened to him, how he'd been duped and used and fattened for the kill, another thought occurred to him: He was going to be their meal. He was Anna's sacrifice. He was going to 'go visit his mother' or 'go on a fishing trip' or 'take a vacation to Europe.' And he was never returning.

He reflected on the months leading up to this, how they'd treated him as one of their own, the entire time mocking him behind his back. He was just like all those others, the ones he'd heard about on the farm, only he'd been groomed right under their noses, not in some far away place.

Anna turned, knelt down, and offered him a sad, sweet smile. She stroked his hair and pinched his cheek.

"You had a wonderful idea, darling," Anna said. "The plan you'd made for preparing me was too good to pass up. And I decided if it was good enough for you, it would be good enough for me."

Tom tried to scream, but nothing happened, his vocal cords frozen. He felt their hands lift him and carry him into the kitchen, where the chef was waiting. Tom tried to move, tried to raise a finger, tried to do anything other than lay there, helpless and weak, but there was nothing he could do.

He felt everything as the chef's cold hands stripped him of his clothes and then rubbed warm, melted butter into every nook and cranny of his body, across his fat belly and flabby arms and legs.

He lay there, weeping furiously inside, fearing what was to come, as the chef then shaved his body, cleaning Tom of any hair. And when that was finished, the chef, with a sigh and a grin, rubbed his body down once more in warm, melted butter.

Then Tom was wheeled out to the banquet table and placed in the midst of them, the hungry rich, the people he'd called his friends but now realized were liars.

The sharpening of the knives, their blades scraping together, stirred him from his sudden hatred and brought back the fear, worming from the pit of his stomach up to the back of his throat. Still, he couldn't move, he couldn't scream.

"Who would like the first portion?" Anna asked sweetly.

"I would," Chuck added.

Anna carved a large chunk from Tom's right thigh. He felt every slice, every awful, painful moment. He could see, when the cutting was done, the bloody plate handed over his body to Chuck, who accepted it gratefully and had himself a bite. Tom watched as Chuck chewed then swallowed a piece of him, a piece gone forever now, and stared as his blood dribbled down the corners of his mouth as Chuck groaned with pleasure. He sucked back the excess blood and smacked his lips together, resembling a fish once more.

"A wonderful idea you had, there, Tom," Chuck declared. "Steak Tar Tar!"

The Club cheered, agreeing heartily.

Dozens of knives lanced into his flesh as the greedy rich cut out portions for themselves. He tried again to scream, one last time, when he felt the cold blade of Anna's knife slide under the base of his penis and, with a quick flick of her wrist, slice off his manhood.

The last thing he saw was Anna grinning; slurping up his bloody penis between her teeth as if it was a thick noodle of spaghetti.

YOU ARE WHAT YOU EAT

ANTHONY GIANGREGORIO

"Wow, it's really coming down out there," Stella Ryan said as she peered past the yellow curtains of the living room and out into the storm. "I guess this is just another excuse for you to sit on your ass and do nothing, Walter."

New England was being pounded with a snow storm the likes of which it hadn't seen since 1978.

The roads were buried under three feet of snow and it would be days before cities would be able to dig themselves out, if not longer.

For the time being, people were trapped in their homes and at work, wherever they had been when the storm hit.

Walter sat in his living room chair, the material worn and stained from years of use, and he stared at his wife's wide back, his eyes drilling into her. He hated her with every fiber of his being but he never told her this. He never said one word to contradict her, for Walter was a beaten man.

Stella turned to look at him, her lips turned down into a deep frown. "You know, Walter, there are plenty of things you can do around the house while we're trapped in here. There's that broken chair, the loose step, and that fixture in the second floor bathroom needs to be tightened down."

"Yes, dear," he said as he drank half his beer to try and dull her voice as it penetrated into his very soul.

"Why I ever married you I'll never know," she said. "Mother told me not to, you know. She said you were worthless. But did I listen? No, of course not." She turned her heaving bulk and waddled over to his chair. She was a good three hundred pounds and the exertion of crossing the room had her huffing and puffing. She reached into a candy dish next to Walter and scooped up a handful of M&M's, then proceeded to shove them into her mouth. A few made it to safety, falling to the rug but the rest went to their chocolately doom, sliding down her gullet as she continued to complain. Walter could almost imagine their tiny screams.

"Mother told me to marry that nice Will Thompson from down the block, but did I listen? Oh no, I had to marry you."

"Yes dear," he said.

She continued, not paying him a bit of attention. "And now we're trapped in the house for days. I hope we have enough food. I told you to go shopping yesterday on your way home from work but you didn't listen, did you."

"But I had to work for fourteen straight hours," he protested meekly. "I had to cover another shift. And you had me up the night before thanks to..."

"Thanks to what?" she asked.

"Nothing," was his reply. He knew better to say the reason he was kept up was the fact she had had gas that would have put a longshoreman to shame. Though he knew what would happen, the previous night she had eaten three bowls of baked beans. That night, the music had begun and the aroma had been overwhelmingly atrocious. Even with the sheets jammed over his nose, as he buried his face in the bedclothes, the smell of her farts permeated his sinuses, making him think he was sleeping in the middle of a trash dump.

And thanks to her body fat, the farts had to work their way out of the crack of her ass, seeping, the sound like a bird was slowly dying in the folds of her flesh.

Walter had curled up into a tiny ball, squeezed his eyes shut, and had wept softly.

He was a small man, just a little over five feet, and she was almost six feet in her slippers. With her added girth, she was a behemoth, the Goliath to his David, and she had succeeded in making him a meek little coward.

After ten years of it, Walter's spirit was firmly broken, the man a former shell of what he'd once been before marrying her.

As she finished off the M&M's—what had been an entire two pound bag—the phone rang and Stella waddled over to it, her arm fat swaying back and forth in a fluid motion. Walter watched her go, thinking the folds of fat moved like a Lava lamp, almost hypnotic in its evolution.

Stella answered the phone and smiled. "Hi, mother, no, he's sitting on his ass as usual. Uh-huh, yes, we're totally trapped here.

The TV said it will be days before they can get the roads clear. No, Walter isn't helping, he never does. Yes, mother, I love you, too. Okay, I'll call you later, bye."

She hung up and shifted her bulk to glare at Walter.

"That was my mother; she wanted to make sure we were okay."

"And are we?" he asked softly.

"I guess so, for now. Now, be productive and make me something to eat? I'm starving," she said as she went into the kitchen, sitting down on the heavy duty chair Walter had bought just for her. In the past, he had found a normal wooden kitchen chair just couldn't handle her girth and so he had searched high and low for a heavy duty one. The one she rested on was made of solid oak, with reinforced wooden slats. The legs were three inches thick and thick dowels held the legs together. For added support, metal straps were weaved into the chair, so that a woman twice Stella's size could use it comfortably.

At least that was what the brochure said, but Walter had noticed in the past few months whenever Stella sat in it, the chair groaned softly, as if it was letting out a heavy sigh. Perhaps it was his imagination, but either way, he knew better than to mention it to Stella.

In the past, if angered, she wasn't afraid to hit him if she deemed it necessary. With so much weight behind her, even a light slap would send him across the room, and he would have to make up something at work to explain where the bruises came from.

He began tinkering in the kitchen, getting out a loaf of bread, a stick of butter, and a pound of cheese so he could make her half a dozen sandwiches for her *snack*.

While he worked, she continued her tirade.

"Mother said you would always be a loser, you know. She said I would never get the things I deserved if I married you."

"Yes, dear," he said as he placed the heavy skillet on the stove and dropped the stick of butter into the pan.

"She told me, 'Stella, he's a loser and will always be a loser'. But did I listen? Oh, no, I had to feel sorry for you. Pity, Walter, that's what it is, just pity." She glanced over her bulbous shoulder at him, her eyes squinting so her face looked like Playdoh with two marbles stuck in the center where her eyes should be. "You're nothing but a waste of space, Walter, a joke. In fact, Mother and I laugh about how pathetic you are all the time."

Walter's hand gripped the handle to the skillet harder as his internal rage began to build. As he stared at himself in the stainless steel backsplash behind the stove, he saw his jaw set and his eyes go hard.

Maybe it was the fact that he knew he was trapped with her inside the house—snowed in—for days, but something snapped inside him, and before he realized what he was doing, he let out a scream that shook the plates in the dish strainer and had Stella trying to turn around, wondering if Walter had burned himself.

He felt like he was at a movie, as he watched himself pick up the skillet and turn to face Stella.

It was like everything went to slow motion, and as she slowly turned to see him, her mouth opening slowly, a banana jammed in there from the bowl on the table as she couldn't wait that long to eat, Walter used the skillet like a bludgeon and brought it down onto the top of her head like a hammer to a nail.

The half-eaten banana in her mouth was catapulted outward like a rocket, the gooey white and yellow mush splashing the cabinet a few feet away to drip down in a snail trail. Meanwhile, the heavy skillet was doing what gravity had intended, nay demanded, and as the bottom of the hot pan struck Stella's head, her skull cracked like an eggshell and flattened her cranium like a giant stepping on an empty soda can. Hot butter from the skillet splashed the kitchen walls as brain matter soon joined it, the mishmash of fluids becoming a Rorschach painting worthy of any museum.

Stella made no sound as her head imploded and the frying pan stayed on top of her neck stump, the hot metal sizzling as the odor of burned bacon filled the kitchen and brains oozed out of the sides.

Walter stood immobile; his hand still on the handle, his breathing coming in gasps, and that was when Stella teetered on her chair.

As Walter watched, the body toppled to the floor, sliding out from under the skillet, which now had Walter holding it out at arm's length.

As the body landed heavily, resembling an enormous bag of pudding, he dropped the skillet and went to his knees.

He had no feelings inside, neither happiness nor horror, just total numbness.

With the clang of the skillet still reverberating in his ears, he stared at his very dead wife, while the wind howled outside in an accusing tone, the snow drifts growing higher.

Walter stared at his dead wife as blood pooled across the kitchen floor for hours, and may have continued to do so for hours more if not for the ringing of the telephone. Pulled from his fugue state, he crawled to the kitchen wall and pulled the phone off the hook.

"Hello, Stella, is that you? Hello?" a voice asked.

Walter didn't speak at first, only cradled the phone to his ear.

"Hello? Who is that? I can hear someone breathing. Walter? Is that you? Put my daughter on, now!"

Walter swallowed hard, then spoke, his voice weak and faltering. "Uhm, hi, Mona. Uhm, Stella can't come to the phone right now, she's uhm, sleeping."

"Sleeping? Really? It's five in the afternoon," Mona declared. Walter could hear her wheezing on the other end of the phone. Mona was bigger than her daughter and was confined to a bed. Walter had wondered if Stella would ever get like that but he guessed now that wouldn't be a problem. In fact, Stella had just lost some weight. She had no head and that had to be good for a couple of pounds. How much did a brain weigh? He began to giggle as he thought about it; the madness of what he'd done sinking in, but Mona brought him back to reality.

"Walter, you tell my daughter to call me when she gets up, you hear me?"

"Uh-huh," he said simply. He opened his mouth to say more but the phone was rudely disconnected from the other end.

Breathing a sigh of relief, he hung up the phone. Then he turned and stared at his dead wife, at a loss for what he should do next.

At six sharp, Mona called again, and Walter said she was in the shower and would be in there for a while. Mona, not deterred in the least, said she would call back at seven.

At seven sharp Mona called again. Walter stared at the ringing phone, wondering if he should ignore it, but in the end he decided to answer it.

"Hello?" he said dully, knowing who it was.

"Put my daughter on the phone, Walter."

"Uh, I would, Mona but she went back to bed again, this time for the night. I guess she's not feeling so hot."

"I don't care, damn you. Now you put my daughter on this instant."

"Uh, okay, Mona, I'll tell her. Look, I have some water boiling on the stove, as I'm making Stella some tea if she wakes up. I'll tell her you called, bye." He then hung up the phone, cutting off Mona's angry protests.

At five past eight Mona called again, and before Walter could speak, she began her tirade.

"No, you listen to me, Walter, if you don't put my daughter on right now, so help me..."

He hung up the phone, not knowing what else to do. As he stared at the phone, he began to smell something disgusting, and when he turned to look down at Stella's headless corpse, he saw his wife had released her bowels and bladder in death.

Knowing he had no choice but to clean it up, he went to get some towels, already dreading the loathsome task.

Mona called back three more times that night but he ignored the phone and slept restlessly on the living room couch. All the while the storm continued to blow and once or twice the lights flickered, but they never quite went out and the next morning he was thankful for small favors when he turned on the kitchen light to see there was still power.

Stella was where he had left her, only now she had a sheet over her placed there last night, the large piece of linen looking like it was covering a massive pile of dirt. He thought he was supposed to feel guilty over what he'd done, maybe after letting it sink in over-night, but the truth was that he felt fine, better than fine actually. It was like a giant weight had been lifted from his shoulders. He was finally free of the fat shrew, free to live his life how he saw fit.

The phone rang, and without thinking, he let reflex do what it was trained to do and he picked it up. No sooner did he place the receiver to his ear then he regretted his action.

"Walter, you better put my daughter on this phone right damn now?"

"And good morning to you, too, Mona," he said almost cheerily. "Sorry, but she's still in bed. Seems to have caught the flu."

He could hear Mona growling, the noise coming from deep in her throat.

"You listen to me, Walter. That snowstorm may have that city locked down but as soon as the streets are clear, I'm going to send the police over there. Do you hear me? I know something has happened to my baby and I'll see you pay for whatever you've done. So help me if you've hurt my precious angel!"

Walter pulled the phone from his ear and stared at it. Did she know? How could she? Did the mother somehow *sense* the daughter had suffered a tragic end? He'd heard it was possible, but would never have believed it was true.

"Mona, Stella's fine, she's just sleeping, now if you'll excuse me, I have things to do, goodbye." He hung up the phone but, as he did, and glared at the large corpse in the middle of the kitchen, he knew he needed to dispose of the body. For Mona was a lot of things, but a blowhard she wasn't. If she said she was going to call the police then Walter knew she would.

He went to the second floor bedroom window to peer outside and he frowned deeply at what he saw. The drifts were higher than the first floor windows of the neighboring homes, his included. The doors were buried, too, and it would take a lot of shoveling to free people from their trapped residences.

He went back downstairs and stared at the corpse, tapping his finger against his chin. So he couldn't drag her outside and hide her in the snow, there was just no way to get out there. Besides, even if he wanted to she was so big and there was no way he could move her. He thought about rolling her and decided he should give it a try.

Bending over, he tried to push her like she was a large log, but all that he got for his trouble was an expelling of gas, the farts of the corpse a hundred times worse than when she was alive.

Now, as he breathed heavily from exertion, he knew he wouldn't be moving the body anytime soon.

But he needed to get rid of it, and if he couldn't bury it, then what? How do you hide the meat and bones of a three hundred pound woman in plain sight?

How do you get rid of all that dead flesh?

The phone rang and he frowned, assuming it was Mona. Deciding it was time to tell his mother-in-law to go to hell, he picked it up and said, "What the fuck do you want, Mona?"

A man's voice was taken aback for a moment but quickly recovered. "Uhm, is this the Ryan residence? Stella and Walter to be exact?"

"Uh, yeah, it is, who's this?"

"I take it this is Mr. Ryan?"

"Yeah, I asked who you are, pal," Walter said angrily. He hated when people called and didn't identify themselves immediately.

"This is Officer Mac Calhoun of the Baltimore Police Department. We received a call from a Mona Williams stating that she feared there might be something wrong at your home."

Walter felt his heart skip a beat. "Oh, uhm, nothing's wrong here, Officer, you need to ignore my mother-in-law. We're having an argument and she can be quite vindictive.

"Oh, really. She said there might be something wrong with your wife...a Stella Ryan?"

"That's right, yes, but my wife is fine, she's in bed with the flu, and Mona won't take no for an answer when she asked to talk to her."

"I see, well, considering the fact that even if I wanted to I couldn't come by your house right now, I guess I'll have to take your word for it."

"Huh, I guess so," Walter said.

"But as soon as possible, when the more important calls are addressed, I or one of my associates on the force will be swinging by for a visit. It's protocol...I'm sure once we drop by and see that you and your wife have weathered the storm safely, we can leave. Won't take more than a minute." He paused. "You could save us a trip by putting your wife on the phone right now, though."

Walter held in the scream beginning in his throat. With an act of incredible will, he kept his voice calm and in fact added some indignity to the tone as he said, "Look, Officer Calhoun, I'm happy to cooperate, but not if it will jeopardize the welfare of my wife. Now I told you she's sleeping and I won't play the games my mother-in-law seeks to drag me into. If I do then she's already won."

"I see, Mr. Ryan. Well, I have to say I have a mother-in-law, too, but we get along fine, I know that isn't always the case, mind you. Fine, then, we'll check on you when the storm breaks."

"Oh, uhm, that will be fine, Officer, we'll be here when you get here. Hey, it's not like we could go anywhere if we wanted to, right?"

"Yes, right, very true, Mr. Ryan. Okay, well, you stay safe, and take care of that sick wife and we'll be *seeing you real soon.*

The phone went dead and Walter stared at it, his heart beating like a triphammer in his chest.

The way the officer said the last part—as if he was making a solemn promise. Hanging up the phone, Walter turned to Stella's corpse with a determined look on his face.

As panic seized him at the realization he would be caught and sent away for murder, or worse, the gas chamber, he knew he had to get rid of the body and he needed to do it before the roads were cleared of snow.

The only trick was how?

As he stared at the body, his eyes began to drift over the kitchen. First he stared at the sink, the dirty dishes still there from last night, then he looked to the stove, at the burner missing the skillet he'd used to kill Stella, and on the rear burner the tea kettle. Stella always kept water in it, even though she wasn't using it. She said if the burner ever got turned on, then the water would keep the tea kettle from burning on the bottom. Humoring her, he had always made sure to keep water in it.

His eyes continued across the stove to the counter, and the one pound package of hamburger resting on it. Last night the meat had been frozen and he had set it there to thaw out overnight before killing his wife. He had planned on making Stella half a dozen hamburgers for supper but now he figured he wouldn't need it.

That made him chuckle a little and he held it in, knowing if he began to laugh, to let out the panic inside him, he would end up on the kitchen floor a raving lunatic. No, he needed to stay calm and focused, to let loose control would only lead to madness.

The hamburger had him thinking about things he would never have so much as considered a day ago, but now, well, things had most definitely changed. At first he dismissed the horrible idea as ridiculous, but as he continued to wrack his mind for what to do, he found he could come up with nothing else.

He reviewed his dilemma once more.

His wife of over three hundred pounds was now dead on his kitchen floor and the police would be coming in a few days as soon the snow storm was over and the roads were clear. He needed to dispose of the body but in a way that no one would ever be able to find it.

Four days, maybe five, if he was lucky and then he would be caught, sent to jail or perhaps death row.

As he stared at the body, he made up his mind—desperate times called for desperate measures and all that.

Casually, he walked around the corpse and went to the kitchen drawer next to the sink. Opening it, he slowly pulled out a large carving knife. It was his favorite knife, one he used on Thanksgiving to carve the turkey. It had a nice weight and feel to it and he kept it perfectly honed.

With his jaw set tight and his eyes cold, he crossed the kitchen and leaned down over Stella. As he slowly began to cut away her dress, he couldn't help but grin and say, "This is gonna hurt you more than it will me, dear."

The first cut was the hardest, but after taking off a large slice of meat from her left thigh, Walter found it became easier with each consecutive piece. It was a lot like carving a deer, he soon found out.

When he had a pile of meat on a dish taken from the cupboard, he went to the stove and fired up a large saucepan after adding some oil. Olive oil, he figured, as vegetable oil was fattening and high in cholesterol.

As the oil began to heat, he took out a meat grinder from under the sink, attached it to the counter, and began to go to work. One piece at a time, he ground up the flesh carved from his wife into what looked like ground pork.

When it was all ground up to the proper consistency, he dropped it into the oil and began to stir.

As he cooked it, the aroma of cooked meat wafted up to him, and despite the heinous situation, he found his stomach grumbling. Deciding in for a penny, in for pound, he took some spices from the cabinet and began seasoning the meat. An onion and some crushed garlic added to the dish until it was a rich, dark brown.

He scraped it into a bowl and then went back for more meat, now casually carving the corpse up like it was a dead carcass.

He quickly learned to cut different sizes, some to look like pork cutlets, some to look like tenderloin. When he got down to the bone, he used a different knife to scrape away the muscle from the bone.

There was a lot of meat and Walter spent the entire day and most of the night just cooking his dead wife into different dishes, picking at each one as he worked. He made chicken fried steak out of the flesh from her arms and took the meat from her ass to make a hearty stew.

There was leftover tomato sauce in the refrigerator from a pasta meal two nights ago and he took that out, fried up some more of her ground flesh, and added it to the sauce, letting it simmer and boil until the aroma wafted through the house.

Taking a spoon, Walter dipped it into the sauce and scooped up a hearty spoonful. Careful not to burn himself, he slid it into his mouth, letting the tanginess of the meat roll on his tongue. He found his wife tasted a lot like pork, but if he cooked the meat just so, the flavor of veal wasn't out of the question.

Taking the fat from under her thighs, he seasoned it and rolled it into a tight ball, then used thread to keep it closed. He dropped this into the tomato gravy and let it cook until it was a golden tan. Why not, he thought. Italians ate pig skin, what was wrong with him eating *Stella skin*?

By the time he was finished, he was exhausted and there was nothing left of Stella but bones. Every organ had been cooked, most used in meat pies after Walter had taken a recipe off the internet. Kidneys, spleen, even her intestines, once cleaned and then stuffed with her ground meat, to make a luscious sausage–he had a ball. He'd always loved to cook and now was his most important meal ever.

By the time he was finished, he took a step back and admired his culinary skills.

On the counter and the kitchen table were piles of cooked meat, dish after dish of every meal imaginable. Sloppy Joe, pasta sauce, chili, what looked like fried beef tips slathered in Worchester sauce, ribs smothered in barbeque sauce—his personal favorite — as well as what looked like breaded pork chops and fillets.

If it could be made with beef, chicken or pork, Walter made it with *Stella meat*.

Once finished, he took the denuded skeleton up to the bathtub and began cleaning it in the tub, letting it soak in bleach.

As the bones were soaking, he went back downstairs. He was starving and he already knew what he was going to start with first.

The storm finally ceased five days later and it took another four days before the police could find the time to visit Walter.

As Walter sat in his living room, eating a bowl of *Stella chili*, three policemen searched his house from top to bottom for his missing wife.

When the officers were done, Officer Calhoun scratched his head as he stared at Walter, who after letting the three cops in, had gone back and sat down.

"All right, Mr. Ryan, where is she?" Officer Calhoun asked.

Walter shrugged as he shoveled another heaping spoonful of chili into his mouth. He had put on over thirty pounds since the day he killed Stella, his all meat diet doing a number on his system.

"I told you, Officer, she left. As soon as she could, she said she couldn't stand me any more and went to see her mother. If she didn't make it there, I don't know what to tell you."

One of the other officers walked into the room, his nose sniffing the air. "Damn, that smells good, what is it?"

Walter never stopped eating as he muttered, "Chili, it was my wife's recipe. She used to say she put a little of herself in every batch."

"Well, it smells damn good, sir," the cop said and then turned to Calhoun and shook his head. "Not here, Mac. And we checked everywhere." He had a picture of Stella in his hand, one taken from her driver's license. In the picture, the bloated face of a woman squinting at the camera and her large shoulders could be seen. He whispered so only Calhoun could hear him. "There's no way that woman's body is in this house, no way. All I found was enough food to feed an army in the freezer downstairs. Man, his wife liked to eat meat."

"Yeah, I saw her picture, too," Calhoun whispered so Walter couldn't hear him. Calhoun nodded and then scratched his head. He had been sure he was going to find something. He turned and walked through the house one more time and paused when he came to a small den/office in the back of the house. In a corner, covered with a sheet, was a human skeleton minus its head. He turned to see Walter standing behind him, still shoveling chili into his mouth like he would die if he stopped. "Man, you sure like that chili."

Walter nodded. "Yeah, you could say that. I got hooked on this meat I'm using a while back and since then I can't get enough."

"Oh, yeah? What kind?"

"Pork, I guess, why, do you expect me to feed you now, too?"

"No, sir, of course not." Calhoun pointed to the skeleton. "What this?"

Walter shrugged as he slurped a particularly fatty piece of meat into his mouth. "A leftover prop from Halloween, I got lazy and didn't bother putting it into the attic. Lost the head years ago." He sighed and burped at the same time. "Look, Officer, you had your look around, and like I said, she isn't here, now I think it's time you left. And tell my pain-in-the-ass of a mother-in-law to call me when Stella shows up. She must have gotten detoured by a fast food joint or something."

Officer Calhoun glanced at the headless skeleton for a moment and then sighed, knowing whatever he'd hope to find wasn't here. "Very well, Mr. Ryan, but if your wife comes home you need to contact us, as of now she's officially a missing person, one of more than a dozen reported so far since the storm hit."

"I will, now if you don't mind, I'd like to finish my lunch in peace," Walter said, slurping another spoonful.

Calhoun turned and walked to the front door where the other two cops were waiting. One at a time, they filed out of the house, and Walter, with a semi-polite smile, closed the front door on them. He did take a moment to go upstairs to the bedroom window and watch as the squad car pulled away, then he went back downstairs, went to the stove and the large kettle full of chili on the front burner, and ladled another heaping serving into his bowl.

Grabbing a beer from the refrigerator, he turned on the television and dropped down into his favorite chair.

As he shoved another spoonful of *Stella Chili* into his mouth, he grinned, red sauce coating his lips like lipstick. Man, he couldn't get enough of this meat, and he wondered what he was going to do when he finally ran out.

Until then, he had already decided he would have the *Stella Beef Tips* for supper, and after that, well, it was a big world out there. He was pretty sure when he finally ran out of *Stella Meat*; he would be able to rustle up some more.

He casually thought of his next door neighbor, Mary.

"Mmmm, *Mary Meat*," he said to himself. "Has a nice ring to it."

EATING FEAR

DAVID BERNSTEIN

Eighty-eight pound, pimply faced Ryerson Copper, once more reluctantly crept home after school. His ribs ached and his left arm throbbed. Emotionally, he was worse, but he hid it from his parents and Lora, his supercilious older sister.

He'd quit keeping track of the times he was tormented in school. Kenny Boring was simply a bully. He picked on many of the smaller kids, but focused on Ryerson most of the time. Living in fear dominated fourteen-year-old Ryerson's life.

Taking his mother's suggestion, he wrote out a list of things he feared the most. The randomly cataloged register was long: spiders—even the tiniest ones, his neighbor's dog—apply named Lethal, getting up in front of class—his face always turning beat red, foreign foods with strange spices—afraid he'd have an allergic reaction and die, and asking girls out, were all at its top. They were all scary and made Ryerson cringe with fright, but the most petrifying of all fears was Kenny Boring. Fearful of somebody finding his list, he decided to leave the bully's name off.

The next day at school, one without Kenny—who was out sick—he watched a documentary on tribal war rituals. Most of it was of no interest and actually grossed him out, but one particular tribe's custom on overcoming fear stuck in his mind. The tribe's members ate whatever they feared, absorbing the essence the living thing held in its body. Even after battle they would eat the flesh of their dead enemies in order to gain their power. If the idea hadn't been so disgusting, he'd have immediately appreciated its possibility.

That night for dinner, Ryerson's mother had cooked meatloaf, mashed potatoes and string beans, a meal he loathed except for the potatoes.

"Eat up, dear," his mother said. "Don't you want to be big and strong?"

"Big? He's a tiny squirt, Mom," his sister laughed.

"Lora, that's enough. Apologize to your brother."

"Well he is small for his age," Lora said.

"Please, Lora," their father said, letting his fork fall to the ceramic plate. "Say you're sorry."

"Sorry, little brother," she said, clearly not meaning a word of it.

"I hate meatloaf," Ryerson said, arms folded across his chest.

"It's good for you," his mother said. "All those little bones and tendons need nutrition to grow. You are what you put into that body of yours."

And that was it.

The tribe was correct in their thinking, only they took it to the extreme. Ryerson stared at his meatloaf and string beans. This was a small, but critical step in gaining the prowess he desired. He picked up his fork, jabbed his food with it, and began eating as if the meal were a jungle feast of flesh and intestines. Each bite became less and less nauseating. By the time he was finished, he imagined the essence he'd absorbed.

After dinner, Ryerson did a little web browsing and found an article of keen interest. It stated the number of people taking antidepressants was multiplying drastically each year as if doctors were giving them away like free candy. Fear and anxiety were rampaging their way across the human population, hitting all age groups. What was the cause?

Apparently, one reason, according to the article's author, was from eating meat. The article stated that slaughter houses for cows, chickens and other fleshy critters had a collected aura of fear in them. The animals could smell nothing but fear and death, sending their bodies into a nervous state, disrupting the peaceful essence within. They were, spiritually, being poisoned before dying, their bodies becoming sickened from the worst fear of all—death.

That night, Ryerson lay in his bed, thinking about the fear-eating tribe and the internet article. Was it really so crazy to believe in such things?

The next day Ryerson saw a small house spider crawling along the windowsill and captured it in a glass jar. Its legs scurried around the jar's base, hopelessly going nowhere. What was it feeling? Was it afraid, or just confused with its predicament?

Ryerson held the jar up to his open lips and tilted it, the spider tumbling down into his moist mouth.

Ryerson crushed it between his tongue and the roof of his mouth. His stomach retched, but he continued, holding back the urge to gag as he swallowed it. Dizziness began to descend. Was it the insect's fear he was feeling? Surely, it was too small to offer anything substantial. He sat on the sofa by the window, and a minute later, his head cleared, leaving him a feeling of victory.

For the next couple of days, Ryerson went around his house collecting spiders of all sizes and devouring them. By the third day, he no longer feared them. He put one in his hair and let it crawl around, thinking nothing of it.

After a few days of spider eating, he decided he needed a variety in his diet and began eating any insect he could get his hands on. Grasshoppers, ladybugs, caterpillars, beetles, earthworms, and a number of other insects whose names he didn't know.

Another week passed and Ryerson was merrily hunting for bugs along his property line when Lethal came running and growling as if the dog was going to attack.

"Lethal, get your butt over here!" Mr. Melman, Ryerson's next door neighbor, shouted. The dog growled louder, and exposed its large canines, appearing ready to kill. Ryerson peed himself, his jeans becoming wet, the warm liquid running down his legs.

"Good, boy," Ryerson said meekly.

"Lethal," its owner yelled. "Get over here, now!"

The dog, clearly wanting a piece of Ryerson, backed away, returning to its owner's side.

"Don't you know not to come near the property when Lethal's off his chain?" The man began laughing. "Did you piss yourself, kid?"

Ryerson looked down at the large wet spot on his jeans. Shame fell over him like a tidal wave, almost knocking him to his knees. The man turned and walked away.

That night, Ryerson lay in bed listening to Lethal bark at something, a small animal maybe. He hated that dog—feared that dog.

And then a smile crept over Ryerson's face.

The next night Ryerson snuck out of his house, taking his .22 rifle with him along with a backpack containing matches, lighter fluid, a couple of potatoes, a foldable camping shovel, survival knife, and utensils for eating.

Lethal was in his doghouse in the Melman's backyard. The night was mildly cool, a soft breeze present. The sky was clear, with enough moonlight for Ryerson's purposes. He approached the property line and sure enough, Lethal came charging out of his doghouse going as far as the cable he was tied to would let him.

He ducked behind a small shrub that bordered the property line. He waited while Lethal kept barking. As he figured no lights came on in the Melman house, they were apparently accustomed to Lethal's rants.

Ryerson crept closer with gun in hand. He stopped two feet from Lethal, whose enormous strength seemed to strain the cable, and he wondered how long it would hold under such strain.

Taking the potato out of his bag, he stuck it on the end of his gun like he'd read on the internet. Ryerson held the gun up, steadied it against his shoulder, pointed it at Lethal's menacing head, and fired.

The potato exploded, and pieces of it flew everywhere, the gunshot hardly making a sound, the makeshift silencer doing its job well. Lethal's left eye exploded along with a piece of his scalp. The canine fell to the ground violently, shuddering as if electrocuted. Ryerson walked up to it as the dog sputtered a few more times before falling still.

It was dead.

Ryerson quickly undid the clasp that held its collar to the cable. The dog was heavy, had to weigh at least ninety-five pounds, but he managed to drag it into the woods behind his house.

The woods were dark, frightening, but not as much as before. The insects that inhabited it were no longer a problem. He began to see the forest for what it was, a feeding ground. He'd have to get his hands on some snakes, especially the rattlers.

Gathering wood, he started a fire using the lighter fluid to get it going. He used his survival knife to gut the dog, clean the good parts, and then cook them over the fire. He'd learned from his grandfather how to gut and clean a fish, dogs weren't much different.

The dog meat was phenomenal once it was cooked. He savored each bite and wondered why such beasts weren't consumed locally.

Looking at his watch, he saw that three hours had passed since he'd set out. He had school tomorrow, but still he lingered.

After burying the bones and other uneaten remains, he sat looking into the sky, feeling the dog's power flowing through him. But it wasn't enough; he was still afraid of dogs, but not as much as before. During the next week, he ate four more dogs taken from the neighborhood. By then he wasn't afraid of them anymore.

Another item checked off his list.

Over the next month, Ryerson began eating anything he could get his hands on, even buying traps at Green's Hardware. He ate possum, snakes—rattlers were especially empowering, birds, a hamster—bought at a pet store, and mice. Insects, of course, were always a welcomed snack.

His mother began worrying about him. He ate less and less at the dinner table, but he was nonetheless, getting larger.

"I eat when you're not home," he told her. "I read that six small meals a day is the healthiest thing to do." That seemed to satisfy his mother's concern.

Ryerson's confidence was soaring at home. Even his sister had noticed a difference in his attitude. He no longer took abuse from anyone, including her.

"Way to go little brother," she said one day after dinner. "I don't know what's come over you, but you're doing well. You have an aura about you these days. Keep it up."

Home life was grand, but school still sucked. For some reason, he still felt small there. The bullies still picked on him, and the girls continued acting as if he didn't exist.

One day, on the way to his locker, Kenny Boring charged into him, sending him to the floor, the books Ryerson was carrying went flying. The entire hall was filled with students, all of them gathering around for a look, many laughing at his misfortune.

"You clumsy ass. Watch where you're going," Kenny said snidely.

"Sorry," Ryerson said, softly. When he began getting up, Kenny knocked his hand out from under him.

"Oops. Looks like you fell again." Kenny taunted while laughing to his friends.

"My fault, sorry. I'll wait till you leave," Ryerson said meekly.

"What was that, dickhead?" Kenny leaned in, putting his hand to his ear. "You'll wait till I leave?" Kenny nailed him in the ribs, knocking the air out of his lungs. "Weakness is like a disease, Ryerson. It needs to be stamped out." Kenny picked up one of Ryerson's textbooks, opened it and dropped a huge yellow globular of mucus on page 245. He closed the book and tossed it to the floor. "Happy reading, dipshit."

As Kenny left, the hallway cleared out. Ryerson sat there for a long time, even after the kids had gone. It was the end of the day, time to go home. He gathered up his books—including the one with the wet snot in it—and went to his locker, placed them inside and went home.

That night in bed, Ryerson realized his next step to overcome his fear. It wouldn't be an easy one, but it needed to be accomplished. He wasn't going to spend his life at the bottom, not anymore.

The following day, after the last class let out, Ryerson followed Kenny home, staying out of view, ducking behind parked cars or trees when necessary.

Kenny lived on the poor side of town, his house, a sorry structure, looked dilapidated and was horribly unkempt. His bedroom was in the back of the house on the first floor, and from what he could see of it through the bedroom window, just as untidy as the outside.

Ryerson had told his parents he'd be studying at the library for the next couple of weeks after dinner until closing, but he would really be outside of Kenny's bedroom—the blinds were always open—watching and learning. After two weeks of studying his prey, it was time to strike.

On Monday, Ryerson followed Kenny into the school bathroom. Previously, fear had often prevented him from entering such a domain with a person like Kenny, but after eating all the vermin he feared had instilled the courage he needed.

"Kenny, may I have a word, please?"

"I don't believe it, Ryerson," Kenny said, as he seized the opportunity, putting an arm around Ryerson's neck, then tightening his grip to cut off the blood supply.

"I'm here to offer you a deal," Ryerson said.

Kenny snickered. "I think I'm fine with the way things are."

"Money," Ryerson said, his vision blurring.

Kenny, loosening his grip, keenly inquired, "What's this now?"

"Let me go and I'll tell you."

"No, tell me and I might let you go."

Ryerson hesitantly whimpered. "Okay. I want to pay you to leave me alone."

"A payoff?" Kenny laughed.

"Yes."

Kenny let go, patted Ryerson on the head, and fixed his collar. "That's my language, buddy."

"I'll pay you weekly to leave me alone."

"Okay, but I want a large sum up front."

"How much?"

"A hundred big ones, then twenty a week."

Acting upset, Ryerson said, "Wow, that's a lot." He didn't care how much, of course, but he had to make it seem like he was shocked.

"Miss a payment and I kick your ass twice as much as before."

"Deal," Ryerson said, holding out his hand.

Kenny took it, held it and asked, "You have the hundred now?"

"No," Ryerson said, meekly.

Kenny pulled Ryerson to him, punching him in the gut, and causing Ryerson to fall to the cold tiles.

"Next time you want to make a deal with me, come prepared," Kenny said. "Until you pay me, you're still fair game." Kenny went to the urinal, unzipped his fly, looked at Ryerson lying on the floor, and relieved his bladder. When finished, he paused to admire himself in the mirror, then left the bathroom.

Ryerson got up slowly, his stomach sore and queasy. The angst he endeared only adding to the determination to make his life better.

The following night, Ryerson grabbed his backpack after making sure it was stocked with the usual supplies. He left his house a little after seven p.m., and rode his bike to Kenny's house.

As usual, Kenny was in his room watching television, his window shades open. There was a pleasant breeze blowing and the sky was serene and clear. Ryerson even saw a shooting star on his way over.

He watched Kenny for over an hour, while Ryerson ate Pepper or Piper, unable to recall the dog's name. It was delicious, and added to his courage and resolve to go through with his plan.

When it was time, Ryerson approached Kenny's window. He stood there staring into Kenny's bedroom for five minutes, Kenny completely unaware of his presence. Finally he knocked on the glass.

"What the hell?" he heard Kenny say.

Ryerson waved and Kenny came over to the window and opened it.

"Ryerson?" he asked, looking bewildered. "What the hell are you doing here?"

"I've come to pay you."

"You creepy little shit." Kenny rubbed a hand through his hair. "Okay then, pay up." Kenny held out his hand.

"Come out here," Ryerson said, taking a step back. "I don't want to take a chance of someone coming in your room and seeing me."

"Stop screwing around or I'll beat your ass."

"I'm serious. I got the cash, one hundred dollars."

"Good point, Ryerson. I don't need anyone thinking I'm sneaking boys in my room." Kenny said with a grin, then turned around and began climbing out of his window.

Kenny's right leg came out first, then he put his knee on the sill before doing the same with his left leg. His ass and lower legs were now outside. Next, Kenny lowered himself so that his stomach rested on the sill, his legs dangling while his feet found footing against the house.

Ryerson watched, his pulse rate already racing. He took deep, calming breaths and pulled out his hunting knife—he wanted to use the .22 but couldn't get it out of the house with his parents still awake.

Kenny dropped to the ground, his back to Ryerson. "Before you pay me I think I'm going to kick your ass one more time for making me jump out of my window." Kenny turned around with an even wider grin on his face, that is until he saw the hunting knife.

Ryerson slashed at Kenny's neck, hitting his trachea and cutting through the boy's voice box. Kenny's eyes wet wide in shock as he put his hands to his throat.

"You're mine, Kenny," Ryerson said, an evil sneer on his lips. He could tell Kenny was trying to scream, but with his throat sliced, he only managed to spit blood. Kenny reached forward to grab at Ryerson, his expression one of panic and fear. Ryerson plunged the knife into Kenny's chest, sinking it deep into the left lung. Blood spewed from the wound, splattering Ryerson's face. He smiled and lapped it up. Kenny's life was slipping away fast and he stumbled forward.

Ryerson pulled the knife free and struck again, this time hitting Kenny in the appendix area before slicing across his lower region. Kenny's guts came flowing out like water from a burst dam. Those parts were mostly inedible anyway so Ryerson didn't mind. Ryerson watched as Kenny fell over—dead. He dragged the body off into the woods before returning to Kenny's house. There was a mess to clean up at the window.

Ryerson wore rubber dish gloves and began picking up Kenny's pieces. There was too much blood, something he could do little about. The police would eventually investigate the scene, but they'd find nothing belonging to Ryerson to link him to the boy's disappearance.

That night, Ryerson had his first human meal. The essence from the human body was extraordinary to say the least. He didn't know if he could ever go back to eating animals in the forest or bugs again. His desire for human flesh was overwhelming.

After the splendid and fulfilling dinner, Ryerson buried Kenny's bones, hair, intestines and whatever else he couldn't finish. He went home that night a new boy.

The next day Ryerson was told by his mother that a classmate was found, at least parts of him, mutilated near his house. He acted shocked for his mother's benefit, and then snickered to himself, before reminiscing about the delectable meal.

The next day, Ryerson walked the halls of Waterville High with his head held high. For some unknown reason, bullies began dropping off the face of the earth—a few teachers, too. Ryerson had built himself a solid foundation from within. His aura emitted strength and confidence. His fear was exorcised like a demon at a church function. His school life had blossomed

The bullies, what remained of them, now left him alone. The girls asked him out and followed him wherever he went. He was given preferential treatment in class and his grades soared—eating a few nerds helped with that. No one was safe from his clutches, food was everywhere.

Ryerson had grown tired of his sister's attempts at bullying and teasing him. He'd grown to hate her and decided to make a meal out of her before setting off to college. Absorbing her energy would only add to his power, making him a stronger individual.

After he had eaten and disposed of her body, his parents became grief-stricken; once sturdy individuals, they were now reduced to depressed fodder. Phone conversations and letters had become pathetic drivel about how much they missed their daughter, each constantly praying she would turn up.

When he couldn't take it anymore, he ate them during his Christmas break from college, leaving their hearts intact, not wanting to absorb their weakness.

The knowledge and power he'd acquired over the years proved its worth as he became one of the world's most influential speakers—eating his way to the top. Soon he would sink his teeth into politics, eventually head for the presidency.

Shortly before his thirty-fifth birthday, Ryerson decided he would take a trip and visit the tribe he'd seen on television as a child. Through his numerous resources, he managed to set up the trip. He could have taken a crew with him, but this was a personal journey he needed to make on his own. Maybe he would eat the tribe's chief, a meal like no other, the chief's body giving Ryerson all the power he'd need to become a big-wig politician, and finally the President of the United States.

Ryerson was given a map with the location of the village. He acquired it by contacting the company that did the original documentary. He was warned not to go alone, that they were savages and dangerous—he disagreed.

He found his way there after a two day trek through the jungle. He'd hired a local guide, one who spoke the tribe's language. He had decided to eat the guide on the way out.

Upon entering the village, he was held at spear tip. The tribal chief came to him, leading him through the village and he was fed delicious foods, meats and vegetables. His guide explained how vegetables were essential to a balanced spirit and that Ryerson's was severely unbalanced.

"They sense your power. It's in your eyes, your posture, even your presentation," the guide said. "Every living thing has power. You have more than anyone the tribe has ever seen. It exudes from you like a fiery sun. The tribe leader would like you to eat meat as well as fresh vegetables."

Ryerson thought himself a genius for making the trip. The tribe would teach him all they knew, making him even stronger.

One night, at a tribal ceremony, Ryerson was given a special meal with rare herbs.

"Drink this, it will give you great balance," the guide told him.

After drinking the liquid Ryerson felt dizzy and passed out.

He awoke hanging naked from a wooden pole, his wrists and ankles tied.

"What's going on here?" he asked, but the guide was nowhere to be found. Ryerson began demanding to be set free. He was told he was the most powerful human they had ever come into contact with, so why were they doing this to him? After ranting for a while, he saw the guide emerge from one of the huts, dressed in full tribal garb; he spoke a few words of the tribe's language to two men of the tribe.

The two men grabbed the pole Ryerson was hanging from and carried him, placing him between two Y-shaped sticks protruding from the ground. Stacks of wood piled neatly under him.

"I don't understand! I'm all powerful! Why are they doing this?" Ryerson yelled.

The guide walked up to him. "We are at war with another tribe. As the tribe's leader, it is my duty to do everything in my ability to see that we win."

"You're the tribe leader? But I thought you were my guide."

"Yes, I am both, for who else would see to the tribe's prey?"

"Prey?" Ryerson asked, perspiration forming across his face.

"Yes. We were going to eat you tonight before battle, taking the fear out of my people and empowering us to victory."

"Were?"

"Yes, were. A man with your power should have presented a dangerous and difficult capture. But you simply walked in and laid down for us."

"So why am I tied up?"

"A meeting has been arranged to try to work out the differences between the tribes. Food and drink will be served."

"You said you *were* going to eat me, as in, *was,* past tense. So am I free to go?"

"No, you misunderstand. We aren't eating you, they are. You will be a false peace offering, poisoning the other tribe with your lazy and overconfident ways, ensuring our victory to come."

Later that night as Ryerson began cooking over an open flame, he began to scream.

STEW MEAT

JOHN GROVER

Madeline stood over the pot, stirring, the rising steam causing her nose to run. She wiped it with a tissue from her pink-laced apron.

"Another hour and it'll be ready," she chirped and walked to the fridge, opening the door. With a wide smile, she reached for the plastic bowl on the first shelf. Humming merrily, she brought it over to the counter just to the right of the stove and its simmering pot, and popped open the lid.

She reached into the bowl and removed a handful of severed human fingers, knuckles and bones removed with precise expertise. Licking her lips, she let them plop into the broth; a pocket of spittle gathered at the corner of her mouth.

Next, she lifted a liver out of the bowl that was washed and cleaned with great care, not a speck of blood contaminated it. Chunks of evenly cut flesh followed into the pot, the first layer of skin stripped neatly from each piece.

Her humming continued as she covered the pot with its lid and preheated the oven for her world famous baked bread.

After about an hour, Madeline removed the cover and gave her stew one last stir. "Dinner's ready!" she called.

George, her husband, strolled like a sloth into the kitchen. Yawning, he took a seat at the kitchen table as Madeline placed a large steaming bowl in front of him.

"Mmm," his eyes widened with glee. "That smells good."

"Oh, Georgie," she giggled. "You say that every time."

The two sat together and devoured the human stew as if they had been stranded on a desert island. Slurping, gnawing, chomping resounded throughout the room and to any average person the display unfolding at this dinner table would be a nightmarishly sickening sight. But to George and Madeline, this was just another home cooked meal.

Every single drop was suckled with a voracity that couldn't be measured, a consumption that would astound the senses. A sane person would go instantly mad in the presence of such insatiable appetites. The delight expressed on their faces was unlike any other pleasure on Earth. What needs were satisfied by this craving of human flesh was a mystery… even to themselves.

All that they knew, all that they understood, was that they loved every sumptuous morsel, right down to the last bite. George wiped his face with a linen napkin, brushing away the piece of carrot that hung on his cheek, the ochre-colored broth coating his chin, and the piece of flesh that dangled from his lower lip.

"I do love your stew," he said, his mouth still full of meat.

"I have some bad news," Madeline said.

George looked up, concern etched on his face. "What is it?" he burped, all color seeming to drain from his face.

"We're out of stew meat," she said.

"Oh, damn," was all that George could muster. "Well, you know what to do, dear."

"Of course."

Yes, she knew exactly what needed to be done. It wasn't her favorite thing in the world but it was for the greater good. It took some preparation and there was no time to waste. She had resisted telling him all day; she just wanted to let him enjoy his meal before breaking the news.

How he loved her stew. She wanted him to savor this meal for it might be some time before she was able to make it again, actually if tonight didn't go well, it might be even longer.

She drew in a deep breath before taking the pot to the sink to wash.

George shot her a glance. "Honey, you know I like to lick the bowl," he said.

"Just stop it, Georgie, there's no need to make a pig of yourself."

"You're no fun," he winked before leaving the kitchen to return to his newspaper. "Great meal as usual," he called.

* * *

For the next few hours she got ready, primping and polishing. Great attention and care was taken in order to fashion a vision of utter perfection.

Downstairs in the cellar, George did his part. He sharpened the cleavers and carving knifes, tested the chains and shackles, checked the meat freezer and cleaned his worktable.

The cellar windows were painted over with black paint and a single light bulb dangling on a chain was all that illuminated George's work. A fridge hummed in the corner, primarily used for leftovers, and an awaiting meat grinder sat in the back of the room.

Hearing a noise on the stairs, George looked up, forgetting his work as he gazed upon his stunning wife.

Even in her fortieth year, Madeline was still a stunning beauty. Her green eyes were mesmerizing and her raven tresses ravishing, a perfect compliment to the silk skirt suit that she wore. Her lips were luscious red, moist and inviting, and her perfume was simply euphoric; the sales clerk had said it was made with actual human pheromones. The clerk had been a tasty one as she remembered.

"Magnificent, simply magnificent," George said, smiling with pride.

"Thank you, dear," she said, stepping off the stairs and joining his side.

"Remember the last one?" he asked, resuming the sharpening of the cleaver in his hand.

"Ah yes," she smiled.

"What a tough one. Put up a hell of a fight. So big and strong."

"Yes, but the meat was tender and robust. Near perfection," she said.

"You'll do fine tonight," George said, brushing her face gently with his hand.

"I know," she said and left the cellar.

* * *

It was almost dusk when Madeline drove away from the house and vanished from George's sight. He always worried about her on these nights, but he had the utmost confidence in her abilities and choices. She was an old pro now.

He muddled about their suburban home, bored and hungry. Sure there was ice cream in the freezer, cake on the counter, and cookies in the cupboard but nothing came close to the taste of that juicy meat, stewed in its own juices. He could still smell it in the air, though dinner was long over.

The craving was nearly insatiable these days. It's all he thought about. The more he ate the more he wanted. It was amazing how addictive it was once you started. George wandered around, trying to occupy himself but soon ended up down in the cellar once again.

He approached the huge meat freezer in the corner, the dim light washing it in charcoal shadows and alabaster shades. George lifted the lid and gazed inside. There was nothing left. Walls of frost glinted red from some blood that had dripped from a few of the packages. In the farthest corner, he spied a sliver of flesh. It beckoned to him, taunted him like the last morsel of a grand buffet that was about to be thrown away by the careless staff.

"Oh no, you don't," George reached in, his large belly squishing against the cold receptacle. His fingers wiggled as he reached in, and before long he got a hold of it, pulled it into his palm, and stood up. It was a bit frost bitten and hard as a rock but he didn't care.

He popped the shred of pink flesh into his mouth as if it were a piece of Popsicle and sucked...licking the savory essence of it. The first human Popsicle he'd ever tried. Hmm, perhaps he was on to something. Maybe he'd ask Madeline to whip up some frozen delights with the next batch of meat they procured.

George was about to suck down the last of it when the doorbell rang. It was the front door. He turned to look through the nearest cellar window but remembered he couldn't see out of them.

"Damn," he mumbled. He turned out the light and ascended to the main part of the house. He walked down the hall and opened the front door.

"Hello, Mr. Sattler," the Girl Scout said from his front step, decked out in her uniform, her arms stuffed with boxes of cookies.

"Well, hello there, Jenny," George said with some surprise. He wasn't expecting his next-door neighbor's daughter to pop by. She was a naturally curious girl and a bit nosey for her own good.

"I'm selling Girl Scout cookies... would you like to buy some?" Her smile was wide and beaming. Her eyes were filled with innocence and glee.

George sighed and stepped aside. "All right I guess. Come in so I can see what kinds you have and I'll get some money."

She glided past him and the aroma of strawberries wafted under George's nose. His stomach growled suddenly. God he was hungry. "Put the cookies on the kitchen table and I'll take a look."

Jenny did as he asked. She glanced around the room. "Where's Mrs. Sattler?"

"She's gone out...ah...shopping."

"Oh, well here they are...mint chocolate, caramel clusters, pecan butter, oatmeal raisin, chocolate chip..."

George stood behind her, eyeing the cookies then giving Jenny the once over.

He wondered what she tasted like. Never mind the cookies. She had meat on her bones. Well, not a lot of it...but she was beginning to fill out. He could tell she was starting to get a belly, he noticed it at the front door. Seems she's been eating more cookies then she was selling. The thought made him giggle inside.

"Wonderful," he said. "Would you like some lemonade?" George started over to the refrigerator and opened it.

"No thank you," Jenny answered. "What's that smell?"

George thought it might be the remnants of the stew from earlier. The pots were still drying, the aroma still vaguely in the air. Could she know what the odor really was? Impossible.

"It was dinner, but now we're all cleaned up. Let me see. Do you have any marshmallow bars?"

"Nope. Not this year. This is all I have."

"Okay, Jenny, I'll take three boxes of caramel clusters. Let me get some cash." George walked into his bedroom and fetched his wallet. Damn girl...why did she have to come to the door now? The craving was almost unbearable.

He walked back to see her nosing around his pots and pans. She turned to watch him enter the kitchen, her fat cheeks covered in freckles. George felt his mouth water and his pulse race. He wiped his mouth quickly so that she couldn't see.

What if she just disappeared? Who would know? The freezer downstairs would hold her without any problem. It was meat after all. Tasty, succulent...damn it, no!

He and Madeline had agreed. No one they knew. No one in the neighborhood. Adults. Mostly male. Men had the best meat. The juiciest. The plumpest. The most flavorful. This was wrong.

"Okay then," George announced. "Time to go."

"I just want to count everything."

"Count it on the way home, Jenny. I really need you to go." He ushered her out of the kitchen and down the hall back to the front door.

"I'm sorry; I didn't mean to bother you."

"It's no bother, Jenny. I'm happy to buy your cookies, I'm just really busy."

"Okay. Well, say hello to Mrs. Sattler for me."

"I'll be sure to." George opened the door and practically pushed her out. Before she could even open her mouth, he closed the door in her face.

He was sure she would tell her parents how rude he was but it was much better than the alternative. George wiped the sweat dampening his brow. He walked to the kitchen, grabbed a box of cookies, went to the living room, and planted himself in his favorite plush chair. This would have to do for now. He was glad he resisted but it was getting harder and harder all the time.

Thank God for Madeline. She always kept him in line. She was so calm and collected. She handled everything and kept the house stocked and running. Outside it was pitch-black. The sun gone. All was quiet, except for the sound of George chomping down cookies.

"Madeline, please hurry back."

* * *

Madeline stood across the street from the Baxter Lounge, the bar she frequented on occasions such as this. She held her breath for a few moments then finally exhaled and started across the street.

She was always on edge on these nights. She was never fully at ease to be the one looking for and bringing home the meat. At least George did all the messy stuff, all she had to do was bring them home and clean up afterwards.

George had thought it best that she go out and get the meat, the males always had so much more to offer; more fat which added so much extra flavor, more meat per pound, and they tasted a bit better, too.

The thick, smoke-filled air struck her head on as she entered the bar, and she wondered sometimes what that did to the meat she and her husband ate.

The interior was dark and noisy as usual, people huddled together at the bar's counter—at tables—talking, laughing, drinking, trying desperately to find companionship, to find a way to fill the void that gnawed away at the inside of them.

Madeline observed this so often and she counted her lucky stars that she had someone at home like George.

She went to a small table near the door and gave an order to the cocktail waitress that had made a beeline right to her the moment she sat down.

It wasn't long before a lonely stranger worked his way over to her.

"Hello." His smile was wide and friendly. Actually he was quite a sharp dresser. He wore a dark-gray three piece suit, his wing tipped shoes were professionally polished, and his chestnut hair was groomed meticulously, not a strand out of place.

Madeline gave him the once over, taking note of how handsome he was and what great shape he was in. His shoulders were broad and his arms bulged with muscles. She almost started salivating right there in front of him.

"Hi there, yourself," she said, lifting her hand to him.

"I'm Jerry," he took her hand and kissed it.

"Madeline." A half smile crossed her lips as she invited him to sit down.

Together they talked and drank and laughed, much like the other patrons of the crowded lounge, although Madeline's intentions were surely quite different from all the others who searched for someone to chase away the blues.

"Madeline, you're a special lady, I can tell."

"Now, how can you tell that, Jerry?"

"Just the way you smile, the way you laugh. I have a sense of these things."

"My you're a charmer, aren't you?"

"Is it working?"

"It just might be." She gave him a seductive wink and took his hand into hers. "What say we find out just how good that sense of yours really is?"

"I like a woman who doesn't beat around the bush." He let her lead him out to her parked car across the street. After she had unlocked the door, he opened it for her and watched her climb in. Her every move was calculated and precise and it turned him on.

"I'll take you back to get your car in the morning," she reassured him.

"The morning?" he said with a smile as the remark escaped his lips.

* * *

George hid on the cellar stairs when he heard the car roll into the driveway, leaving the cellar door slightly ajar. The adrenaline pumped through him as he waited, his breath growing heavy.

In his right hand, he clutched a large carving knife.

The front door creaked open and the couple stepped into a living room drenched in darkness. Feeling for the light switch, Madeline lit up the room with one stroke of her hand.

"There we are," she sighed.

Jerry stopped her, and without warning, planted a kiss on her. They stood against the wall, enjoying the touch of one another.

George crouched in the darkness, lurking and watching. He watched them kiss as the anger surged through him. He couldn't wait to hack into that piece of meat, the meat that was pawing his wife right now.

"How's that sense now?" Jerry asked her, staring into her sparkling eyes.

"It's pretty damn good," she said. "Come on, let's get more comfortable."

She led him into the kitchen, just a few feet away from the cellar door and George's waiting blade. Sitting him down in one of the kitchen chairs, she opened the refrigerator and fetched a bottle of wine. She could see that he wasn't totally off guard yet, that he was still very much in control. She needed to make this as easy for George as possible.

"More?" Jerry asked. "Where do you put it all?" he laughed as he opened the bottle for her.

After pouring two tall glasses, they consumed even more alcohol, washing the night into the morning hours.

Madeline sat in the chair closest to the cellar, she could feel her husband's presence behind her, and her heart fluttered as thoughts of fresh new meat whirled in her head. George had been waiting for so long, he was quite patient but this seemed to be taking longer than planned.

She watched Jerry's eyes study her, sweeping up and down her body then glancing around the kitchen. The alcohol she poured into him seemed to be having little effect.

One more time she poured him a full glass of wine. He smiled at her pleasantly as she poured herself another as well, but only half of what she gave him.

He reached for the glass and knocked it over with a staggering hand. "My God, I'm so sorry," he said. "I'm so damn clumsy."

"Oh, think nothing of it." She stood up, lifting the glass off the table.

"Let me help you."

"It's no bother, really," she said, turning to head for the sink and a dishrag.

Before she could take another step, Jerry leapt from his chair, snatching the wine bottle from the table and bringing it down hard on the back of her head.

The bottle shattered, and wine splashed like a tidal wave, soaking her back and dripping onto the floor. Madeline fell over face first and was rendered unconscious.

Jerry stared at the cellar door, eyes piercing the crack and the splinter of darkness between it and the frame. "All right, big boy," he said to George. "Come on out."

George stepped out of the door, his face aghast. "Madeline..." he gawked at her, tears streaming down his fat cheeks.

"You two thought you were going to put one over on me," Jerry said, holding the broken wine bottle in one hand. His gaze was fixed on George as he reached into his suit with his free hand.

Out of his suit coat Jerry pulled a serrated dagger. "Like I told Madeline, I have a sense of these things."

"You son of a bitch!" George screamed. "I'll kill you for hurting Madeline!"

"C'mon, big boy. You think you got what it takes?" Jerry prodded, bracing himself.

George charged, his knife held high, but he was no match for Jerry who sidestepped him while driving the dagger into George's stomach. Jerry seemed to be quite an expert, George realized. He wasn't just another piece of meat.

With the dagger in George's gut, Jerry slashed his throat with the wine bottle, then watched as the big man fell to his knees.

Driving his deed home, Jerry withdrew the dagger and then plunged it into George's chest.

George coughed up some blood, quivered a bit, and dropped his carving knife to the floor. A moment later he fell onto his face, a sigh escaping him.

Jerry waited a moment and then tapped George with his foot. Satisfied, he walked over to Madeline and turned her over. "Thank you, my lovely," he whispered. "I knew you were special. You've solved all my problems."

He smiled while driving his dagger deep into her chest.

*   *   *

Three days later.

Danvers Street Butcher Shop.

"Here you go Pearl, two pounds of stew meat," Jerry said as he handed the white bundle to the gray-haired woman standing in front of the counter.

"Thank you so much, Jerry. I'm so glad you reopened your shop," the old woman croaked as she gently laid the package into her shopping basket.

"Well, thank you. I don't think I'll be having any more problems for a while. I've gotten a new supplier for my meat."

"Such a nice boy," the old woman said before exiting the crowded shop, and rightly so, for it sold the best quality *meat* in town.

CANNIBAL CAMPING TRIP

ANTHONY GIANGREGORIO

The Land Rover pulled into the parking lot for the camp ground in upstate New York at half past two on Saturday afternoon.

No sooner did the vehicle come to a stop, then the doors were opening and the Johnson family stepped out, stretching and yawning after the long drive from New York City.

Doug Johnson turned to look at his family with pride and admiration.

His wife, Tina had just stepped out of the passenger seat and was smiling at him as she wiggled her right leg, which had fallen asleep. Behind her, his oldest daughter, Alicia, was standing and holding her cell phone up to the sky, as if it would magically work because she raised it two more feet over her head.

"Dad," Alicia said, stretching out the word. "There's no signal up here, how am I supposed to survive for two whole days with no phone service?"

Doug chuckled at her, thinking of that saying about how a cell phone can only be separated from a teenage girl's hand when it's taken from her dead body.

"Well, I guess you're just going to have to rough it, honey," he said with a grin, Tina showing him one of her own.

"Alicia wants to talk to Jamie, that's why she's mad there's no signal," Doug's youngest daughter, Amy, said with a contemptuous smile. "They're in love. They're gonna go all the way next week at the Prom."

"Shut up, you little twit!" Alicia snapped as she spun on her sister, who danced away laughing.

"Girls, girls," Doug said and looked at Amy. "Stop trying to get your sister into trouble. She and her mom talked about next week and I have total faith in her judgment."

"Thanks, Dad," Alicia said and stuck her tongue out at Amy.

Doug laughed, always finding it amusing how Alicia would act so much younger around her sister.

Tina walked around the Land Rover and gave Doug a hug. "Where is everyone, honey? This place is empty," she said.

Doug took a real look around for the first time since pulling into the parking lot. "Hey, you're right, it is empty. Wow, that's weird." He shrugged it off as soon as he spoke. "Hey, more woods for us, I guess. Maybe the campers skipped this week and we got lucky and will have the forest to ourselves."

"Great," Alicia said as she raised her hands up and then down in frustration. "On top of everything else, there's no one else to talk to but you guys."

"We love you, too, dear," Tina said as she pulled out a pack of cigarettes, took one out, and lit it. Doug frowned, took the lighter from her hand and put it in his pocket, but said nothing to her. She had agreed to not smoke in the house or the car so he had to leave her alone. It was her choice, he kept telling himself. She eyed him angrily but then her mood shifted and she turned away, taking another drag as she did so.

Doug clapped his hands together to get his family's attention. "Okay, so enough chit-chat. Let's get the packs and tents and get hiking. It's a good two hour walk to the glade where we'll be setting up for the night."

"Why do we have to go so far in?" Alicia asked. Why can't we just go over there and set up." She pointed to a copse of trees just off the gravel parking lot.

Doug sighed. "Because it's not real camping if the car is a stone's throw away, honey. We need to be deep in the forest, away from man and civilization. We need to have to rely on our wits."

"And what we brought with us, like food, water and magazines," Amy said with a sly grin. She was a wise-guy and Doug loved her for it, but sometimes it did get annoying.

"Yes, dear, and what we bring with us."

Doug went to the back of the vehicle, popped the rear hatch, and began taking out the camping gear. Fifteen minutes later, he pressed the button on his key ring, locked the Land Rover, and led his family into the wilderness.

"Are we there yet?" Alicia whined for the hundredth time.

"I think so. It should be just around that bend at the top of the path," Doug said as he led his family ever onward. Tina was quiet, too tired to speak, and Amy had run out of energy to talk almost an hour ago. Only Alicia seemed to have the energy to complain and she did so at five minute intervals.

Ten minutes later, they crested the bend in the path and each of them let out a gasp of amazement at the vista before them.

There was a wide glade, and to the left of it, was the edge of a cliff, overlooking a massive amount of forest and surrounding mountains. It was truly breathtaking.

"Wow, Doug, you said it was beautiful, but I didn't believe just *how* much when you told me," Tina said as she dropped her pack and walked to the edge. It was a very steep facade and if a person was to fall, there would be no surviving the drop.

"I know, huh? Mac in accounting told me about this place. Said he found it by accident. We're so deep into the mountains that no one else knows about it."

Alicia picked up a candy wrapper and shoved it under Doug's nose. "No one, huh? Looks to me like people have been here."

"Well, what I meant to say is, not many people know about it. It's way off the hiking trails and unless you want to take a chance and go free-hiking, the odds of finding this place is pretty slim."

"So then, Dad, what's with the path?" Amy asked. "If there's a path then people must come up here."

"Good point, honey. But that's not a people path we were on, that was an animal path. See, animals are a lot like people and they pick the easiest path to use. Then others follow, and before you know it, there's a discernable path in the woods. Usually you see them by streams and lakes where animals go to get water."

"Oh, okay, makes sense I guess," Amy said as she went to join her mother.

"Don't get too close, Amy!" Doug called. "Tina, keep an eye on her," he said.

"I will, I got her!" Tina called back.

Alicia dropped to the ground, not very interested in the view. Doug didn't mind. He had seen her eyes go wide when they first crested the bend and knew she was impressed.

"So, Dad, do we make camp here?" Alicia asked.

"No, honey, we have to walk a little bit more. It wouldn't be safe to make camp here for obvious reasons."

"Great, more walking."

He chuckled, knowing his daughter's mood swings. "It's not far. I promise; no more than ten minutes. Mac told me there's this wide circle devoid of foliage and there's logs set up around it. At one time someone set up a camp there but it was years ago, maybe longer.

"Fancy words there Dad, *devoid*. Why not just say no trees and junk?"

"Because I'm trying not to talk down to you now that you're older, that's why. It's a compliment; you should take it as such."

"Whatever. God, Dad, you're such a goofball."

Amy came running back and hugged her father. "Wow, Daddy, it's beautiful. It makes you think you could just jump off and fly away."

"Well, I suppose so, but you know you can't, right?"

"Of course, Daddy, I'm not a kid anymore," she said and trotted off to join her sister, who snapped at her impatiently as siblings will to one another.

Tina returned and wrapped her arms around Doug, kissing him on the cheek. "Oh, Doug, what a gorgeous view. It was certainly worth the hike to see it. I'm glad you decided to take us on this trip. I think it's just what our family needs."

"I couldn't agree more, honey. So what do you say? Do you want to stay here a little longer, or do you want to keep going to the place Mac told me about and set up for the night?"

"Sure, let's go. Once we're unpacked we can make some smores," Tina said.

Doug picked up his pack and looked over at Alicia who was fiddling with her cell phone. "If it didn't work down by the Land Rover, honey, it's sure not gonna work way up here. Just put it away, will you please? Would it kill you to be a part of this family for just a few days?"

"Yes, Dad, it would. God, I should be with Kathy at the mall today. She said Jamie is going to be there and I wanted to see him."

"She likes Jamie a lot, Daddy. They want to kiss and stuff," Amy said and pretended she was kissing her hand.

"Knock it off, ya little runt."

"Alicia, watch your mouth!" Tina snapped.

"What, Mom, I said *runt*. God, everything I do I get in trouble."

Doug began walking. "Come on, let's forget it ever happened and keep moving. You'll feel better once we have a fire going and your tent is set up."

"Doubt it," Alicia said and began walking. Tina and Amy took up the rear as the Johnson family continued their hike.

A short time later, Doug and family reached the circular area empty of plant life and set up their tents. One tent for Doug and Tina and one for Amy and Alicia. Doug managed to get a fire going after more than fifteen minutes of work, and when he finally did, Tina clapped and cheered him, boosting his failing spirits.

They sat around the fire, talking and laughing and even Alicia was getting into it. Doug saw the little girl who used to run to him when he arrived home from work every night. The short-tempered teenager had melted away, and he relished her change in personality, knowing once they returned home and her cell phone worked, and she was bombarded with the massive machine that was corporate America, filled with sex, sex and more sex, she would revert back to the annoyed teenager she had been for the past two years.

So for now, he laughed with her, listened to her talk, and tried to imagine that this was reality and what was left behind was all a dream.

As night fell, and the fire began to die, the family of four each went to their tents to get a good night sleep.

Doug was amazed when Alicia went to him and gave him a goodnight hug, something she hadn't done in years.

Amy was right behind her and she hugged him and then went to Tina, then with a round of "Goodnights," everyone turned in.

As Doug stretched out on his sleeping bag, Tina curled up beside him, he closed his eyes and listened to the sounds of the forest. He could hear crickets chirping softly, and the wind blowing through the trees, and though he was used to the sounds of traffic buzzing by his bedroom window as he slept each night, he found the sounds of nature lulling him into a deep sleep, the long hike up to the camping spot also helping to knock him out almost as soon as his head touched his small pillow.

Doug awoke to screams of his wife and daughters, and for a moment, he didn't know where he was.

For almost a full ten seconds he was lost, his mind trying to figure out where he was, what was happening, and if he was dreaming.

As his mind cleared, he saw the flap to the tent was open as well as a long tear in the material of Tina's side of the tent. It was as if a knife had sliced into the material.

As his mind focused, he saw Tina's legs, kicking frantically, as she was dragged out of the gash in the tent. She was screaming for help and Doug didn't know what to do. He was in shock, not understanding what was happening. In the background of his panic, he could hear Amy and Alicia yelling for Mommy and Daddy.

The tent flap was open, and it wasn't empty. In front of the tent, stooped over, was a human figure, the face lost in the shadows of the night, but Doug's nostrils were assaulted by feces and the odor of an unwashed body.

With his brain frantically trying to make him snap out of it, the dark figure reached inside the tent and grabbed his stocking feet, then yanked, dragging Doug out of the tent like he was nothing but a stuffed doll.

He slid across his sleeping bag to find himself staring up at a half-moon, the night sky clear of clouds, a few stars winking down at him as if they were watching his drama with amusement.

He heard Tina cry out to his left and his head turned to look for her. He saw her pulled to her feet by two shapes hidden in the night. Tina was a fighter and never stopped struggling, and she got lucky and her right hand snapped out and struck one of the figures in the nose. Even over the cries of his children, Doug heard the distinctive snap of a breaking nose and one of the figures fell back, sputtering blood from the same nose.

But Tina's victory was short-lived as the other figure pulled a knife, and in less than a second, slid it across her throat, almost severing her head from her shoulders, the blade cut so deep.

Doug could only lay still, his eyes wide in utter horror, as he saw a gout of blood shoot out of his wife's open throat to splatter the ground like warm rain. Her body twitched and spasmed and the figure holding her stepped away from her, Tina's body falling to the cold ground to writhe in its death throes.

"Tina!" Doug yelled, but only managed the one word before he was smothered by the figure that had dragged him from the tent. Something hairy covered his face and he sucked in the funk of old meat and sweat.

Acting on instinct, he fought and kicked to try to extricate himself but the figure was larger than him and he was overpowered.

Rolling on the ground, he got lucky and managed to squirm free of his captor. No sooner did he do this then the figure was grabbing him again. He kicked out with his right foot and felt the satisfying squish of testicles under his heel. The figure moaned in pain and fell to the ground and Doug rolled to his knees. A few feet away, he saw Alicia and Amy being dragged into the woods by more shadows shaped like humans. His girls were screaming for him, yelling for their mother, but no help was coming.

Doug jumped to his feet, preparing to run and save his girls, to take them back from whoever had them, but before he took two steps, another shape came at him from behind and brought a large wooden club down onto the back of his head.

Doug saw stars then, small pinpricks of light flashing before his eyes. As he fell to the ground, slipping into unconsciousness, two things followed him into the abyss; the dead eyes of his wife as she lay on the ground in a pool of blood, and the haunting cries of his two daughters.

Then the lights went out.

Doug returned to the land of the living somewhat slowly. Once more he didn't know where he was and it took the constant scraping on his back to pull him back to the real world.

When the next pain struck him, he became fully awake.

The pain came from the countless rocks and branches littering the forest floor, which were cutting into the skin on his back.

He looked up to the see it was still dark, and as his body flowed over a thick patch of twigs, he realized he was being dragged across the forest floor. He looked down at his feet to see two men pulling him, each one holding a foot. His shirt was now nothing but rags, and with each yard they dragged him, more of the skin on his back was ripped away.

Wincing, he held his tongue, not wanting to alert his captors he was awake.

By the way he was being dragged, he had a feeling his captors assumed he was dead, and for the moment he had no reason not to want to perpetuate that assumption.

Moving his head to the right, he spotted another man walking. This man carried a burden, but in the darkness it was hard to see what it was. He could see the burden was draped over his shoulder like it was the carcass of a slain deer. The part Doug could see swinging loosely, like a ball on a tether, swayed with the cadence of the figure's gait.

Then the figure passed under an opening in the canopy of trees and the thinnest bit of moonlight cast a pale glow on the figure. Doug controlled his reaction to scream when he saw that the part of the man's burden that was swinging, was actually Tina's head, hanging by a thin bit of flesh, constantly moving back and forth like a macabre pendulum.

He heard a screech of pain and his head snapped to the left to see three more figures, each carrying a burden.

In the gloom of the forest night, he immediately knew it was his daughters, both awake but gagged by the sounds of their muffled cries.

His entire body welled up with panic for his daughters, then the loss of Tina filled him with grief and he fought the choking urge to yell, to kick at his two captors and fight to save his little girls' lives.

But though filled with fear and rage, he remained calm, knowing he was outnumbered and acting irrationally would only get him killed...like Tina.

His eyes went to her swinging head once more and he felt choking sobs rising up in his throat. His wife of over twenty years was now dead, and he had been there to see her die. He hadn't protected her and now she was gone.

But his daughters were still alive. If he could save them, escape the woods, they could still be a family. They could mourn Tina's loss but continue. They had to, for the memory of his wife. He knew she would want him to do everything in his power to save her little girls, her babies. The only question was how? How could he hope to prevail over the greater numbers of his attackers?

One of the figures spoke to another one and Doug didn't recognize the words. They seemed like English but were garbled, like they were being spoken by a retarded person, the syllables low and guttural, dragged out when they should be short.

His head felt woozy and he almost fainted, only his force of will keeping him awake.

Looking back up at the night sky, he saw the moon wasn't where it had been before. He didn't know what time it was, but he could tell he'd been out for a while. Where he was being taken, along with his family, was far from his original campsite.

As he scanned the surrounding woods, all he saw was isolation. Nothing looked familiar, no paths, nothing.

Wherever he was, he was far from civilization. He knew the woods went on for miles upon miles and it wasn't far-fetched to believe that these people, whoever they were, could somehow live in the mountains somewhere, never found in the endless miles of forest by man.

Of course, as he thought about this, he realized how ridiculous it sounded. That was the stuff of horror books, where the inbred family lived in the woods and would attack unwary travelers to kill and take their valuables.

Somehow he didn't think they wanted his wrist watch or his Land Rover. If they did, then why carry Tina's corpse through the woods? Wouldn't it have been easier to dump her body off the path or perhaps bury it?

His head hurt, and the more he tried to rationalize the actions of his attackers, the more it didn't make any sense.

Thirty more minutes of being dragged like a sack of laundry and the trees began to open up. He saw ramshackle buildings, no more than shacks, each resembling small tool sheds. They were built in a rough circle, the interior of the circle made up of mud, rocks and a large fire pit in the center.

As the two men dragging him reached the edge of the circle, each one let go of his feet. His right heel struck a sharp rock when it fell and it was all he could do not to cry out. The man on the right turned around to look at him and Doug closed his eyes and feigned death. The man grunted, satisfied his prey was harmless, then looked back to the other man.

Opening his left eye a small amount, Doug saw his daughters and Tina's corpse being carried into the circle. Tina's body was dropped to the ground without respect, her arms flapping over her side to lay still. It broke Doug's heart see his wife handled this way but he forced his anger down, knowing he was vastly outnumbered and he needed to bide his time; for what he didn't know yet.

His daughters were carried to the edge of the circle where wooden posts were embedded in the ground. Each girl was tied to a post with their hands behind their backs. Their clothes were quickly cut away until they were stark naked, tears running down their cheeks as they sobbed in terror.

The two men who had been dragging Doug took a step away from him, one peeing on a tree while the other called out to another figure lost in the darkness.

And that was when Doug saw his best chance to escape.

Jumping to his feet, he picked up a fist-sized rock as he stood. Before the man who was urinating knew what was happening, Doug smashed the rock into the back of his head, the man's knees giving out as he fell into his own urine pool.

The other man heard Doug's attack and turned to see the supposedly dead prey very active. He yelled out and Doug dropped the rock, then he began to run, the shouts and alarm of the others in the camp sounding out behind him.

"I'll come back for you, Alicia, stay strong!" he yelled and hurdled a fallen tree to dash into the underbrush.

Behind him, he heard the footfalls of a half dozen figures and knew he needed to run for all he was worth. He knew if they caught him, they would make sure he was dead this time. There would be no second chances.

The low-hanging tree branches slapped his face and arms as he charged through the forest. In the darkness, trees seemed to jump into his path, and he deftly avoided them, more than once striking one with his shoulder. The pain was excruciating, but he shrugged it off, knowing to pause was death.

Behind him, his pursuers grew closer, their footfalls growing louder.

For more than fifteen minutes, Doug ran at full speed until his lungs began to labor and spots danced in his vision. A shooting pain had sprung up on his left side and he knew he was at the end of his rope.

Behind him, the whooping calls of his pursuers grew ever closer.

It was when he was about done for and he knew only a few more yards and he would collapse, that the ground fell out from beneath him and he found himself falling down a steep incline. Though he tried to control his descent, he was soon falling upside down, then right side up, then sideways. Branches and brush slowed his descent, and more than once a sharp branch jabbed his flesh mercilessly. His head struck a rock and he began to lose consciousness.

He yelled out once or twice but he had no time for such frivolity. And then he reached the bottom and splashed into a deep stream, the cold water snapping him back to full alertness. The current wasn't strong, more than enough to pull him along, and as he swam to the surface, sputtering and coughing, he caught the briefest glimpse of his pursuers on the ridge slightly behind him. As he floated downstream, they began to follow him, running along the ridge.

Doug knew he was still far from free.

Sucking in a deep breath, his heart pounding like a steel drum in his head, he dove underwater and went to the bottom. His hands found a mud slick rock bigger than his body, and he held onto it, then closed his eyes and counted in his head. His plan was that his followers would continue running downstream, assuming he was still moving with the current, and when he finally resurfaced, they would have no idea where he was.

He stayed under water for nearly two minutes, and as his head broke the surface and he swam to shore, he could barely focus, he was so oxygen deprived.

A small copse of branches and leaves had built up along the shore and he moved into it, his head now hidden from view. With the darkness all but complete, he knew there was no way he could be seen and he waited, never moving, only half his head exposed, his mouth hidden in the water as his nose touched the surface.

Once or twice, he heard yells and shouts, but soon it was lost amongst the steady gurgle of the stream.

He waited for over an hour, and with his body shaking from the cold temperature, he climbed out onto the shore and slowly made his ascent to the top of the ridge.

He sat there, his eyes darting back and forth as his blue lips trembled from the cold, but there was no sign of his pursuers.

Ten minutes later, his heart beat slowing, he knew he had lost them. But he couldn't leave, not yet. His daughters were still in the camp. And though he wanted to run back to civilization as fast as he could, he knew he couldn't leave his daughters. After what those monsters had done to Tina, he knew his girls were in grave danger.

So, shaking off the cold, and only in his stocking feet, he slowly got his bearings, crossed his fingers he was going in the right direction, and began to make his way back to the camp to save what was left of his family.

It took more than an hour for Doug to find the ramshackle camp again. Over the course of that hour, he panicked more than once, thinking he wasn't going to be able to locate it.

It was pure luck that allowed him to discover it once more.

As he was creeping around in the dark brush, trying to retrace his steps, he accidentally blundered into one of the members of the camp.

The woman was as shocked to see him as he was to see her, but Doug was the first to go into action. She had been squatting to pee, and it appeared these people picked any old place to leave their waste, and before she could yell out and sound the alarm, Doug's hands reached out and wrapped around her dirty neck. She fought back like a wildcat, kicking and scratching, one of her knees going into his crotch, but he never let up and eventually she began to sag in his hands as she lost consciousness.

By the time she collapsed at his feet, her face was a dark blue; when Doug got a better look at her, he saw she was filthy, in her early twenties, and look like she had Down Syndrome.

The first thing he saw was the necklace she wore, and on closer inspection, he was horrified to see it was made of human ears, more than one with the earrings still attached. The second thing he saw was the knife hanging from her belt, a man's belt if he was correct.

Because it was dark, it was hard to see clearly, but he'd already seen enough.

Taking the knife from her, he looked down on the unconscious woman and knew right there he needed to decide what to do next.

His moral compass began a battle in his head of what he should do with her. If he left the woman be, she would wake and alert the camp he was near, but if he killed her to silence her, then he became a killer, a murderer that was no better than the attackers who had taken his family...and killed Tina.

But then, they had kidnapped his daughters, slaughtered his wife without mercy, and tried to kill him. He hadn't asked for this; they had been the aggressors. His mind raced with right and wrong and he may have spent another hour wrestling with the decision if the woman didn't make it for him.

As he sat over her, trying to decide what to do, her eyes snapped open and she let out a guttural growl. Without thinking about it, moving purely on instinct, for survival, Doug slashed at her throat with the knife, slicing her jugular and causing her beginning yells to become low gurgles.

Blood shot from her neck to coat her small breasts and more than two pints splattered on him before he fell away in disgust, now covered in the sticky plasma.

He stared at her as she twitched on the forest floor to then lay still, her eyes glazing over to then stare up at the night sky. He looked at the bloody knife in his right hand, the arm beginning to shake as he realized what he'd done, but as time passed, his hand grew strong and his jaw taut as resolve filled him.

He had killed this woman and he was fine. He was still Doug, no better or worse. It was as he gazed down on the still form that he truly realized to kill wasn't such a bad thing. It was easy actually, no harder than crossing a street or cutting the lawn. It was a chore that he needed to do to save his daughters. The taboo of 'Thou Shalt Not Kill' had been shattered and he felt free, more alive than he had in his entire life, and he knew it was time to save his family and get revenge for the death of Tina.

Thinking this way, he knew he could now kill others of the camp if he had to, and he was fairly confident that would be the only way to rescue his girls.

Standing tall, blood sluicing down his shirt and pants, he turned and trotted off into the forest, heading for the camp which by luck or fate, hadn't hear the woman's cries.

He knew before the night was over, either he would be dead or his new knife would taste more blood.

It was still more than two hours before dawn when Doug reached the perimeter of the camp and crouched low behind a thick patch of blackberries. Through the thin branches, he was able to see the fire in the center clearly.

But whatever courage he'd felt before reaching the camp quickly vanished as he stared at the macabre tableaux before him.

At the fire, ten people sat, each eating like they were starving animals.

The meat was raw, and at first he didn't know what they were eating, but when a body shifted to the left, he saw the corpse of his beloved wife, Tina, sprawled in the dirt.

Her head was now fully severed from her corpse and it sat on a rock like a bizarre trophy. Her torso had been gutted, the organs extracted, and as Doug watched mystified, two men picked up the torso and rammed a pole through it, then placed the torso on a spit over the fire. A woman with a malformed face began sprinkling what had to be spices on the meat while the others continued chopping up the arms and legs like it was a carcass after a hunt.

Not able to withstand the horror, Doug knelt over and puked, his eyes squeezed tight as vomit left his mouth to splay his feet and tears slid down his cheeks.

He didn't know how long he sat there in the brush, crying, but in time he was pulled from his grief by the screams of his little girls.

Scanning the camp, he watched them appear from out of the darkness, dragged by their hair by two more men. Doug saw that the brows of both men protruded heavily; giving them a Cro-Magnon look. After seeing the features of the woman he'd killed, he was starting to get an idea who these people were, though it seemed so far fetched as to be unbelievable. Still, the reality was before him.

His naked daughters were in tears, their faces covered in streaks of dirt and grime and Doug wracked his brain for a way to save them. But there was nothing feasible he could do. If he charged into the camp, he would be quickly overwhelmed and brought down.

Alicia was first as she was dragged close to the fire, only a few feet from where Tina's corpse was gutted. Doug squeezed the knife hilt so tightly his knuckles turned bone white, but there was nothing he could do.

Alicia was tossed to the ground, and without so much as a hesitation, the man dropped down over her and slit her throat. As blood shot out of her torn carotid, he began to gut her, dragging the knife from her neck to her groin, cutting off extra skin when feasible.

Doug stared in utter shock, his mouth opening and closing as he slipped into a state of absolute terror. From where he hid, he had a perfect view of his daughter's death, and as he watched, the man reached into her gaping chest cavity, cracked the ribs, and pulled out her still beating heart. With a throaty yell, he sank his teeth into it, tearing and chewing at the engorged muscle. When he was half done, he tossed it to a woman who yelped merrily and began feeding. The man then pulled out organ after organ, handing them to the greedy camp dwellers, each ripping and tearing at the organs with their teeth, blood sluicing down their chins to cover their naked chests.

Doug was frozen in place, his entire world crumbling beneath him. He felt nothing. He was alone in a void where there was no light, no sensation.

Alicia was cleaned, gutted, her limbs severed, and her torso placed on a spit next to Tina's. As the torso was lifted onto the spit, Doug spotted a tattoo of a dolphin at the crease of her back, right where her butt would begin. His daughter had always loved dolphins and he hadn't known she even had a tattoo.

For some reason, seeing that tattoo caused him to fall to the ground, crying harder, his shaking shoulders scraping the dirt. He may have stayed like that forever if not for the screams of his younger daughter, Amy.

Peering through the brush, he could only watch helplessly as she was also killed. For some reason, the man who dealt with Amy was more merciful. He took her small head in his hands, then twisted sharply, snapping her neck and ceasing her cries.

But Doug found out this wasn't so merciful when the man picked up Amy, hung her by her feet, then slit her throat to let the blood seep out into a cracked ceramic bowl beneath her. His little angel, his sweet daughter, was being drained of her blood like she was common cattle. It happened so fast that Doug barely had time to register it. One second she was screaming, then she was hanging and dripping her blood into a bowl.

His mind raced with everything he'd seen, and as he watched the cannibals eating his family, their malformed faces flickering in the firelight, he found himself about to pass out from the pressure.

With the visions of his family being slaughtered fresh in his head, he gladly welcomed death, in fact, he prayed it would come soon, as he slid into unconsciousness once more.

But he did awaken, and as he slowly sat up, he moved a few branches aside to see the camp was quiet. He saw a few bodies lying prone around the waning fire and by the subtle twitches of their limbs he could tell they were asleep.

Looking up at the sky, he saw he had less than an hour before dawn would arrive.

Looking back at the camp, he could see the remains of his family, their bones set in a pile near the fire. Their heads were used as trophies, the flesh peeled away so only red, grinning skulls remained. He tried not to think about what those skulls truly were; his lost family.

The time he was unconscious had helped him. Though only fading wisps of smoke, he faintly remembered terrible dreams as his mind tried to process the carnage he'd witnessed, the absolute grief no man should have to experience in one lifetime.

But whatever his mind had rationalized, whatever it had decided while he was unconscious, he now felt only one emotion fill him from head to toe.

Revenge.

Pure...unadulterated...revenge.

Coming to his knees, he crawled into the camp, careful to stay away from the flickering firelight.

It took him more than ten minutes to reach the first sleeping figure. It was a man. The lips were twisted and the nose was crooked, but as the sleeping man shifted and blew out a snort, Doug knew his assumption was correct.

For some unknown reason, these people were all mentally retarded. The distorted features of their faces sealed the deal along with their jilted speech patterns. How these people ended up in the middle of the mountains, miles upon miles from civilization, was a mystery; one he wasn't in the mood to figure out.

Where normally he would want to help these unfortunate people, after what they had done to his family, all he wanted to do was kill them.

Creeping over the sleeping figure, he raised the knife, then in a fluid motion, placed his free hand over the deformed mouth and slid the knife across the exposed neck.

The eyes went wide on the retarded man's face but with Doug's hand clamped over the mouth, nothing but a few muffled grunts slipped free. It took less than fifteen seconds for the flailing arms to grow weak, to then fall back to the ground.

Doug was splashed with hot blood but he ignored it; in fact he relished it. The warm spray was a baptism of murder, one he would continue until every evil being in the camp was destroyed.

When he was sure the man was dead, he crawled over the corpse to the next sleeping figure.

It was a woman and her small, pint-sized body showed the stunted growth of a dwarf. The protruding jaw and large forehead added to what he'd already come to accept as fact. These were what the civilized world called 'special people', but now they were only killers and murderers, and worse, cannibals, feeding on the flesh of their fellow humans.

He fell on top of her, plunging the knife into her chest, right over her heart. He felt the blade slide in and the subtle resistance as it passed through her ribcage, then the pressure lessening as the tip of the knife cleaved her heart in two. The woman's eyes snapped open and she elicited a gasp, but nothing more escaped her lips. Her head rose a few inches as she spasmed, and other than releasing her bowels, she gently lowered her head to the ground to lay still.

Doug grunted at his handiwork, amazed at how truly easy it was to kill another human being.

Guilt filled him for a fraction of a second, but when he glanced at the skulls and pile of bones that was his family, he brushed it off and renewed his vow of slaughter.

After killing each of the sleeping figures around the dying fire, he then began entering each of the ramshackle huts. One at a time, he crept in like a thief in the night to steal their lives one at a time. By the time he was finished and every occupant of the camp was dead, he was bathed in blood from top to bottom, the sticky plasma becoming a new skin.

If for even a moment he regretted his actions, when he came upon the last hut he knew his action were righteous, and not for his own personal vengeance.

For inside the last hut were shelves upon shelves of bones and grinning skulls. To the left of the doorway were piles upon piles of wallets, wrist watches and shoes. All kinds were prevalent, from high heels to hiking boots, the menagerie of footwear told a gruesome tail of murder and carnage.

He took a pair of hiking boots that fit him and exited the hut.

He had killed close to twenty men and women this night and he felt nothing but sorrow. One, two, ten, twenty, what did it matter?

His family was dead and gone and he was alone.

Fresh tears spilled from his eyes and he fell to the ground, weeping softly.

Time passed, the sun rose and still he lay immobile, too weak to move. When he finally pulled himself up, he wondered if he should just torch the place, burn it all to the ground. But though lost in grief, he still was a part of civilization and when he returned with his incredible story, he would need proof of what happened.

With one last glance at the camp, he turned and began walking, knowing he would have to try and pay attention to the direction he went in so as to bring back the authorities. As for the slaughter of the camp's residents, he would keep that a secret for himself.

It was as he reached the edge of the camp, traversing a section he hadn't passed before, that his foot came down on a small pile of leaves in the center of the path.

Suddenly, there was a metallic sound and his leg felt like it was on fire. He yelled out in pain, and in the nearby trees, birds took flight, disturbed by his outcry.

Doug fell over, landing hard and yelling out once more as his ankle was twisted and his leg felt like it had been dipped in acid. His knife was gone, tossed away when he felt the bite of pain, and it was now lost somewhere in the leaves carpeting the forest floor. It could be anywhere and would take far too long to even attempt to search for it.

The knife could be a few feet or ten feet, he had no way to know for sure, let alone what direction to begin his search.

Looking down, he saw he had stepped into a bear trap, the metal mouth with its sharp teeth now clamped tightly over his ankle, trapping him. He reached down and tried to open it, but the second he touched it, blinding pain filled his vision and he lost consciousness.

When he came to, the sun hadn't moved very far and he figured he'd been out for a short time. Breathing heavily as fresh tears of pain leaked down his cheeks, he tried again to free himself.

Once more he failed miserably and slumped to the ground exhausted.

When he had the energy to try again, he decided to see if he could just drag the bear trap with him. As he dug around the trap, he found it was attached to a long metal chain, and when he pulled it, he saw it had quite a lot of play.

Maybe something in the camp could help him get free.

He began crawling back to the camp, one inch at a time. Each time he dragged his body, blinding white light filled his vision, but after the first ten feet or so the pain began to dull, though it was still agonizing. He figured it was his pain receptors on overload.

One excruciating yard at a time he crawled back into the camp, and when he was only a few inches from the first body, the chain finally went taut, causing him to cry out yet again.

But he managed to reach the body and pull it to him. He yelled out in glee to find a knife on the corpse. It wasn't big enough to pry open the trap with, but it was something.

Through his pain-addled mind, he wondered what the bear trap was for and why there was such a long chain on it, but then such matters were forgotten.

There was nothing close to him that he could use to pry the trap open and he slumped to the ground in defeat, soon fading into a fever-induced sleep that had him waking and passing out again and again over the next day.

On the second day, he awoke to darkness, and other than insects arriving to feed on the corpses, all was silent in the camp. No predators had arrived yet, though a few birds hopped about. He threw rocks at them and they flew away.

He was so thirsty it hurt and his leg throbbed with a steady rhythm, like a motor on a ship. With nothing else to do, he slept, sobbed over his lost family, then slept some more.

Days passed and he began to grow weak from hunger. He knew a man can only go for a few days without food and water and he knew he was close to his breaking point.

But he didn't want to die, not yet anyway.

His stomach was already bloated from hunger and his throat was raspy as he barked out laughter. Looking down at his foot, even in the darkness, he could see it had swollen in mass. Soon gangrene would set in if he didn't attend to it.

He knew there was only one thing he could do.

Sitting up, he took off his blood-soaked, dirt-covered shirt and tied it around his leg just a few inches above the teeth of the bear trap, the makeshift tourniquet cutting off blood flow to the foot. Then, with gritted teeth and a scream on his lips, he began to cut at his leg, sawing back and forth as pain filled him.

He passed out.

When he came to, he went back to work, cutting and hacking at his leg to severe his foot from the bear trap. He passed out three more times, and each time he woke up, he went back to work. The bone was the hardest, as he had to chip away at it with the tip of the blade. Each time the tip struck bone, his vision dimmed and he shuddered in agony.

He lost count how many times he passed out, and if time still mattered, he would have guessed it took him a full day to severe his foot from his leg.

But finally, with one last hack of the knife to bone and flesh, he pulled his leg free.

But he knew he was far from done yet and he crawled to the fire pit, pulled out Tina's cigarette lighter still in his pocket, and lit some kindling.

He was sweating profusely and had the shakes by the time he was finished, but a small fire was now burning in the center of the pit.

Without pausing, he sat up, spun around, and stuck his leg into the flames, searing his open wound and cauterizing it. He passed out yet again and it was only luck that his leg fell out of the fire as he collapsed to the ground.

Smoking, the redolence of charred flesh filling the area, Doug slid into oblivion once more.

When he woke up, he knew even with his leg cauterized, he would still die of hunger. He remembered when he had crawled through the camp to kill its occupants, he had found no other food source other than human flesh.

At first he balked at the idea, but as the hours passed and he felt the constant gnawing of hunger and grew ever weaker, he knew he had no choice.

Dammit, he wasn't going to die here. Not after everything that had happened.

If for nothing else then to let the world know what had happened to him and his family. He needed to survive, to escape this charnel house of death.

He let his eyes play over the corpses, now bloated from days in the sun, and his stomach roiled inside him. No, he wouldn't be eating them; he would die due to eating the rancid meat if nothing else.

Then his eyes spotted his severed foot, still lying in the middle of the bear trap.

Crawling across the ground, he picked up his foot. He stared at it, studying it like a connoisseur would a particular cut of meat. The foot was fresh, it had been on him only hours ago.

He brushed the dirt off the top where he had sliced it off, took off the boot and sock, and stared at it. He saw his toenails needed to be clipped and that made him laugh. Hell, he could bite them shorter with his teeth now.

Another tinge of hunger pain ripped through him and he grunted, then, his resolve firm that he would survive, he bit into the heel of the foot, his teeth sinking into the soft flesh. Pulling his head back, he began to chew.

He didn't know what he was supposed to expect, but he knew it probably wasn't what he tasted.

As he took another bite and the raw meat slid down his throat to fill him with energy, he didn't gag, and instead took yet another bite.

The more he ate, the more he grew accustomed to his decision, and by the time he was almost done, his eyes were closed and he was savoring the taste.

He thought of that old saying about how it would taste like chicken.

And he laughed to himself, feeling better with each bite.

It didn't taste like chicken at all, in fact it taste just like...

CLEANING UP FOR DINNER

MATT NORD

The life of a cleaner wouldn't usually be considered full of excitement and that was the life of Carl Hannigan. That was until he took the job cleaning the house over on Hertz Avenue.

Carl owned a small cleaning business, Mac's Cleaning Service, with a moderate amount of clients, mainly commercial; business offices, doctors' offices, a couple banks, a large car dealership. Business was going pretty well, especially considering how the economy was still pretty much crap.

Lucky for Carl, crap was his business. People still made a mess and they were still willing to pay someone to come in and clean up after them. The fact that people were messy and lazy was what kept him in business.

Most of Carl's business was at night. After everyone else had gone home for the day, a crew would come in and wash windows, sweep and mop the floors, disinfect bathrooms, empty the trash, and dust.

That left the day hours open for the most part. Usually, that was when office work and banking was done, supplies were purchased, and invoices were sent out. Of course, this was also when people wanted their houses cleaned.

Carl didn't usually take house jobs. He hated cleaning houses, but money was money. Because he didn't take on too many house jobs, let alone new ones, he usually would just go by himself and clean, keeping all of the profit. There were plenty of hours for his employees at night, and despite the fact that house cleanings were a pain, he also liked to keep busy on occasion.

He pulled the express van into the driveway of the house on Hertz Avenue. It was a bit further out than he normally went, about fifteen miles outside of town, but it was fairly early in the day, and even though it was scheduled to be a four hour job, he knew he would return in plenty of time to get back into town and restock the van for the night shift.

The house was fairly large. Carl started to think of the reasons he didn't enjoy cleaning somebody else's house. They tended to be a lot more picky than businesses. It wasn't that he wanted to cut corners and do a half-assed job; it was the inane little things people wanted done that annoyed him.

"The kitchen sink is full of dishes. You do wash dishes, right?"

"I left the linen on the end of the bed. If you could just make the bed, that would be great."

"My kids left their toys all over their room. Pick them up and put them away."

The general public just didn't get it. A cleaner and a maid service are two different things. Why don't I just stick around and cook dinner for you, too? If they wanted a butler, then hire a damn butler!

One time he had a person demand a discount because after dusting a table, a couple photos were slightly out of place. How insanely anal can you get? If there was one thing that cleaning houses had taught Carl, it was that people were crazy.

He sized up the house as he began unloading equipment: vacuum cleaner, dust rag, mop and bucket, and cleaning kit. He walked up the sidewalk, trying to carry everything at once. The kit was precariously sitting on top of the bucket, which he was pushing along with the mop.

Halfway up to the front door, the right wheel of the mop bucket caught on a particularly wide crack in the sidewalk. As it started to tip forward, the cleaning kit began to slip. Carl moved to grab it, letting go of the vacuum. Unfortunately, the momentum caused the vacuum to fall to the ground. The bucket fell on its side, and while grabbing the edge of the kit, all of its contents spilled to the ground.

"Shit," Carl mumbled. Just his luck but all part of a day's work.

He picked up everything and continued his trek to the house.

He set everything down on the front stoop and reached for the doorbell. The door opened when his index finger was two inches away. Standing before him was an average-looking, middle-aged woman wearing a plain brown dress and large eyeglasses. She looked like a stereotypical librarian. In fact, the stuffy look he received upon her opening the door lead to a quick flash in his mind of her behind a desk, stamping books and shushing children.

Carl stifled a smirk. "Hello, Mrs...."

"Are you Mac?" the woman asked.

"Uh, no," he replied. "I'm Carl. Carl Hannigan."

"I thought I spoke to Mac the other day."

Oh, boy, he thought. This was a common thing he had to deal with. He didn't know if people were being smartasses or if they were just plain stupid.

"No, ma'am," Carl replied, "you spoke with me."

"But the man I talked to said he was the owner of the company."

"Yes, ma'am. I'm the owner."

"So, you're Mac."

It took everything he had not to roll his eyes.

"No, I'm not Mac. My name is Carl Hannigan. I own Mac's Cleaning Service," he said, a little slowly.

"Then why is it called Mac's?" the woman inquired.

"Well, I purchased it from a man named Robert Mackenzie. He went by Mac; named the business accordingly, I suppose." Carl didn't know how much longer the ridiculous conversation was going to go on.

Just let me clean the damn house, lady, he thought to himself.

"So, why isn't it Carl's Cleaning then?" the woman asked.

"Well, I suppose that would make sense," he replied, "but everybody knows Mac's Cleaning. I figured why buy it if I'm not going to cash in on the brand name?" He gave her what he thought was a charming grin.

Apparently, she wasn't impressed. "Uh-huh." She turned and walked back into the house. "Well, come on. You've got some work to do."

He was a little taken aback. Not that he should have been. He'd gotten used to being made to feel like 'the hired help.' That was, after all, what he was.

But I'm also a business owner, bitch, he thought to himself.

Carl picked up his equipment and followed her into the house, half-surprised she didn't tell him to use the 'servant's entrance.'

"Now, there's a lot to be accomplished and not a lot of time to get it done. As I told you over the phone, I'm having a dinner party tonight, and I've had a few additions to the guest list. I do appreciate the fact that you were able to come on short notice. You are going to help me make this party go off?" the woman asked, while making her way through the house, pointing at specific rooms she wanted special attention given to.

The tour ended in the kitchen. Carl looked around in amazement. So far, it was the largest room he'd seen in the house. Embedded in the center of the far wall was the largest oven he'd seen outside of an industrial-sized bread oven he'd once cleaned in a bakery.

"Wow," he said. "What do you cook in that thing?"

She smiled. "It's custom made. I use it for occasions such as tonight. I cater to a... specific group of friends."

He looked over at her. She was staring at him. The look gave him an uneasy feeling.

She looked back at the oven and said, "I'm going to need you to clean that out, but not until later. I want you to start with the bathrooms, then dust the rooms I showed you..."

"Okay."

"...then sweep, vacuum and mop. You do have Murphy's Oil Soap for the hardwood, right?"

"Yes, ma'am," Carl assured her.

"Also, there's a room that I didn't show you that I need you to clean. Don't worry about the upstairs at all," she said. "We won't be going up there tonight."

"Okay," he said. "Oh, before I forget, I'm going to need a check before I leave today."

"Fine, fine, I'm not worried about that," she said, waving a hand in his general direction.

Well, I am, lady, he thought to himself. He'd been jilted in the past, and small claims court is too much of a pain in the ass to deal with.

The job went smoothly after he finally got started. He didn't see his client for the entire first two hours. The first floor was huge, and there were plenty of things to be cleaned and dusted. The odd thing was that they really didn't need to be. The house was pretty much spotless. Still, he went around and cleaned everything she specified. He didn't know which of his rich client's might have nanny cam's watching.

Whatever, he thought, I'm getting paid by the hour.

After he'd finished most of his work, he went to the other room she'd mentioned. The door was shut, but the knob turned when he tried it. He reached for the light switch and the room lit up. Carl was confronted by what looked like a room from a museum of natural history. Masks, weapons and clothes from what he assumed had to be some sort of African tribe.

There were also several framed photographs hanging on the walls and sitting on tables. All of the furniture appeared to be handmade. He looked around with interest at everything. There were even three 'shrunken heads' hanging from a hook on the wall.

They have to be fake, he thought to himself. He started to wonder how many of the items would say 'Made in China' if he turned them over. He picked up a small statue and went to turn it over.

"I can assure you, they're all authentic."

Carl jumped a bit, almost dropping the item he was holding. He managed to regain it, then set it back down on the table.

"Really?" he asked. "It's an amazing collection. How on earth did you get all of this stuff?"

She looked slowly around the room and then back at Carl. Again, he felt uneasy as she looked at him, like a fly trapped in a spider's web.

He looked at her again, thinking how much she looked like a mousy librarian or schoolteacher.

She spoke after a while. "I was a missionary to the Fangres tribe in Africa for several years. They were gifts from those I served."

"Wow, that must have been...interesting," he said.

"It was very... enlightening. My compatriots called them heretics and idol worshipers. I prefer to think of them as more... misunderstood," she replied. "Now, enough idle chit-chat. You've got more work to do. I've changed my mind. I don't need you to clean in here."

She turned and left the room, calling to him over her shoulder. "Just come with me to the kitchen. I want you to finish up in there."

He glanced back around the room, his eyes resting on the apparently real human heads. Real, huh?

Carl picked up his cleaning kit and headed back to the kitchen. She already had the oven open for him. Obviously, that was her main cleaning concern.

He didn't like to use the harsh oven cleaners for this type of job, especially in someone's house. While in the army, he'd pulled plenty of KP duty, and had found that nothing worked better than soapy water, a steel cleaning pad, a green pad, and some good old elbow grease.

He looked into the oven and again noticed it really didn't look too bad. There was a bit of burned-on food at the bottom, mainly towards the back, but other than that, it shouldn't take much to get it looking nearly new.

The oven was pretty deep, so when he'd taken the racks out and got to cleaning it, he found he almost had to crawl inside in order to get to the worst of the filth.

"It's funny, Carl," the woman said. "Looking at you as you work inside the oven reminds me of a story the tribal elders would tell. It's about a warlock who ate the tribe's children, and was later tricked into the fire himself."

Carl stopped scrubbing so he could listen.

She began stepping closer so she could lean into the oven. "You probably know the European tale of Hansel and Gretel, yes?"

"Yeah, of course," he said a bit shakily.

"Well, same basic concept," she said, looking in behind him. "Don't forget the very back."

He scrubbed harder, faster, almost feeling hands pushing him deeper inside. His mind was telling him that the walls of the oven were getting hotter.

Then, he was finally done, and crawling back out of the oven, pulling his cleaning bucket along with him. He took off the latex gloves he was wearing and wiped the sweat from his brow. The woman was standing nearby, looking down into the oven.

"Looks wonderful," she said.

"I'm glad," Carl replied. He paused for a moment and then said, "You know, I thought for a second..."

"That I was a witch, and was going push you into the oven and cook you, clothes and all?"

He chuckled uncomfortably. "I..." was all he got out before the blade sliced his throat open. Blood sprayed over the counter and bathed the woman in red. He grabbed his neck, trying in vain to stem the flow, but warm blood pulsed between his fingers.

"That's ridiculous," she laughed. "I'm not a savage. I have to clean you before I cook you."

She reached for him, easily bearing his weight to the floor.

She looked around the kitchen, her eyes taking in the blood splatter. The last thing Carl heard before fading into the black empty was, "You've made quite a mess, dear. Too bad you won't be around to help me clean it up."

THE FIRST KILL

MARK M. JOHNSON

Cool blue eyes watched them through the two-way looking glass. Although he couldn't see them in the darkened room, the prisoner's eyes still seemed to shift back and forth between the two detectives.

His hands remained chained to the table, despite his lawyer's protests. Still, he wore a bemused smirk on his handsome face, as if his arrest were some kind of practical joke. He tossed back his head, shifting his long, blond locks from his handsome face, and laughed.

Detective Ron Novak, a large man with a slight pot belly, crew cut black hair, and a cold cup of coffee in his hand, walked up to the glass. "Smug asshole, do you think he'll crack?"

Detective Joe Neidermeijer, the taller and thinner of the pair, pursed his lips and shook his balding head. "Doesn't matter, Ron, we've got enough physical evidence to serve up that filthy rich bastard on one of his silver platters, and he knows it."

"Still," Detective Novak sighed; he took a drink from the cold cup and grimaced. "It'd be nice to seal it up with a nice juicy confession."

Detective Neidermeijer grimaced, "Bad choice of words."

Detective Novak glanced over his shoulder and sighed. "Yeah, sorry."

In the interrogation room, the attorney slid his chair back and stood. He smoothed his five thousand dollar suit and then turned to the two-way mirror, motioning for the detectives to return to the room.

"Here we go," Detective Neidermeijer said.

They left the viewing room and paused outside the door to the interrogation room. Something unspoken passed between them and then they opened the door and walked into where the bloodsucking lawyer and his murdering client waited.

"Gentlemen," Mr. Stein offered his hand, which both detectives ignored. Stein dropped his hand and nodded. "Detectives," he said, correcting himself. "My client, against my advice, wishes to make a conditional confession."

"Tell your *client*, he can shove his conditions right up his ass next to that silver spoon!" Detective Neidermeijer snorted.

"Hold on, Joe," Detective Novak said, placing a hand on his partner's arm.

Detective Neidermeijer shook off the hand and glared down at the chained prisoner. "No, Ron! Fuck him and his goddamned confession." Joe took another step closer and jabbed his finger in the prisoner's face. "We got you, motherfucker!"

The prisoner gazed up into Joe's eyes impassively and grinned. "Yes you do," he said in the silly Irish accent of the Lucky Charms leprechaun from the TV commercials advertising the sugar infused breakfast cereal. "And a fine bit o' police work it was, if I do say so me-self!" He giggled manically and danced in his seat. "They've got me lucky charms, they do!"

Shifting into the richly emotionless monotone of a TV news anchor, the animated glee on the prisoner's face melted into deadly seriousness. "Late last night," he said, mimicking a recent news report. "Twenty-nine-year-old, multi-billionaire and globe trotting playboy, Dominic Sebastian Whittington, was arrested after the discovery of a hidden mausoleum on the grounds of his home near Dallas, Texas. The mass tomb is believed to contain the remains of at least one hundred or more missing young women." He paused and grinned, showing off his perfect glaringly white teeth for dramatic effect. "Many of the remains showed signs of what the authorities are describing as, 'cannibalistic mutilation'. The authorities have declared the entire, four-hundred square yard estate a crime scene."

"Oh, yeah," Detective Neidermeijer said. "You're fucking bat shit, right? Is that a preview of what we're gonna see in court, rich boy?"

"Detectives, please," Mr. Stein said, pulling their attention away from his performing client. "The remains discovered on my client's property are not of local victims, or so he claims. If you meet his meager demands, he's willing to help in the identification process."

Detective Neidermeijer narrowed his eyes and looked back to the rich killer shackled to the table. "What the fuck does he want?"

Mr. Stein smiled benignly, "He simply wishes for the two of you to sit and listen to his story and confession—over drinks."

Detective Neidermeijer laughed harshly as he continued to stare down his amused prisoner. "Fuck you, asshole!" he shouted, and leaned closer to the prisoner's bemused face. "I got better things to do than listen to this freak boast about his kills!"

"Joe," Detective Novak said and motioned towards the empty seats across the table from the smiling prisoner. "It's worth a listen."

"It's fucking bullshit, Ron, is what it is!" Detective Neidermeijer grumbled as he moved to one of the empty seats and sat down heavily. Detective Novak sat beside him, looked across at the rich boy killer, and motioned for the nut-job to take the floor.

"Thank you, Detectives," Mr. Stein said and retook his own seat as he dialed a number on his cell phone. "You can bring it in now," he said into the phone.

The prisoner's eyes flicked to his attorney and then back to the two men responsible for his arrest. "I'll take a top shelf long island iced tea, please."

"You've got to be shitting me," Detective Neidermeijer laughed, and then stopped short when someone knocked on the door.

Detective Novak rose, stepped to the door, and opened it. He spoke briefly with someone and then turned to look at his partner with an incredulous look on his face. "There's a fucking bartender here, with a portable bar and a waitress."

Detective Neidermeijer smiled and gazed back at the prisoner. "Big money motherfucker, huh?" He looked back at his partner, "Fuck it, let 'em in, I could use a drink."

"Okay, let him in," Detective Novak said and stepped back while holding the door open. A smartly dressed bartender along with a stunning blond server entered the room with a large-wheeled cart. Detective Novak closed the door behind them and returned to his seat.

"Long island top shelf," Dominic ordered; he looked down at his manacled hands and sighed. "With a straw."

"Yes, sir," the bartender replied and began mixing the drink. The server set the drink down in front of Dominic minutes later and stepped back. "Anyone else?" she asked.

Detective Neidermeijer grunted, "Jack Daniels, neat," and reached into his pocket.

"The drinks are on Mr. Whittington," Mr. Stein said.

"I ain't drinking anything that freak pays for," Joe said and flipped through the bills and tossed a few of them onto the table.

"Thank you, sir," the server said as she placed Joe's drink down in front of him and scooped up the cash. The server stepped back and looked expectantly at the other two men. Detective Novak waved her off and Mr. Stein smiled and shook his head.

Dominic took a sip from his drink and sighed contentedly. "Ah, that hits the spot," he said and smacked his lips.

"Okay, asshole," Detective Neidermeijer said to the prisoner. "Lets get this freak train rolling."

Dominic smiled devilishly. "I'm going tell you a little story about a fishing trip I went on with my father when I was fourteen." His impish smiled faded. He took a long slow drink from his glass, and his eyes misted over with memories of the past.

"Once my father told me that everything that he had would be all mine someday; his legacy to me." Dominic looked up over the rim of his glass into Detective Neidermeijer's eyes. "Are your parents going to leave you anything?" He frowned sadly. "Or are they dead already?"

Detective Neidermeijer hissed and gritted his teeth. "Watch it," he growled.

Dominic shrugged. "My father left me a little over sixteen billion dollars, and that's just the available cash assets." He took a long slow deep breath and blew it out in a whistle.

"Now that's a lot of wealth, you know what I mean? There's almost nothing you can't do with that kind of money. I didn't want to sit around waiting for the old man to grow old and croak forty or fifty years later to have it, so I...moved things along."

Dominic began to sway back and forth as he broke into song. "So, just sit right back and you'll here a tale, a tale of a fateful trip, that started from this Texas port, aboard this fishing yacht." Dominic sang out, mimicking an old TV show theme song. He looked up again at his audience for any reaction or response, and let out a sigh when he saw they were unimpressed. "Okay, on with the story," he sighed in mock disappointment.

"It was the annual fishing trip, my Father, Benjamin Theodore Whittington, loved to fish for sharks. I don't really know why. Maybe it was the feeling of power you get when you hunt down and kill something that can kill you also." He smiled softly as he drifted back into the memories of days gone by. "Every year, we went out in one part of the world or another. When I was ten, I watched him pull a massive great white shark out of the ocean off the coast of Australia, now that was something to see let me tell you!

"On the last trip, we went out closer to home, or at least closer to one of our homes. We have places all over the world, you see. I've lived in almost every one of them at one time or another. I'm kind of from everywhere and nowhere at the same time.

"My mother died in childbirth. Doesn't that make me a natural born killer?" Dominic laughed softly at his personal joke. "So, it was just me and my father together against the world. But I hardly ever saw him. He had me shipped off to the four corners of the earth for just about everything. I also had a small army of handlers and nannies, so in all reality, I hardly knew my own father." Deep inside the dark corners of his black heart, something stirred when he thought of his father. A dark storm gathered in his eyes and something moved inside him, some inexplicable emotion at the bottom of his black empty heart.

"I had it planned right from the start, so it was definitely pre-meditated—premeditated all to hell. We were out in the middle of the Gulf of Mexico when I put my plan of tragedy, death, and destruction into action." He took another pull on his drink, though he kept his eyes closed, lost in the past.

"I used that shit that veterinarians use to put the family pet down, sodium pentobarbital. It really wasn't difficult to get a hold of when you have almost unlimited resources. I had eight syringes loaded with massive overdoses of it, enough in each to kill a horse. I only needed six really, but I wanted to err on the side of caution, you see. We were on a five day fishing trip in the gulf, so I waited until the first night to move them onboard the fishing yacht Dark River. Don't you just love that name for a boat? Anyway, onboard there was my father and I, my father's little brother, Nicolas, my late mother's older brother, Bradley, and my father's two cousins, William and Gregory, and our fearless yacht owner, Captain Barnaby.

"They were all dead the moment they stepped onto that boat, every last man in my entire immediate family all in one place. The entire group of heir's to the family fortune in one hit, how lucky is that?" Dominic's eyelids clenched shut tighter, his brow furrowed as the excitement of the memory took hold.

"I did the captain first. I waited until after three in the morning to be sure everyone would be out. They were all early risers, so I was confident they would be out by then. When I crept up to the captain's room, I saw the light under the door and realized he was still up, so I had to think fast to stay on schedule. I'd seen the way he was looking at me when no one else was watching, so I got an idea.

"When I opened the captain's door and walked into his room, I was wearing nothing but my briefs. I had the syringe hidden in one hand and my other hand was over my crotch. He was lying on his bunk when I opened the door. I think he'd been diddling himself, because he jumped up and I could see his hard-on just before he pulled his boxers up. I think he said something like, 'What the hell are you doing boy?' I just stood there trying to look like a frightened, confused little boy. I never said a word to him. Hell, I was struggling not to laugh.

"Captain Joe Barnaby was somewhere in the neighborhood of sixty or so, balding with an old captain's paunch. The guy was an old Texas sailor, with the whole salt of the sea southern accent. I'd taken a big chance on him being a little boy lover. I would have been in some very deep shit if he had tried to march me down to my father's cabin to tell him I was a little ass-fucking fairy. However, it just so happened that I'd hit the nail on the head with this one. He rushed past me, and after looking out of the door to check the hallway, he closed the door and smiled at me with a heat in his eyes. He just kind of slithered over and got down on his knees in front of me. Can you believe that shit?"

Dominic opened his eyes, glanced over his glass at the detectives, and was delighted to see he had their undivided attention. Satisfied, he closed his eyes again and returned to his story.

"Well, I was hard already, and that's what he saw. I'll just bet he thought I was hard for him. Shit, I know that's what he thought, because he said so. 'Oh, damn, boy, ya'll all ready for me, ain't ya?' He drawled at me, barely able to keep his hands from shaking as he pulled my briefs down.

"I was hard on account of the thrill of killing someone for the first time, you see. I let him go to work on me for a minute, and then, just as he was getting into it, I popped the cap on the needle and slammed it into his neck! Oh, man, what a reaction I got. He fell back and I pulled the syringe out, looking at me like, 'what the hell did you just do?' Then he just fell over and that was it; my first kill! And then I went and jerked off right on his dead body. Damn that was a good time!"

Dominic peeked out through closed eyelids, and upon seeing that he had disturbed the two cops with his story, he continued.

"The rest of the guys on the yacht went like clock work. I snuck in and stuck 'em in their sleep and that was that. Kind of like an anticlimax after all that crazy shit with the captain. I looked at it like a job that had to be done, with the quick and efficient professionalism you would expect from a blossoming killer such as myself. By four-thirty it was all over, my father and I were the only living people on the boat." Opening his eyes quickly, Dominic caught them with looks of confusion on their faces.

"Ha! Gotcha!" he called out to them as if they were school playmates. "I bet you thought I took out my dad the same way I got the others, didn't you?" He did a little dance in his seat and then returned to his tale. "Well, I wasn't going to let the old man off so easy, I had far more grandiose plans for him. Like I said, all of the guys on this fishing trip were early risers. My father was no exception. You could set your watch to him. Honest, he was nothing if not punctual, a man of ritual and habit. Just like every other day, he was up at five and in the shower. By twenty after five, he'd brushed his teeth and was getting dressed for the day, and that's when I went for him.

"From the moment we reached the middle of the gulf, we were chumming. Do you know what chumming is? Have you seen the movie Jaws?" He mimicked the theme from the film, but the detectives said nothing and he sighed in disappointment.

"Anyway, we were dumping fish guts, parts, and blood into the water the whole previous day and night. It's a big part of shark fishing. It's how you draw them in. It's the bait. Well, I stood outside of my father's room, and got myself all worked up and excited looking. Then went running into his room, acting like the enthusiastic little boy on a shark fishing trip I was supposed to be.

"I hollered, all out of breath. 'Dad, Dad! I was out chumming and I saw a big one! He was circling the boat, and came right up off the starboard quarter! I swear I looked right in his eyes, you gotta come see, hurry!' I was pulling on his arm, dragging him down the hall and up onto the deck. 'Okay, okay, I'm coming,' he's saying. I got him over a beam to starboard and pointed down excitedly into the water, 'There, that's where I saw him!' "The sun was just starting to come up over the horizon and the water was dark and murky. He was looking deep into that dark water, when I pointed down right next to the starboard hull. 'There!' I screamed. 'There he is,' and that gullible fucker bent over and looked hard into the water; he really wanted to see that shark. I took a few steps back, planted my foot right into his ass, and kicked him over the side."

Dominic laughed quietly at the memory, and then continued. "He went over screaming like a mad man, and who can blame him? His son had just tossed his ass into the gulf in the middle of a blood slick. I didn't waste any time. The ladder he would need to climb back onto the boat was only a short swim away at the stern. I ran up to the wheelhouse and cranked up the motor, then pulled away and left him treading water."

Dominic giggled. "Oh, boy, was he pissed, you should have heard the shit he was screaming at his little boy. I got about a hundred yards or so away from him and stopped. I let him tire himself out trying to catch up to the boat. When he got within thirty yards or so, I tossed him a life vest."

Dominic looked up and sighed. "The life vests have these little flashing lights and transmitters attached, so that the coast guard could find you if you went overboard. The life vest I tossed to my completely enraged father had this little amenity torn off. Without saying a word to him, I tossed out the life vest, then ran up to the wheelhouse and put a little distance between us again. My dad was in excellent health and a superb swimmer, so it didn't take long for him to catch up to the yacht. I really had to stay up on deck for the first hour. The entire time he was out there screaming for help, I never said a word. I just smiled at him, and waved like nothing was wrong. Boy, did that ever drive him fucking loopy."

Dominic slapped his hand against the table, jingling his chains and guffawed, "What a hoot!" He sighed and took another drink before returning to the past. "After an hour of driving the yacht away from him every few minutes, he finally got the idea and stopped trying to catch up to the boat. He just kind of floated out there, silent and pissed off. This gave me some time to drag all of the bodies of my dead relatives and the little boy-loving captain onto the main deck. While I was bustin' my ass in this rather arduous task, my father started calling out for help again, calling for the captain and his other buddies that he thought were still alive on the death boat. By this time, the sun had gotten high in the sky, and it was really heating up out there.

"You really should've seen the look on his face when I started chumming again, with the body parts of the people he was calling to for help. That was the first time I ever had the chance to dismember a human body. Let me tell you, it's not as easy as you think it's going to be," he chuckled.

"Of course, I did have a little experience in cutting up the bodies of small animals from biology class in school and all, but I had never dismembered a human body from head to toe before. He was floating out there, screaming for the captain. That's why I went to work on Barnaby the pedophile first. When I held up that fat ass, little boy fucking freak's head for my dad to see, he finally shut up. And when I tossed the head out into the water right next to him, he started calling out to Jesus."

Dominic swayed from side to side in his seat and laughed quietly. "Oh, man, that was some funny shit, my dad of all people, calling out to Jesus. For the next couple of hours, I just got into chopping up the bodies; I was wearing only a pair of shorts and deck shoes. By the time I had most of the hardest work done, I was totally covered in blood and sweat. I must've looked like a fucking lunatic to my dad, who was still out there bobbing around in the water, calling out to God. And that's when I got to thinking about lunch."

Dominic paused and smiled again; his eyes glittered with excitement as he caught the reluctant expectation in the eyes of the two detectives sitting across from him. "Yes, it's exactly what you're thinking. All that fresh meat just lying there on the deck, and I found myself wondering what it would taste like."

"So, you're saying you ate your own relatives?" Ron whispered harshly.

Dominic laughed heartily. "Barbecued aristocrat, you'd be surprised just how decadently delish it really is."

"I'll pass, are we done yet, fuck nut?" Joe grunted.

"Oh, no, Detective, there's more," Dominic giggled. "As I was indulging in my pulled flesh barbeque sandwich, I broke the silent treatment I was giving my soon-to-be-dead father. 'You have two choices,' I hollered out to him between bites. That got the babbling fucker to shut up, all that calling out to God and his forsaken son was getting on my nerves by then anyway. 'You're going to die today,' I told him, 'but how you die is up to you.'

"'Why are you doing this, son?' He had the nerve to ask me, I mean really, I'd just murdered and dismembered all of his closest friends and family, and then tossed their body parts into the gulf. Fuck, his own brother's body parts were floating out there with him, and he's asking me why? 'The sharks will be here soon if they're not already,' I said to him, 'you can either float there and wait for them to find you, or you can ditch the jacket and drown yourself. It's up to you.' He just floated out there, all quiet like, thinking about it for a few minutes, and then he started cursing me to hell and back. Holy shit, man, I never imagined he could talk like that, the filthy words that were coming out of his mouth would've made a sailor puke.

"'Well, that's fine and all,' I said, 'but one way or the other you're still gonna be fish food before the sun sets.' 'You go to fucking hell,' he said to me. 'Everybody has their dues in life to pay,' I told him, 'and today your number's up.'

"Right there, at that moment, as if on queue, the first dorsal fin broke the surface about fifty yards off to the south. He saw it too, and it shut him up real quick. He watched it circle around, then another, and another, and in the next fifteen minutes we had at least six. Then the feeding had started."

Dominic bounced in his seat like an overly excited child as his memory took him back. "He looked around at the bloody, splashing water where the sharks were feeding on the chum, and then he looked up at me. I should be dead right now with the look he threw my way, I don't think I've ever seen a colder more raging hate-filled pair of eyes."

He sighed deeply and his eyes softened. "Then, without another word, he slipped out of the jacket and went under. 'You fucking coward!' I yelled out to him, but he was long gone. If you knew my father as I did, though, you would know that there was no fucking way he was going to go down without a fight. No way was he gonna take his own life. He wasn't going to go gently into that good night. So I sat back on one of the deck chairs and waited. Now, I have to give credit where credit's due! It had to have taken a lot of balls to swim under water through all those sharks, and then just sit there in that bloody water on the end of the deck ladder for almost an hour. But that's what he did. So I just sat there on the deck waiting, the sounds of the feeding sharks, seagulls, and waves lapping up against the side of the boat lulling me into a half-sleep. Then I see it, his hand slowly coming into view over the edge of the deck as he climbed the deck ladder. I let him get almost all the way up, until I could see the whole upper half of his body. He saw me laying there, looking like I was asleep, still covered in all the blood from my hard work of body dismembering. Then I sat up and pulled a gun out from under my leg where I'd been hiding it. I was pointing his own gun at him."

He giggled again like a small child pulling the wings off a fly. "The same chrome-plated pearl handled 9mm Smith & Wesson revolver he always carried with him everywhere, was now in the hands of his killer, who just happened to also be his only son. He just hung there for a second, looking into my eyes with this grim determination."

Dominic's eyes widened as he once again saw his father in his mind's eye. "Then screaming like a madman, he leaped up onto the deck from off the ladder. But before he could get over the edge and onto the deck, I put three rounds into his stomach. He fell back over and into the water, and right into a shitload of hungry sharks in the grip of a feeding frenzy. I stood on the edge of the deck, watching them rip him apart, it took about two minutes of him screaming and the sharks hitting him every few seconds, and then it was over. I was almost hypnotized by watching the sharks eat him, I just stood there in absolute awe at what I had accomplished. Then it was time to finish up. I went down and got cleaned up a bit, then headed back to the wheelhouse and got the yacht underway. For the next day and a half, I motored that bloody yacht across the gulf, almost one hundred miles from where I put everyone into the water. Then I put the finishing touches, on my little patricide adventure.

"Using my extraordinary talent for mimicking voices, I put in a quick SOS call to the coast guard in captain boy fucker's Texas drawl. Then set the timer on the little bomb I had brought along; I put it next to the fuel tank. Just to make it look good, I dumped a little fuel on the deck, lit it up and walked through it and got myself a little burned up, but not too bad. Then I grabbed myself a life-jacket, activated the homing device, and jumped into the gulf."

Dominic sighed and sat back as if he were exhausted from the telling of his tale. "Now you have to admit, I was taking a very big chance jumping into the water like that. I mean, I could have been eaten by sharks just like I'd done to my dad. I swam as far from the boat as I could in the five minutes I had left on the bomb's timer. Then in a fucking blaze of glory, that bastard blew! Man, what a sight, there was one muffled explosion, then nothing for a few seconds, and I'm thinking I screwed up. Then, *kaboom!* That bitch went up like the Fourth of July! Five minutes later it was gone, nothing but black smoke in the sky and a debris-laden oil slick on the surface of the water.

"I was out there for almost four hours before the first helicopter flew past, those incompetent assholes flew past me twice before they found me. Then it was over, a terrible tragedy, almost an entire family lost, with me being the only survivor. Everyone felt so bad for me, and I played the role of the grief-stricken son perfectly. I'm telling you, I should have won the Oscar for my performance."

Dominic went silent for a full minute in an introspective trance, as he slowly shook off the cobwebs of the past and found his way back to the present. When he finally opened his eyes, he found the two detectives and his lawyer looking at him with what he thought was stunned, silent admiration.

"I know, fucking amazing, huh?" Dominic asked his audience.

Detective Neidermeijer shook his head. "I think I'm gonna throw a party after they hook you up to the lethal injection machine and end your miserable life."

Dominic shook his head in mock sadness. "They're not going to kill me, Joe," he whispered conspiratorially with a smirk. Then he leaned forward and whispered louder. "You know all those bodies you found; all the sweet young ladies that I fucked, and then bit to death? He laughed and sat back with a self-satisfied sneer on his handsome face. "That's right, boys; it's true, I ate them to death, raw, bitch-Tar Tar." He giggled, clicked his teeth together, then licked his lips lavishly and flashed a smile. "I've developed a taste for it over the years."

"You sick bastard," Ron said.

"Yeah, well, I'll give you that, but those bitches; they're from all over the world, man. Fifteen, no wait, sixteen from Great Britain, fourteen from France, quite a few more from Germany, some from Australia, a shit load from Mexico. A lot of them were vacationing Americans and Europeans. Hell, and that's just in the first year. I reaped those sweet little tasty young morsels from all over the world. You and me, Joe, we're gonna be solving a lot of unsolved missing person's cases." He laughed merrily. "Plus, I'll bet there'll be enough extradition requests to keep me alive for years."

For the past few minutes, Detective Neidermeijer had nearly grinded his teeth to dust and then the weakening dam holding back his fury burst. He thrust himself upwards, knocking back his chair as he stood. Reaching behind him, he snagged the chair and lifted it high over his head, aiming for Dominic's head.

"Joe, no!" Detective Novak shouted and grasped the chair before Joe could bring it down. "It's what he wants, man, think!"

Dominic never flinched at the chair hovering threateningly over his head. "Aaaand in this corner!" he shouted, mimicking the familiar old voice of Howard Cosell. "We have the chained and helpless, Dominic Whittington."

"I'm going to be there, when they pump you full of poison," Joe said coldly as he allowed his partner to pull the chair from his hands. "Right or wrong, I still ought to plug you now and save the tax payers some money."

"Well, Joe," Dominic continued in the famous sports caster's voice. "What's right isn't always popular. What's popular isn't always right. And you can quote me on that!" He broke down into uncontrollable laughter that mimicked a famous psychotic joke-ster. "Oh, come on, Joe, why so serious?"

A ringing cell phone broke into Dominic's insane laughter and he fell silent. "I believe that's your phone, Detective Novak," he whispered in an expectant tone.

Detective Novak looked down at the phone on his belt, realizing that the prisoner was right. He unclipped it, looked at the un-known number on the display and then lifted it to his ear. "Detec-tive Novak," he said. "Baby?" he asked with deep, unsettling worry creeping into his voice. His face blanched and he stopped breath-ing as his face twisted with confusion.

"Jenny!" he hollered. A storm of rage blew in, settling in his eyes as his grip threatened to shatter the little cell phone. "Who the hell is this? Hello? Hello!" His breaths came in gasps and the phone beeped in his hand, announcing the arrival of a photo.

Joe put his hand on his partner's shoulder. "What's going on Ron? Who was that?" Detective Novak held the phone out to where they both could see the photo that had appeared on the screen.

"Your own partner was fucking your little sister," Dominic purred. "And you didn't even break his nose for it." He shrugged his shoulders and laughed softly. "At least he made an honest woman of her, and that niece and nephew of yours, Joe, they're really gorgeous kids."

Detective Novak placed the phone down on the table and stalked around it towards the shackled prisoner.

"Detective, so help me if you place your hands on my client!" Mr. Stein shouted as he jumped to his feet.

Joe slammed his hands onto the lawyer's shoulders and forced him back into his seat. "The game has changed, asshole. If you want to live through this night, I suggest you shut the fuck up," Joe growled.

Detective Novak kicked the chair out from beneath Dominic and grasped the prisoner's throat with both hands as Dominic fell to his knees.

"Where are they?" Detective Novak asked as he started to squeeze Dominic's neck.

"Don't know," Dominic gasped.

Detective Novak's face twisted, as grief-stricken fear and inconsolable rage fought a war to a stalemate in his shifting features. "Where are they, you bastard?" he screamed. "Where are they?" he yelled repeatedly as he drew back a clenched fist to then pummel Dominic's face with it.

Dominic fell limply to the floor under the enraged detective's assault, only his manacled hands preventing him from sliding all the way to the floor.

"Ron!" Joe shouted as he came around and pulled the raging man away from the beaten prisoner. "You're gonna kill him."

"They took Jenny and the kids, Joe," he sobbed in a blind rage as he struggled with his partner. "I'll fucking kill you," he growled tearfully at Dominic. "I swear to God Almighty, I'll fucking kill you!"

Mr. Stein rushed around and helped his client back into his chair. "I'll have your badges for this," he said sharply. "This is unacceptable, this is..."

Detective Novak interrupted the chastising lawyer with an avalanche of obscenities. "You can have my fucking badge," he spat. "You can have it after I cut your client's throat with it."

Dominic spat blood from his busted mouth, and leaning forward, he reached into his bloody mouth with his fingers. After feeling around inside for a few seconds, he laughed. "I can't believe I still have all my teeth!" he mumbled with his swelling lips. "Those were some impressive blows, Ron. Beaten quite a few helpless prisoners, have you?"

Detective Novak struggled in his partner's arms. "You're fucking dead, I swear, if anything happens to them..."

"No, Ron," Dominic snarled loudly. "Something already has happened to them. And they *will* be dead, unless I get what I need from you and your partner. Right fucking now!"

"What do you want?" Joe asked venomously as he continued to hold his weakening partner back.

Dominic smiled, showing his bloody teeth. "I don't really need to tell you what my people can do to that lovely woman and your kids, do I?" He sat back in his chair and spat a wad of bloody phlegm onto the floor. "No, I'll just let your imagination run wild on that one."

Detective Novak's heart rose into his throat and he screamed in agony. He struggled against his partner's hold for a few more seconds and then went limp.

"What the fuck," Ron sobbed out with frustrated rage. "Let me go, man, I got it, I'm okay." He gently pulled free of Joe's hold, his breath coming in deep shuddering gasps as he regained control of himself. His face twisted with violent wrath, as tears gathered in his raging eyes, and his body trembled with barely contained violence as he leaned over the table. "What the hell do you want from me?"

Dominic leaned forward and gazed into the watery, bloodshot, wrathful eyes of Detective Novak. "First," he said softly, "I want to assure you, that I have no interest in your family other than the unfortunate need to use them in this circumstance. Your wife's a bit too aged for me, old bitches are a little gamey. Your daughter's a bit young, I never touch anything under sixteen, and it's not quite tenderized yet. Hey, even I have standards! And the boy, well, let's just say I don't swing that way."

This gave no obvious comfort to Detective Novak; his raging eyes misted over and spilled onto the table. "What do you *want!*" he shouted, punctuating his question by pounding his fist on the table.

Dominic smiled. "Freedom, of course. Rebecca?" He addressed the server by name as she stood in the corner of the small room. Ron turned and looked over his shoulder at the bartender and his server, whom everyone had forgotten. They both stood with their backs against the wall behind the prisoner. Despite the horrid details of the prisoner's story, and the violence perpetrated on him by Detective Novak, they both appeared unnaturally at ease. The server locked eyes with Dominic at the mention of her name and nodded. With the cold efficiency of a professional killer, she retrieved a small silenced pistol from behind her back and executed the bartender with a single shot to the head.

"Jesus Christ!" Joe shouted, reaching instinctively for his weapon, but his hand found nothing as no weapons were allowed in the interrogation room. "Shit!" he gasped as the woman turned her weapon on the two detectives.

Dominic laughed and whooped as he bounced in his seat. "Holy shit! You should have seen your faces, guys," he snickered. "Priceless!"

The killer waitress, kept her eyes on the stunned detectives as she reached into a pocket and tossed a handcuff key onto the table.

"No need to worry, boys," Dominic said as he quickly freed himself with the key. "She's not going to kill you, unless you force her to." He stood and hurried over to the bar cart.

"How the fuck did you get a gun in here?" Joe growled.

"Really, Joe?" Dominic heaved a sigh. "You'd be surprised what a few million dollars cash bribes can get you." Using some soda water and a towel, he cleaned himself up, grimacing as he wiped the blood from his swelling lips. "I just need you to sit down and be quiet, and marvel at my ingenuity as I make my daring escape." He giggled again as he stripped out of his clothes and began dressing in a spare bartender's outfit stowed in the bar cart.

Detective Novak watched the gun-toting server with fiery eyes as he took his seat. His partner followed suit, his eyes moving from the silenced weapon in her hands to the dressing serial killer. "Where're you gonna run to, asshole? We've frozen all your money!" Joe said.

Dominic glanced up as he buttoned his shirt, beaming with happiness. "That's not even a tenth of my holdings. I was prepared for this, Detective. Where did you think that anonymous tip came from?" He chuckled softly. "I led you to me. I was getting bored with the same ol' same ol'. Oh, man, this is going to be so much fun!" He turned to his attorney as he pulled the jacket over his shoulders. "Stein, what's the time?"

The lawyer looked down at the Rolex on his wrist, "Quarter past ten at night," he said, and then noticed the two detectives glaring at him. "I had no prior knowledge of my client's intentions here," he said smugly.

"Not to worry, Steiny. Oh, and you're fired," Dominic said casually as he nodded to Rebecca. The pretty killer turned her weapon on the stunned lawyer and put a round through his head, splattering the detectives with brains and blood.

"Fuck me!" Joe gasped.

His partner merely wiped the blood spatter from his face and continued to glare at Dominic.

"I've wanted to do that for years! I fucking hate lawyers," Dominic said in a singsong voice. He retrieved two sets of handcuffs from the bar cart and tossed them to the detectives. "I'll need you to cuff yourselves to the table legs now, if you don't mind." The two men complied reluctantly while Dominic smiled down at them.

Dominic walked around the two men and took the Rolex from his murdered lawyer's wrist. He held it up and began counting down. "Three, two, one," he said, and then the lights went out. After a brief moment of complete darkness, the emergency lights came on, casting the interrogation room into murky shadows.

"Right on time!" Dominic yelled and cackled like the wicked witch of the west. "Well, that's my cue, boys." He walked back around the table. "But before I go..." Dominic suddenly grabbed his chair, picked it up, and swung it savagely into Detective Novak's face. Ron cried out and fell back to the floor, his face a bloody ruin.

"You bastard!" Joe shouted.

"Tit for tat, Detective, just returning the favor," he said, gesturing to his busted lips.

"I'll find you," Detective Novak mumbled through his broken teeth and crushed lips. "And when I do, there won't be an arrest."

"I sincerely hope you try your best, Detective, it'll keep this interesting," Dominic said and then unceremoniously followed his female assassin out of the door, closing it behind him.

Seconds passed, and then the door opened once more.

Dominic leaned in holding the silenced pistol. "Oh, yeah, about your wife and kids." His mouth twisted in a cruel grin and he winked mischievously. "I lied," he said as he smacked his lips

The first shot took Detective Joe Neidermeijer in the face just above his nose, and he fell without a sound. The second shot blew off the top of Detective Ron Novak's head, cutting off the detective's blood-curdling scream.

Dominic tossed the gun with his fingerprints all over it onto the floor. "Let the games begin," he giggled, and closed the door behind him.

COOKING WITH GRACE

WILLIAM TODD ROSE

Hand-delivered by courier to the office of Ms. Grace Agnolotti, The Packer Building, 1400 Central Avenue, Suite 856 at 1:34 PM, Wednesday August 13th.

Dear Ms. Agnolotti,

In response to my initial emailed query you responded, and I quote: "As the editor of such culinary masterpieces as *Sinfully Delicious* and *The Caramel Sutra*, I do not appreciate my valuable time being wasted with such a ludicrous proposition. Packer and Sons is not in the habit of publishing 'gag' books or pandering to a sensationalism-crazed public with such ill conceived attempts at humor. Furthermore, I find your book proposal to be in extremely bad taste and pray that this abortion of a manuscript never sullies my desk with its presence. If such a document even exists to begin with, which I personally choose to believe not to be the case, then call me an optimist."

I apologize for any confusion my letter may have caused and wish to assure you that this was not an attempt to poke fun at the fine publications of your company. In fact, all eight volumes of *Cooking with Grace* line my kitchen shelves and are what inspired me to take up the knife and cleaver to begin with.

Within those sacred pages, I found something larger than myself. Something that actually made sense. The world is a chaotic whirlpool and the events that swirl around you are always trying to suck you down into the darkness of the vortex. You might think you have a firm grasp on the lifeline of reality but sooner or later an undertow comes along and wrenches it right out of your hands. You find yourself drowning in a sea of confusion, not knowing whether to swim or die, while all the flotsam and jetsam from your shipwreck of a life rips bloody gashes in your too-frail skin.

But a recipe...now that's the way life should be. Measured quantities. Clear, concise instructions. Time-tested outcomes.

So I assure you that my letter was written with the utmost levels of sincerity. I have spent many hours perfecting the techniques and ingredients detailed within the pages of *A Feast of Fools*. Not all of my little experiments were successes, of course, but these failures should not detract from the passion invested in the work as a whole. This is not a mere cookbook; it is my heart and soul, laid out for all to see. As such, I promise you that the manuscript is very, very real.

But, perhaps, you require an example of my expertise. If nothing else than to prove that I am not the jester you, and so many others, originally thought.

SWEET AND TART FANNY ROAST
Ingredients:

- 1 chunk of fresh buttock flesh (about 2 ½ to 3 pounds)
- Salt and pepper
- 2 tablespoons canola oil
- 1 medium onion, sliced
- 2/3 cup cider vinegar
- 2/3 cup apple juice
- ½ cup packed light brown sugar
- ¼ teaspoon ground allspice
- 1 tablespoon bone meal mixed w/ 2 tablespoons cold water

That, however, is just a teaser. After all, if I gave you the entire recipe, what would stop you from simply stealing it and calling it your own creation? I can advise you, though, that what separates my book from all the others currently on the market is that I do not simply address how to prepare the dishes within with it. As you stated in volume three of Cooking With Grace, nothing is more important than fresh ingredients. In light of this, I have also shared the benefit of my experience with the armchair gourmet on how to best hunt and butcher the meat for themselves. In the chapter "A Clever Ruse for Your Rue" I go into painstaking detail concerning the various means of gaining a component's trust in an overtly suspicious society. Chapter 7, "A Pound of Flesh" will be of particular interest as well. For example, few people realize how greasy and slippery the web-like fat on a still-warm cut of meat can be; but with my practical suggestions, the reader will cut their prep time in half. Perhaps another excerpt is in order, if nothing else than to further substantiate my technique and knowledge. In this section, I am instructing my students on how to best remove the silverskin which, as you know, is the thin membrane left on certain cuts of flesh once the excess fat has been trimmed away.

"Slide the tip of a sharpened knife under the shiny tissue layer and angle the honed edge of the blade upward. Next, you will want to slice back and forth while ensuring that the silverskin is pulled taut. Continue to slice the skin off using this method until all has been removed."

Are you beginning to see now? Is the realization dawning upon you that your life has been touched by the presence of a grand master?

I look forward eagerly to your reply.

You have my email address.

Write Me.

Sincerely,

xxxBuTcHeRxxx

Hand-delivered by courier to the office of Ms. Grace Agnolotti, The Packer Building, 1400 Central Avenue, Suite 856 at 11:02 AM, Wednesday August 21st.

Dear Ms. Agnolotti,

I realize that only a little over a week has passed since I last wrote. I have no doubt that you are discussing the prospects of *A Feast of Fools* with the other editors at Packer and Sons. I can only hope you are championing my masterpiece with the ardor it so rightly deserves. However, this letter is not a thinly veiled attempt at forcing you to reply to me. I realize that in the publishing world these things sometimes can take a while. And for now I am patient.

No, the true purpose of this letter is to let you know that I recently bought a copy of *Living With Grace: One Woman's Climb To The Top*. If the truth be told, I actually camped outside of the bookstore the night before it hit the racks. It was a cold night for this time of year. By the time they opened the doors at nine the following morning, my clothes were so drenched from the rain that it felt as if I had a fully grown person draped over my body. For the next few days, I had quite the case of the sniffles. So bad, in fact, that a badly timed sneeze alerted a potential *ingredient* to my presence that I was hiding in the closet. Needless to say, the menu of *coq au vin* and crisp greens I'd planned for that night was definitely no longer an option. I hated wasting perfectly good meat, but it insisted on waving that little taser around while blocking the door.

But I digress. As I was saying, I picked up a copy of your autobiography the very first day it was on sale—I find it safe to assume that I was, in all likelihood, the first person in my city to hold a copy of the book in his hands. I took it home and devoured every word, finishing it well before dinner time that evening.

Bravo, Grace—may I call you Grace? I feel like I know you so well that formalities seem stiff and awkward now, even when written.

Bravo!

I must say that I never realized how interesting of a life you have lead. When your husband died, leaving you and little Angelique to fend for yourselves in a town that didn't give a rat's ass, I found myself actually worried that things might end badly for you. The long hours flipping hash in kitchens where there were more cockroaches than talent; the frustration of having this beautiful dream of culinary school dashed against the rocks of poverty; those nagging thoughts of just ending it all during your self-described 'dark period'; you became a believable character and I was pulled into your world like never before.

I also thought the pictures spread throughout the book were a nice touch. However, I do have concerns. Angelique looked extremely pale in the full color ones. And so thin. I also couldn't help but notice the little cracks at the corners of her mouth when I studied it with my magnifying glass...am I correct in my assumption that she's anemic? That would seem to explain the high-iron trend I've noticed in practically all of your most recent recipes. And like with teenagers these days, it's almost like that sort of thing is a fad.

I understand that you love your daughter very much. Despite the long hours you put in at the office, and the constant bickering you describe in your book as hormonal insanity, you want what's best for her. And who could blame you?

Which brings me to the real point of this letter. If you'd like, I would be happy to procure the freshest liver you and your daughter could ever want to taste. I know of a clinic that specializes in the treatment of polycythemia—which is basically the polar opposite of anemia—and would have no trouble finding some iron-rich morsels to gift you with. All you have to do is say the word.

Write Me.
xxxBuTcHeRxxx

Email sent from g.agnolotti@chef.net to fresh4flesh@gmail.com at 11:10 AM, Wednesday August 21st.

THIS HAS GONE TOO FAR, YOU TWISTED LITTLE FREAK! MY COLLEAUGES ADVISED ME TO JUST IGNORE YOU AND THAT EVENTUALLY YOU'D GET TIRED OF THIS BIZARRE LITTLE GAME BUT NOW YOU'VE WENT AND BROUGHT ANGEL INTO IT AND I WILL NOT TOLERATE ANY MORE OF THESE SICK ATTEMPTS AT HUMOR. YOU SIR (AND I USE THAT TERM SO VERY LIGHTLY) NEED HELP. IF YOU HAVE NOTHING BETTER TO DO WITH YOUR TIME THAN SIT AROUND AND DREAM UP WAYS TO HARASS DECENT, HARDWORKING PEOPLE THEN PERHAPS THE WORLD WOULD BE A BETTER PLACE WITHOUT YOU IN IT!

!!!!!LEAVE.ME.ALONE!!!!!

Email sent from fresh4flesh@gmail.com to g.agnolotti@chef.net at 11:45 AM, Wednesday August 21st.

Grace, I know you've been under a lot of stress lately with the upcoming merger and all but you must understand that so have I.

When I first read your email, your message made me long to do things. Bad things. I wanted to taint the meat by rupturing intestines and spewing their rotten poison all throughout the stomach cavity. I wanted to make the livestock scream, to see it cry, to bruise the tender flesh in every way possible. I wanted to revert back to that angry, viscous beast who was trapped within the whirlpool of chaos. You and your thoughtless words did that to me. ME.

I tried to use the self-talk the court appointed therapist told me about when I was a teenager, but it's just as useless now as it was back then. I knew deep down that wasting so much quality meat simply because I was angry with you was tantamount to blasphemy. So rather than frittering my stock away, I decided to put it to good use. Forget chicken soup...there's nothing quite like a good consommé to calm the soul.

Now that my belly is full and warm and I'm thinking more rationally, I've decided to forgive you, Grace. It was a difficult decision, but if we are to have a professional relationship once *A Feast of Fools* has been published then I believe it to be the right one.

xxxBuTcHeRxxx

Email sent from g.agnolotti@chef.net to fresh4flesh@gmail.com at 11:52 AM, Wednesday August 21st.

Fuck you and your so-called cookbook! I've had enough of this shit. I'm turning over everything you've sent to the authorities. We'll see how funny you think it is when the cops are knocking down your door.

Excerpt from transcript of interview between Lt. Detective Ben Maxwell and Grace Agnolotti, 9:45 AM, Thursday August 22nd.

Maxwell: Do you have any enemies, Ms. Agnolotti? Anyone who would have something to gain from harassing you?

Agnolotti: Detective...Maxwell, is it? You don't get to where I am without stepping on a few fingers up the ladder. But this? I can't imagine how anyone could possibly expect to gain anything from this.

(*sound of rattling papers*)

Maxwell: What about your daughter? Maybe a kid at school, jealous ex-boyfriend...

Agnolotti: Angel? No...everyone loves Angel.

Maxwell: Are you sure? I mean, I know you put in a lot of hours at your office. She's home alone by herself, you can never really be quite sure what she's getting into, can you?

Agnolotti: (*long silence*) Are you calling me a bad mother, Detective? Is that what you're implying?

Maxwell: No, no, I just...I just meant sometimes, you know, kids have this secret life. A life parents aren't always welcome to and...

Agnolotti: Look, Detective, Angel and I may have our disagreements. Hell, I think on some level she blames me for her father's death as ridiculous as that may sound. But she's my daughter. I would know. I'd be able to tell. (*rustling sound*) Okay if I smoke in here?

Maxwell: It'd be fine with me, but the Health Department, well they're another story. So what does Angel make of all this, Ms. Agnolotti?

Agnolotti: (*mumbling*) Turning into a fascist society, I swear to God...(*sighs*) She doesn't make anything of it.

Maxwell: How so?

Agnolotti: Because I've never told her. Look, we get cranks and disgruntled authors all the time. Usually they vent for a bit and then we never hear from them again. It goes with the business. But this one...this guy's persistent. And I just want it to stop.

Maxwell: So, do you think that's what this is? A disgruntled author trying to make your life hell?

Agnolotti: (*short pause*) Well, correct me if I'm wrong, Detective Maxwell, but isn't it sort of your job to find that out?

Maxwell: (*sighs*) Yes. And no. I mean, right now there's not really a whole lot we can do. (*rustling sound*) I admit, these letters are downright weird. Bizarre even. But he really hasn't threatened you. We could see if maybe there's a stalking charge we could make stick. Providing we can find the guy. He's obviously fixated with you and your work.

Agnolotti: I don't care. I want it to stop.

Maxwell: We'll see what we can do, Ms. Agnolotti. Here's my card. If he contacts you again, give me a call. I'll be in touch if we turn up anything.

Agnolotti: (*angrily*) Why do I get the feeling that I'm being placated, Detective?

Maxwell: Look, ma'am, we'll do...

Agnolotti: As little as possible, I'm sure. Good day, Detective. Oh, and just a little tip. That black tie? It's way too thin for those lapels. Makes you look like a fucking moron.

```
      Email sent from g.agnolotti@chef.net to
    fresh4flesh@gmail.com at 10:34 AM, Thursday
                  August 22nd.
```

The cops have your letters and emails. They will be all over you soon. They assured me that, because of who I am, they're devoting their full attention to this case. Let it end now and maybe I won't press charges once they've tracked you down. Let it end.

```
      Hand-delivered by courier to the office of
    Ms. Grace Agnolotti, The Packer Building, 1400
    Central Avenue, Suite 856 at 5:34 PM, Wednesday
                  August 31st.
```

Grace,

I have a new recipe for you:
- 1 pound of my special 'veal' cutlets
- 1 tablespoon lemon juice
- salt and pepper
- 2 tablespoons flour
- 3 tablespoons butter
- 8 ounces mushrooms, sliced
- ½ cup broth (see recipe in Chapter 4, "Soup to Nuts")
- 2 green onions, sliced thin
- ½ cup heavy cream

Can you see where I'm going with this? No? Allow me to enlighten.

I've already placed the cutlets between two sheets of plastic wrap and rapped on it gently with the brim of a coffee mug—one of my little secrets. It didn't take long as the meat was already very tender to begin with. I was humming a little song to myself as I brushed them with the lemon juice and imagined that I was God painting flavor into the pink flesh laid before me. Salt and pepper next, sprinkled lightly, and then a nice dusting of flour. Medium heat with melted butter, a nice big cast iron, the sizzle of the meat as I brown each side for two minutes or so.

Can't you practically smell it? That mouth watering aroma? There's nothing like fried foods to really get the taste buds going. You said that. Volume 6, Chapter 8 of Cooking with Grace. *And I know how much you love veal...I know so much about you now. That's why I selected this particular recipe. In honor of you. In honor of us.*

Once the meat was browned, I plated them and sautéed the mushrooms until they were nice and tender. I must admit, though, that I cheated. I made the broth earlier and simply brought it along. But the broth gets added and brought to a boil. Then I reduced the heat and simmered for about five minutes. Which was enough time to harvest some more cuts from my livestock; it is beyond caring. It now simply exists to give life and energy, flavor and scent. Returning to the skillet, I added the browned meat back to the skillet along with the onions and cream. Covered. Cooked for five more minutes.

Do you see? Are you imaging the flavor profiles? Can you even begin to? You've had chicken, lamb, fish, beef, pork, frog, and just about every other creature that exists on our little planet; yet, you've never tasted my ingredient of choice. But you've thought about it, haven't you? Long before you ever heard of A Feast of Fools you wondered what it would be like. If even only for a fraction of a second.

Don't feel guilty. Guilt is a wasted emotion, saved for the weak. For the livestock. After all, there's not a single person in the culinary arts field who hasn't had those same thoughts at one *point or another. But nobody talks about it. Nobody acts upon it. It takes a true visionary to break through the boundaries of taboo, to cast aside societal prejudice in favor of exploration. I am that man. I am the Christ of the cooking world and you could very well be my Mary Magdalene —*A Feast of Fools *our gospel. And yet you've acted more like Judas.*

Do you see?

To help light the way, I've placed candles on the table. But the blood looked so dark against the tile that it had to be cleaned. Funny how candlelight changes things like that, how it alters your perception.

I selected a nice Pinot Gris from the wine cellar—hints of pepper and a slight citrus undertone. I must admit that wine has never been my specialty, but I think this will suit the meal nicely.

Everything is perfect. The livestock is hidden away in the broom closet for the time being, the candles glowing softly, a little Leonard Cohen from the stereo system in the living room.

This is what A Feast of Fools *is about. This moment. This special, magic moment.*

You just need to see.

You just need to understand.

Do you see?

When I was a child, my grandmother had an expression. "The proof is in the pudding." she'd always say. It's probably the only good memory I have of that hateful bitch. Those six little words: the proof is in the pudding.

I've decided to grace you with one last chance. Perhaps for you to truly understand the depth of my vision, you first have to walk in my shoes. You have to know that special feeling that comes with the very first bite. Some people have described it as rubbery or chewy...but they simply lacked the skill to prepare it correctly. I've spent the better part of my life perfecting the technique, honing my talent like I would the blade of my favorite sashimi knife. I have created art. And this amusing little piece, my take on veal with mushroom gravy, is the perfect introduction to my body of work.

I'm sure you know what makes veal so tender...why the meat is so pale compared to a roast of beef or a nice steak.

Do you see now?

The calves are slaughtered young.
They are kept anemic.
It's time to come home, Grace.
The table is set.
The candles are lit.
And this particular meal tastes heavenly.
Like an *Angel*.

SAVING MONEY

MICHAEL D. GRIFFITHS

"So how do you like it?" Pitch asked, while cutting another huge piece from his steak. Swirling it in the bloody grease on his plate, he popped it into his mouth before Talon had a chance to reply.

"Yeah, it's great," Talon answered. He hoped this wasn't a prelude to Pitch asking him to up pony up some money for his share of the meal. Talon only had three dollars to his name and didn't want to part with them.

"I'm glad you like it," Pitch said and some of the other guys at the table laughed for some reason. "Would you like a beer?"

Everything about Pitch lived up to his name. From his dyed hair to his wardrobe, everything was a deep dark black. He kept himself clean-shaven and was probably a few seasons shy of Talon's twenty-five years of age.

"Wow, you have beer, too? What'd you do, roll somebody?"

He laughed between mouthfuls. "There might have been some *rolling* involved?"

Rick, or Rick-the-dick, as most people called him, handed Talon a can of cheap beer. Rick was tall and creepy, in a general sort of sense, which even the outdated glasses he wore couldn't dispel. Local legend had it that another guy called 'Trash' had kept the lanky freak from raping a girl behind Greasy Tony's sub shop. Why Pitch let the guy hang around was beyond Talon. Still, a guy on Talon's budget couldn't turn down free food and beer, so here he was.

The group of five guys and one gal circled the grimy table that was in the main room of the small shack known as the Mutant House. Torn and shaggy show flyers mixed with random posters in an attempt to conceal the dirty brown walls. Garbage mingled with dumpster dived furniture and junk, until it was hard to distinguish one from the other.

Taking another bite of meat, Talon let it melt on his tongue. *Who would have guessed these losers could cook so well?*

"So what do you think you might be eating?" Pitch asked. This elicited more laughter from his buddies and girlfriend, Stain.

"Some kinda steak, I guess."

"It is *some* kind of steak," Mucci giggled beside him.

Talon was starting to feel uneasy. What was going on with these guys? He took another bite and washed it down with a big chug of beer.

"Would you like to know?"

"Ah sure, why not," Talon replied.

"Rick, go grab what's in the fridge."

Moving to the refrigerator, he took a plate out and then strangely waited until he was nearly standing behind Talon before tossing the plate onto the table.

Talon shot to his feet so fast the chair toppled backwards with a clang. He gasped when he saw that Rick had tossed a folded human arm onto the table. Most of the meat had been sliced away, except for the flesh around the hand, which had turned a sickly light blue.

The others were laughing at Talon's reaction, but Rick placed a controlling hand on his shoulder and whispered, "Just stay cool." The words were drawn out and eerie, sounding like some fiend out of an old horror movie.

"What the hell are you guys doing?" Talon managed to spit out.

"Saving money," Pitch said, standing up.

"By eating people?" A deep terror began to well up inside Talon. It was an explosive feeling of horror, which he could barely control, but he knew that if he lost it, trouble would quickly follow.

"Hell, it's not our fault?" Pitch began, as he started to pace through the crowded room. Papers were crushed under his feet and he knocked over an overflowing ashtray. This created a gray cloud that clutched at his combat boots. "We've hit way worse than a recession here, Talon. America is dying. We're living off its corpse anyway, so why not take it one step further?"

"Where did you get the body?" Talon couldn't help but ask, which caused Rick's hand to clamp down on his shoulder painfully.

"Don't worry. It was already dead, if that's what you're think-ing," Pitch said with a dismissive flick of his hand. "Everyone's so hungry that people are dying all around us. Rick found this corpse in the street; no one cared. The city might've gotten the paramed-ics around to cleaning it up eventually. They don't care about us or care that we're starving, they just want to clean up the streets so that the uppercrusties don't have to be disturbed by our reality."

"But who was this?" Talon tried to shrug Rick's hand off his shoulder, but this only made Rick grip him harder.

"Just a bum." Ceasing his pacing, Pitch turned and glared at Talon, staring him down. "Why should we live in poverty, until we end up like those guys, wasting away in the streets? Why should we spend every cent we get just to try to survive and miss out on everything? Hell, you liked that beer, didn't you? Do you think we would be able to afford something even as simple as these cheap-ass beers if we're shelling out money for grub? Hell, no. We'd be sitting here eating some oat supplement, staring at each other. Some Saturday night that would be."

"I hope we can trust you not to narc us out," Rick whispered into Talon's ear. "Cause if you do…" His words trailed off, but Talon knew the implications; the silent threat that perhaps he would be their next meal.

"So I ask you this, Talon, are you with us, or are you just going to continue to grovel for the Posh, washing their dishes at that place you work, watching more food get tossed in the garbage disposal every day than you could eat in a month?"

The grip on Talon's shoulder intensified. "Yeah, I'm cool. I would never narc on you guys."

"We want more than that, Talon. We want you to be one of us. We've already shared one meal; why not make it a lifestyle. No matter what, we'll never starve and we'll certainly have more cash for other stuff."

"I don't know," Talon said. This was wrong, so wrong, and he just wanted to get out and never return, but he had a feeling he wouldn't make it out at all if he didn't tell them what they wanted to hear. Quickly building a plan and fighting down his growing sickness at what he'd eaten, he figured he would play along with them for now.

"I guess you make a few good points," he said. "I hate eating synthetic mush and not even having enough money to wash it down with something more than nasty tap water."

"Now you're talking," Pitch said.

"Wait," Rick said from behind Talon. "Before we welcome him into the fold, I want to see him clean his plate. Can he do it now that he knows what he's eating?"

Pitch must have seen Talon grimace, for he smiled and said, "Come on, Talon. Talk minus action equals zero."

His hands felt like fish caught in the mud while his throat constricted painfully. Dread welled up inside him, building into fear. Looking around the constricted room and feeling Rick-the-dick's grip on his shoulder, left little doubt to the true nature of this test. Fail, and it could be his arm they would be eating tomorrow.

His mouth turned to ash. Could he do this? Eating this meat was the only way to get out of here, but would it go down his throat? Could he make it happen?

Slowly, trying not to let his arm tremble, Talon picked up his fork and stabbed it into his remaining triangle of dripping black meat. It was a big piece, but he believed that it would be better to do it all at once, for he wouldn't wish to have to do it again and again.

Staring at it, he could see the crimson muscle. It looked like human flesh now. Hesitating too long could give him away. Frowning uncontrollably, he shoved the whole piece in-between his teeth in one bite. It filled his mouth and he gagged. His throat tensed, closing like a vise. Flesh splintered and tore, splitting into wet fragments that became caught between his teeth.

He began to dry heave.

Not bothering to hide the menace in his voice, Pitch said, "Don't do it." A steak knife filled his hand and he brought it up like a weapon. "Don't do it."

Panicking, Talon snatched up his beer and downed it. He was barely able to keep from vomiting, but the beer washed away some of the foul taste, and with a supreme effort, he was able to swallow the rest.

For a moment, all he could do was pant heavily. He didn't notice at first that Rick-the-dick had let go of him. "Can I have another beer, please?" Talon asked.

"Sure," Pitch said and tossed him a beer. "Good job by the way. Now you only have to pass one more test."

* * *

Moving through the Stygian night, Talon followed the lanky form of Rick-the-dick. They were passing through the slums of southern Tucson, which were some of the worse parts of the city, and of course, where they all lived.

Streetlights that hadn't worked for a decade stabbed the earth like black daggers. Overhead, the smog obfuscated any hint of the stars he knew lurked above. Leaving the major streets, Rick weaved through the alleys. These grimy thoroughfares had gone from being thoroughfares to hard-bitten squats for all manner of dregs.

Normally, Talon would be put off, entering these suspect areas, but the tall imposing figure of Rick-the-dick kept the others at bay. Gazing left and right, he saw gangs of dregs. Many eyed them as potential prey, but they had chosen to keep their distance so far.

"These places are too crowded," Rick hissed back at him. Talon also thought these folk probably did something with their dead, other than let police drag them away, but he kept his opinions to himself.

The pair moved away from the throbbing seas of dregs and headed for the canals. These canals were dryer than a bucket of sand left in the desert and were now just crumbling monuments to a time when rivers still moved across this part of the city, unless you counted the garbage-choked flashfloods that ripped through Tucson in the spring. These were long gone now, and the canal loomed before them like a dark scar cut into the Earth.

People still malingered here and there, for it was rare to find any sort of isolation within the city limits. They moved closer to the canal. A walkway ran along it, which had once been part of a recreation program, but due to the smog, long gone were the days when one could exercise outside. Such things now belonged only to those rich enough to afford the indoor gyms, or people like him that worked off any nutrition he received through drudgery.

A bridge formed a black arch, which blocked half of the northern city's lights and created a wide shadow across the trail. Rick headed for it. Talon hesitated at the lip of darkness.

"Come on, you wuss," Rick ordered.

Normally Talon wouldn't have gone anywhere near a place like this, but he supposed that he and Rick were the predators now.

To his right, only a thin railing kept path traffic from tumbling into the canal bed far below. To his left, the darkness thickened where the bridge continued into a narrow space between the road and the dirt below. Rick had some sort of light and was shining it into these recesses. Talon hurried closer to the light.

Looking back at him, the grim form of Rick nodded, the light reflecting off his archaic glasses. He motioned with his head and Talon saw a tangled, sleeping form. The man was so filthy he was nearly camouflaged into the dirt.

"Is he dead?" Talon whispered.

Rick's response was to kick the man in the shin while he removed a pair of lead pipes. The man groaned, but made no move to retaliate or even awaken.

"He's still alive, Rick," Talon said.

"That's a situation which can be easily fixed." Then with a snarl, Rick tore the old man from his bedding and violently dragged him to the edge of the dirt.

Screaming began and ended quickly, when Rick laid the lead pipes into the old dreg. Talon couldn't move as the sick crunches filled the air. Rick beat on him again and again, until there was no doubt the old man was dead. Then, crouching over his victim, Rick began to search the man in the faint hope he might possess something valuable.

They were right next to the rail separating them from the long drop into the rocky canal. Without really planning to, Talon rushed forward and gave Rick-the-dick a mighty shove. Rick's eyes grew wide, more with anger than fear, and he clutched at Talon as his body balanced precariously on the railing. Fingers tore strips of hair from Talon's hair, but with a grunt, Talon grabbed the base of Rick's boots and upended him backwards and over the railing.

Rick didn't even have a chance to scream as his body plummeted into the debris-choked canal.

Another person might have just fled back home and hoped for the best, but Talon knew what sort of end that choice would lead to eventually.

He had different ideas.

*   *   *

"Hey, Talon, what're you doing here?" Marty asked. He was one of the cooler guys he worked with. He didn't talk down to Talon just because he was a lowly dishwasher and Marty was a cook. "I thought you had tonight off?"

"Oh, I think I left my cell phone here," he lied. Talon didn't have enough money to own a cell phone, and because of it his dating pool was pretty narrow. No girl wanted a man who didn't have a cell phone, that meant they were dirt poor.

"Well, the lost and found is near the register," Marty said.

That's what he was hoping Marty would say.

Hurrying through the busy kitchen, Talon dodged plates and conversations. He saw a stray steak knife on a table and tucked it into his back pocket. It wasn't too big, but it would come in handy.

Making it to the front, he dropped behind the counter. Sassy was working, which he couldn't decide was lucky or not. He had a hard enough time talking to her normally, but tonight, he was already feeling like his pulse rate had doubled.

The thought that he'd eaten a steak of human flesh splattered across his mind. Did it somehow make him different? Could it scar you? He tried to push such feelings away. There would be plenty of time to ruminate on that horror later. Right now, he just had to make sure he had a later.

Attempting to push his tangled thoughts aside, he moved in behind her, waiting. There were worse places to be. She wore a skintight Chinese dress, and it did what it was supposed to do, gracing her thin figure exquisitely. The scarlet dress matched her heels as well as her lips. She had a short blonde gloss cut, which belled out just over her hairline. Luminescent, light-blue eyes finished the look.

Sassy was able to select men from the cream of the available undercrusties, and sometimes some who weren't so available. Talon knew she was way out of his league, even though they were of the same age. But despite this, she had always been decent to him and they joked around a lot.

Turning to face him, she smiled, "Hi there, Talon, just can't stay away from the fun, huh?"

"You've got me pegged. But I can't hang here next to you while I'm not on the clock, so I have to come in off-shift for the privilege."

He noticed he might have brought some color to her cheeks, and she eyed him slyly, but then quickly said, "Why are you really here?"

"I think I might have left my cell phone here?"

"Really, I didn't know you had one." Throwing her hip out slightly, she looked at him.

"Why, do you want my number?" he asked with a grin.

"Maybe." She pointed a scarlet fingernail towards a haggard yellow box that sat under the counter. "There's the lost and found. If you see a pair of amber earrings in there let me know."

Talon was trying to kill time. He had to stay behind the counter as long as possible. Minutes dragged until he had spent enough of them to search the box three times.

"You know that if you lost it here, some jerk would swipe it anyway," she said from behind him.

"Here, how 'bout these? They match your dress?" he said while holding up a pair of thick red winter gloves,

"Hilarious. If I didn't know better, I'd say you were lingering down there to check out my legs."

"Man, I should have thought of that." He was trying to joke, but things were wearing thin. Then, what he was waiting for happened. One of the waitresses came up with a man's credit card on a plate. Sassy quickly scanned the card. The number was only on the blue screen for a few seconds, but Talon jotted down the info on the back of his hand with a pen.

Thank you Brian Whitney, he thought to himself with a secret smile. The digits disappeared before he could double check that he'd gotten the right number. He'd better hope he did, because his entire plan rested on the number.

After a few more jokes and laughs with Sassy, he was on his way. Dashing out into the dark night, he headed back to the last place in the world he wanted to go.

* * *

"Yeah, he sent me back to get everyone. There's three people that we got," Talon said while gesturing with his hands. "We need help getting them all back."

Pitch glared at him through squinted eyes. "Why three? Rick knows we're only supposed to do one at a time."

"Yeah, well, see, that's the thing. This is way more than what you guys got before. These three were smugglers. They had all sorts of stolen electronics and stuff. We can bury the bodies if we have to. Who cares?"

Pitch had drawn a black-bladed knife and was now playing with it while they talked. Talon tried not to stare at it. "How did you guys take out three guys from the majors?"

"Mostly because Rick is a freak," Talon answered. "The guy went crazy. The whole thing happened under a bridge over the canal. He got two of 'em and I got the third by pushing him over the railing."

"You killed a guy?" Pitch didn't struggle to hide his disbelief.

"Unless he can survive a thirty-foot drop," Talon said.

"Come on, Pitch," Stain was saying, while she tugged his arm. "I've always wanted an Ipod. It would be cool to have a television here too and make some real money. Rick is...nuts like Talon says. I could see him wasting those guys easy."

"I'm still not sure," Pitch said as he pointed his knife straight at Talon's face. There was now only a foot of space separating the tip of the blade from his eye. "It seems a bit on the *too good to be true side* for my tastes." He paused. "Why didn't Rick come back with you?"

"Someone had to guard the rear," Talon said. "He'll be able to scare off any dregs." The others were getting excited and soon Pitch didn't have much choice.

"All right, you morons, we'll check this out. But we're all going." He pointed the dagger at Talon again. "As for you, we'll be keeping a close eye on you."

"As long as I get my share," Talon smiled widely, hoping it looked genuine.

"Oh, we believe in sharing everything," Pitch said. As he spoke, the glowing eyes of the rest of the gang focused on Talon. Trying not to shiver, he could only meet their gaze for a moment, before he turned and led them out the door.

Many of them paused to gather up weapons. Not to be outdone, Talon went to grab a baseball bat but Pitch was faster. He snatched it up and tossed it to Mucci. The dark-skinned youth caught it easily.

"No weapons for you yet, Talon." Pitch turned to Mucci. "Keep an eye on him. If anything goes less than perfect, keep hitting him until he stops screaming."

Mucci pushed Talon forward with the tip of the bat as the group faded into the streets of Tucson.

* * *

We won't go hungry, no not tonight,
Flesh is so tender you don't need a knife.
Eating yer buddies.

The group sung as one, except for Pitch, who led them quickly through the night. Talon had dropped back as far as Mucci would let him. He had given Pitch the basic instructions and the man knew the way.

The night came alive around them as the men continued their eerie chant. Shadows clung to the refuse that lined the road, looking like fields of dead bodies. The taste of the meat bubbled up into Talon's throat, staining his lips, bringing back what he'd done. He could feel it. It clung against the side of his stomach like a solid lump putrefying his insides. He knew he was tainted, but he couldn't worry about that now, he had to see this through.

They were nearing the bridge. In the distance, the lights on the opposite side of the city glittered like the stars the smog hid.

"Keep an eye on him," Pitch hissed back to Mucci, and then began to jog under the bridge. A light could now be seen on the far side. "Rick, is that you?" Pitch called out.

Talon knew he had to act fast. "Hey, look out," he said to Mucci, grabbing his arm."

"What the hell?"

"The guy I pushed over the ledge, I saw him. The fall didn't take him out." Without waiting for a reply, Talon took off back the way they had come. Mucci, uncertain at first, followed. As soon as they reached thicker shadows, Talon spun around and punched Mucci in the face. The young man wasn't expecting such a sudden turn, and the fist broke his nose in an explosion of blood.

While Mucci stumbled backwards, Talon's left hand grabbed the bat and his right hand punched him again. Grunting, Mucci released the bat. The blow caused him to trip over a rock and he went crashing onto his back. Talon raised the bat, like he was going to finish the job, but a helicopter floodlight began to illuminate underneath the bridge. A garbled, electronically-amplified voice began shouting orders and was closely followed by gunfire.

"Good luck, dumb ass," Talon yelled back at the battered punk and began to sprint away. "And thank you, Brian Whitney; sorry about the hassle they'll be putting you through after all this," he muttered to himself. *That guy must have been loaded*, Talon thought. If the reported kidnapping brought out helicopter support, Talon must have picked the right guy to call in the false report with. The cops wouldn't find Brian Whitney there, however, but they would find enough to make sure the trip wasn't a waste. If any of Pitch's crew survived the encounter, he doubted he would be seeing them for a while.

He was almost back to one of the main roads when a large figure blocked his path.

At first, Talon thought it was some random dreg or maybe a cop who had moved around to cut them off, but then he saw the glint of the helicopter lights shining off his glasses. It was Rick-the-dick. The man could barely stand without swaying and blood dripped from the middle finger of his disfigured left arm, slowly creating a muddy black pool where it mixed in the dirt at his feet.

"You son-of-a-bitch. Can you comprehend what you've done?" Rick asked, his voice trembling.

"Rid the world of a bunch of dirtbags, is what I'm thinking."

With a roar, Rick rushed forward, swinging one of the lead pipes he'd managed to hold onto after his fall. Talon still had the bat and used it to block the attack. Moving faster, his backswing took Rick in the temple with a loud *crack*.

Talon raised the bat behind his shoulder, like he was waiting for a pitch, Rick rushed him, the lead pipe raised to split his skull in two. Talon swung the bat. It connected with the lead pipe and sent it flying into the dead bushes lining the path.

Rick called out, "I'll kill you for ruining everything," and leapt forward. His long, lanky arms got past the bat and he began to clutch and pull at Talon. Before Talon knew what was happening, long teeth had buried themselves into the flesh of his shoulder. He cried out in pain as the jagged teeth quickly tore through his shirt.

Dropping the bat, Talon reached back into his back pocket. Pulling out the steak knife, he jabbed it between two of Rick's ribs. The man gasped out and stumbled away, taking the knife with him.

"Try to eat me, will you," Talon spat at him while clutching his bleeding shoulder. "You're the one who's gonna get carved up like a steak."

After yanking out the knife, Rick came at him again, but Talon picked up the bat and swung it into Rick's face. There was a re-sounding *crack* as the tip of the bat broke Rick's jaw; he tumbled off of the path with a wet, muffled groan.

Talon was going to make sure he finished what he started this time. Leaving a vengeful Rick-the-dick alive wouldn't be wise.

Then a noise from behind stopped him.

A low growling could be heard coming from the bushes. Another quickly followed it, then a third. Thin shadows created finger-wide tiger strips on the circling pack of wild dogs; the packs preyed on the unlucky and alone. They scented blood and were more than willing to prey on the wounded or dying.

"He's all yours, boys," Talon muttered, as he slowly retreated down the path, holding the bat in front of him.

Rick reached out a pleading hand and moaned again.

"Sorry, I guess it's your turn to feed some hungry mouths. Only I think this meal won't be over as quickly."

Though Talon tried to forget, the screams as Rick was torn apart haunted him for months; nearly as long as it took him to forget the taste of human flesh.

Eventually it faded, but his friends always wondered, why for no apparent reason, Talon had suddenly become a vegetarian.

BEST MEAT EVER

ANTHONY GIANGREGORIO

"I'm telling you, this place has the best steaks in town," Tim said to his girlfriend as they walked along the avenue.

"I've heard that before, Tim," Alice replied cynically.

Tim was a connoisseur of meat. He would take her out almost every Saturday night to some new steak or rib joint, and it wasn't unheard of for Tim to drive two and three hours to reach the newest restaurant he'd found on the internet.

"No, Alice, I'm serious this time. I heard some great stuff about his place. They've got steaks as thick as your fist and for next to nothing."

"That doesn't sound too profitable." She crossed her arms as they stopped at the corner, the light was red and the cars were buzzing past. She pressed the button on the pole so it would change and they could cross safely.

"You'd think so," he said. "But the owner must buy in bulk or something." He laughed as he clapped his hands together, rubbing them greedily. "Hell, I don't care why he does it. I'm just glad he does!"

The light changed, halting traffic, and they crossed, surrounded by other pedestrians off to who knows where.

"If this place is so great," she said, "then how come you never heard about it before today? I mean, you go to every single one you can find and this one's right in your backyard, so to speak?"

"Yeah, I know, weird, huh? It seems this one just popped up a few weeks ago. No advertisement, nothin'. It wasn't there and then it was."

"So we're going there now?" she asked.

He nodded. "Yes, but like I said, I promised dinner *and* a movie so we'll go see a movie first and then have a late dinner."

"Okay, I want to see 'Impossible Chances'?"

He rolled his eyes. "That new movie with the guy who is kind of a geek but the really hot chick falls for him anyway, right?"

She nodded.

"I don't blame you, it's so original."

"I don't care, I like those movies and you said I could pick," she said.

"Fine," he sighed, "it's your choice, but then we get to go eat."

"Deal," she replied and the two continued on.

Two and a half hours later, the movie now over, the young couple were back on the street making their way to the restaurant.

"God, I can't believe how long that movie was," he said.

"It was for character development."

"Character development? More like developing an ulcer. God, the lines were so clichéd, who wrote that thing, a fifteen year old girl?"

"Are you sure you know where this place is?" Alice asked, changing the subject. She'd like the movie and didn't want to hear him trash it. They'd been walking for almost a half hour and she didn't like the neighborhood they were in. The word 'seedy' came to mind.

"Yeah, I got the directions off the internet; it's only a few more blocks away."

"But you said that three blocks ago, my feet are killing me," she complained.

He frowned. "Hey, it's not my fault. I told you not to wear heels," he said and pointed to her black pumps. "I said 'sensible shoes'."

She frowned. "These are sensible shoes...for me, anyway."

He rolled his eyes as he wrapped an arm around her waist. "Hey, baby, I'm so excited to eat at this place I'll carry you if I have to. Even that terrible movie hasn't ruined my appetite."

She smiled then, her mood lightening. "I just may take you up on that offer to carry me if we don't get there soon." She shifted to the side, her short blouse riding up on her waist, and Tim's eyes went right to the exposed skin, his manhood stirring slightly.

"What're you looking at?" she asked coyly.

Not wanting to come off as a horndog, he pointed to her tattoo. It was of a red butterfly with a carnation in its mouth. He had never seen one like it before and loved to look at it, as it was on her back, and he would stare at it as he made love to her from behind. He was on a first name basis with that tattoo, so to speak.

"Nothing, baby, just admiring your tattoo."

"Uh-huh," she replied but she leaned over and kissed him. "This place better be as good as you say it is."

"Oh, it will be, it will be."

The two walked on, weaving in and out of the pedestrian traffic as Tim's mouth watered in expectation of the steak he would be eating in less than an hour.

* * *

Chef Vito Arturo stared at the almost empty shelves of the meat locker, shaking his head in disgust.

He was out of inventory...again.

Reaching into his pocket, he pulled out his cell phone and pressed the first number on speed dial. Seconds later, the phone beeped and another voice picked up.

"What?" the small voice said through the speaker.

"We're almost out, I need more product," Chef Vito said.

"I'm workin' on it," the voice said. "It's getting' scarce out here. The bums are gettin' wise to me."

"That's not my problem, that's yours," Vito said firmly. "I pay you to keep my supply coming and that's what I want you to do."

"Yeah, well, the supply is gettin' thin. It might be time to pick up and move on to the next city."

Vito ground his teeth, frustrated. "Is it really that bad out there?"

There was a pause, then the voice said, "Yeah, it's that bad. The bums know there fellow buddies are gone, there's almost no one on the streets anymore, they all go to homeless shelters now. Pickings are slim out here, Vito."

Vito sighed heavily, accepting what he knew was inevitable. "Fine, just try to get me one more specimen and then we'll call it a day here. I want to get in one more crowd for dinner tonight and maybe tomorrow, too, then we'll pack it up."

"Sounds good, and I'm sure I can rustle up at least one more," the voice said. "I gotta go, I see a potential target now. Man, he looks down on his luck."

The phone went dead and Vito ended his side of the call, slid the phone back into his pocket, and stepped deeper into the meat locker to study what was left of his supply.

The right side of the cold room was empty, but the left side still had a few items here and there. Vito was already going through the menu in his mind, thinking where he could use what piece of meat for in a recipe.

He went to the shelf and picked up the first cut of meat. It was a human leg, as were all the meat cuts in his cold room. The leg had been from a large male and he stared at it as he pressed the meat with his thumb, testing elasticity.

"Hmm, I could make a nice roast with this one," he said to himself as he set the leg down and went to the next piece of meat.

Four human arms lay stacked like cordwood, each wrapped in plastic. He studied them and decided he could make a nice stew after carving the meat from the bones. The fingers could be used as a substitute for Buffalo wings. He always found it amazing how after he slathered them with sauce and kept the lighting in the dining room low, how the customers never noticed it wasn't chicken they were eating.

He picked up a severed head—one of five— and held it in his hands. The brains could be used in a red gravy. When cooked, the brains resembled tripe and the eyes of each head could be added to a soup; of course he would tell the customers the eyes belonged to lambs.

Setting the head down, he went to the remaining three torsos. The insides had been gutted and were now nothing but hollow cavities. Two of the torsos had been woman and the breasts had been removed to be used in a stir fry. He planned on smoking the torsos, then slicing the ribs and marinating them in barbeque sauce. When they were finished, they tasted better than beef.

Of course, it looked like he might not get that chance now that supplies were growing thin.

The homeless population took a while to catch on, but when they did, they began staying off the streets. Once that happened,

Vito had to move on to the next city. He only took the homeless, as anyone else would be missed and investigations conducted. But no one cared about the homeless and the meat was free, so he had an astronomical profit margin.

It wasn't hard to rent a building that had the necessary kitchen, add a few tables and paint the walls, keep the lighting low to hide any defects, and he was open for business.

He went to a bucket containing livers, hearts, and kidneys of the slaughtered bodies.

The livers would be sautéed with mushroom and onions, the kidneys sliced and made into a pâté. As for the hearts, well, he still hadn't figured out what to do with them. As the major organ in the human body, the heart was all muscle, so it was very tough and chewy. He'd tried steaming it, frying, boiling, and roasting it, but no mater what he attempted, the heart always reminded him of eating rubber.

Vito had begun eating human flesh back in Vietnam. He was a POW for more than five years and in that time, when he and the other prisoners were starving, they had no choice but to do things so extreme the average American would have preferred to die than do them.

At first it had been foul, and he had fought to keep the meat down, but as time went by, he found the taste had grown on him.

The people he and the other prisoners ate were of their own group, ones that died from sickness or other ailments. But for each one that died, the rest of the group thrived, and by the time he was rescued, he actually had some meat on his bones, and didn't look like an emaciated POW should look. Of course, the meat on his bones, so to speak, wasn't actually his, but he was alive and that was all that mattered.

When he returned to the states, he found he still craved human meat, and no substitute would suffice. Always the entrepreneur, he figured out a way to feed his habit and make a living at the same time.

The voice on the cell phone was Matt, another POW who had acquired the taste for human flesh. Together, they were a team. Matt found them and Vito cooked them up, and the two maintained their hunger. Vito reached out and took the bucket of organs, then carried it out of the meat locker and to the stainless steel table in the center of the kitchen. It was time to begin preparing the house special for the dinner rush that would be arriving in only a few short hours.

He pulled out the livers, set them on a cutting board, and began chopping them into pieces, his stomach already rumbling with hunger from the odor of fresh human meat.

But there was no time to eat right now. He needed to get the torsos into the oven, trim the meat from the leg, fry up the kidneys for the pâté, and chop the fingers for the mock Buffalo wings.

He smiled to himself as he worked, thinking how truly stupid the customers were. Slap some ground meat on a bun and tell them it was beef and no one ever questioned it, they just dug in, for all purposes nothing but ravenous dogs in a feeding frenzy.

He chuckled at the thought.

The customers were just so damn gullible.

Tim and Alice arrived at Vito's well after the dinner rush. Stepping inside into the small foyer, the restaurant was empty, no other diners present. It looked as if the place was closed for the night.

"Are you sure this is the place?" Alice asked. "No one's in here."

Tim made an aggravated face. "Well, of course not. We took so long getting here we're just lucky it's still open. Guess we're the last customers of the night."

"Oh, so you're blaming me that the movie was filled up and we had to wait till the next showing, is that it?"

"Yes, Alice, I am. We could have gone to see that new action flick; we didn't have to wait for an hour and a half to see that stupid movie. And for your information, it was terrible."

"Well, I'm so sorry you didn't like it as you've so plainly stated, but we did something I wanted for once," she argued while crossing her arms over her chest. "You know, I didn't even want to come to this stupid restaurant, I did it for you, to make you happy. I don't even eat meat that much, you know that." She looked hurt and Tim felt bad.

"I'm sorry, baby, I guess I have been a little bit of a jerk. Look, we're here now. "Hopefully, I can get them to make me something, even if it's to go. I didn't come all this way for nothing."

He looked up to see a man in a dirty apron walking from the back of the restaurant. He had dark hair and his Italian descent was obvious to a blind man.

"Can I help you folks?" the man asked. "I'm Vito, I own this place."

"Uh, hi, yeah, uhm, I heard a lot of great stuff about your meat and I was hoping we could get a table." Tim wrapped an arm around Alice's waist.

Vito scratched his head. "Geez, pal, I'd like to help you, but I'm cleaned out. I get limited amount of stock and it's all gone."

Tim wasn't about to give up that easily. "Oh, come on, sir, surely you must have something lying around. Look, like I said, I came a long way to get here. I just found out you even existed and I was really hoping I could get a steak or a burger or something. I've just got to try out your food."

Vito shook his head. "Sorry, like I said, I'm all out."

"But you don't understand," Tim protested, "I've been dying to come here, you can't send me home, not without at least trying some of your meat."

Vito had a feeling this guy wasn't going to take no for an answer so decided he might as well just give the man what he wanted and send him on his way. He scratched his head and smiled at Alice politely. "Well, I'm supposed to get a short order delivered tonight but I don't know exactly when that might be. The order could show up in five minutes or forty-five."

"I don't care, we'll wait!" Tim yelled happily, excited that he wasn't going to be turned away.

Vito mulled it over for a few seconds as he let his eyes play over Alice. She was an attractive woman and he was a red-blooded man.

Finally, Vito sighed. "Fine, have a seat, you two, and I'll get you some drinks. My waitress has gone home for the night so I'll be serving you."

"That's fine, that's fine, really, we're not fussy," Tim said as Vito led them to a table near the kitchen doors.

"What do you want to drink while you wait?"

"A couple of beers would be great," Tim said.

"Okay, two beers comin' right up. You care what kind?"

Tim shook his head. "A beer's a beer, right, Alice?"

She shrugged. "Whatever." She wasn't pleased at all.

Vito nodded and left to get the beers and returned a minute later. After setting them down, he grinned once more. "You two get comfortable. When the order arrives I'll whip you up somethin' tasty. All right?"

"Yes, yes, thank you again, you've been great. I'll be sure to tell my friends about this place."

Vito nodded at that, knowing by the time this guy's friends arrived, he would be long gone and setting up in another city.

"I'll be in the kitchen. I have some more work to do. If you need anything, just yell. We're informal around here. But don't come into the kitchen." His face grew hard. "We don't allow the customers into the kitchen."

"Okay, thanks," Tim replied, barely noticing Vito's change in demeanor as he walked away, pushing through the swinging door to the kitchen to disappear. A few seconds later, pots and pans could be heard rattling as he worked.

Tim opened his beer and sighed happily. "Well, we're here and we're gonna eat. All's right with the world."

"Is that what you think?" Alice asked. "Look at this place, it's a dump," she waved her hand around her, signifying the restaurant. Tim looked at the other tables, the floors, and the walls. There was new paint on the walls, but even in the dim light, he could tell it was tossed on haphazardly. Some of the tables had broken legs hastily fixed with duct tape and the table he sat at was wobbly and had chips on its top. Some of the chairs didn't match and the floor was dirty, but Tim shrugged it all off. "It's ambience," he said. "Any good restaurant doesn't need a lot of fancy shit, the food speaks for itself."

"That's your answer?" she asked.

"Yes, it is, now drink your beer and try to relax, I want to enjoy this and so far your being a drag."

She sighed and took a sip of her beer. "I know I am, but...well, Christ, this place is a dump."

"Maybe, but it's got the best meat this side of the city so be nice. I went to your movie so let me have this, please?" He batted his eyes like he was trying to romance her.

She grinned slightly, and a small chuckle escaped her lips. "You know I hate it when you do that, you look so goofy."

"I thought you loved it when I was goofy?"

"I do," she said.

He reached for her hand and took it gently into his.

"We good?" he asked.

"For now."

The couple sat quietly in the empty restaurant and drank their beers while in the kitchen, the clatter of pans filtered out like New Wave music.

An hour later and Tim was growing impatient. Vito still didn't have his meal ready and it was going on midnight. And Alice was angry, and for the past twenty minutes had been demanding to leave.

"No, it can't be that much longer," Tim said.

"I don't care, I want to leave. I'm hungry and I'm tired of waiting."

"Look, we've been here this long, what's a little longer?" he asked.

On the table in front of them were three more beers each. Vito had apologized twice and said the delivery should be arriving soon, but the delivery man wasn't answering his phone.

Alice stood up, crossing her arms over her chest. "No, that's it, I've had it. I've been asking to leave for almost a half hour and it's clear you have some sort of obsession over this place, well fine, I'm going to the bathroom and then I'm leaving."

"Oh, come on, Alice, don't be that way," he said, reaching for her arm.

She pulled it away and took a step backward. "No, forget it, it's too late now. I'm leaving and there's nothing you can say to talk me out of it."

His face grew dark. "Fine, go then, I'll eat by myself, thanks for nothing," he said and waved her away.

She made an aggravated noise from deep in her throat and headed off to the bathroom, leaving Tim to mull over her actions. As far as she was concerned, she was already gone, and was now forgotten as he stewed in his frustration.

Alice went to the rear of the restaurant, assuming that was where the bathrooms were. She wanted to go before she left. It was so gloomy, the lights on so low she could barely see, let alone read anything, and she found herself stumbling around. She found a small hallway and she took it, now her bladder letting her know it needed to be emptied. Those beers had caught up to her and she hurried down the hall, searching for the doors marked Women's Room.

She could hear the clatter of pans again, and before she realized it, she reached the end of the hall, pushed through a small door, and found herself in the kitchen, to the far right of the swinging door Vito used after talking to them.

As she moved into the kitchen to ask Vito where the bathrooms were, she saw the man was standing at a table in the center of the room. He was cutting something.

A shelf of pans was in her way and she slowly moved closer, hesitant about bothering the chef. Would he be mad that she was in his kitchen? Perhaps, she had known some cooks to get very upset if you entered their domain and he had said they weren't allowed in his kitchen. But she was a woman and an attractive one, too. Usually she would just show some skin and bat her eyes and most men would melt and do anything for her.

When she reached the shelf, she peered through the stacked pans to see Vito more clearly, and when her eyes went down to what he was cutting up, her eyes went wide with shock.

It was a human head, the skull cracked open like a pineapple. The brains were on a butcher block cutting board and Vito was chopping them into small pieces where he then placed them in a steaming kettle.

Alice's eyes went to the head, seeing the empty eye sockets, the eyes now gone. The mouth was hanging open and the tongue was missing, the visage locked in a silent scream for all eternity.

Her mouth fell open, mimicking the severed head, and she felt her breath lodge in her throat. What she was seeing was a mistake, a gag, it had to be. But as she watched in horror, Vito picked up the head, scooped out the remaining brains and set the empty head to the side, to then take out another, fresher head. She watched in absolute terror as he used the cleaver and chopped at the skull, the process reminding her of how someone opens a coconut.

She felt her mind swirling as he cracked the skull and once more scooped out the brains. She saw the head was female, a ragged, aged face, like a cocaine user or someone withered by sickness. She had no idea she was looking at one more street person, the visage corrupted by living on the streets.

She knew she needed to leave now, to get Tim and run for the front door; they needed to tell the police what was happening in this house of horrors. But as she went to turn around, a handle of a pot was extended on the shelf and she bumped it with her shoulder.

The pan rattled and Vito looked up immediately, his eyes seeing her instantly as she looked back at him in petrified shock, for all purposes resembling a little girl caught taking a cookie from the cookie jar before dinner, her hand in the jar upon discovery.

Like a striking panther, Vito was moving, and before she knew what was happening, he reached her, locking her right wrist in his hand like a vise.

He shook his head as he glared at her and she saw genuine regret in his face. "I'm sorry you saw that, honey. Now you leave me no choice."

She opened her mouth to scream, to call out to Tim to come save her, but before she could utter a signal screech, Vito's fist came around and sent her into the dark oblivion of unconsciousness.

As she fell into oblivion, she realized she'd found a place to go to the bathroom, as warmth slid down her leg.

Tim looked up when Vito exited the kitchen.

"Good news, my delivery finally came, I'll have your meal ready in about ten to fifteen minutes."

"Well, it's about time. My girlfriend already left and I have to tell you, I was about to leave, too."

"Then my guy came just in time. So let me get you another beer and in a few minutes you'll be eating the best meat this side of the city." He left then, returned a moment late with another beer, flashed Tim a smile, and went into the kitchen.

Tim pulled out his cell phone, dialing Alice's number. She only left a few minutes ago and maybe she was still close by and would return if asked nicely. He frowned when it went right to voice mail and he left her a brief message, apologizing, asking her to come back, and that he loved her. He set the cell phone on the table and took a sip of his beer. Well, at least it would be worth it in the end as Vito was making his meal.

Twenty minutes later and Tim was growing impatient once more. He was about to get up and go to the kitchen and tell Vito he was tired of waiting and was finally leaving, when the man pushed through the swinging door with a plate of steaming food.

"Ah, at last, I was about to leave," Tim said as Vito set the food down in front of him. Tim breathed in, the savory aroma of the meat causing his taste buds to water.

"I'm glad you didn't. This is a very special cut. Tender to the point it'll melt in your mouth." He raised his hands in front of him like he was pushing an imaginary person. "Eat, go, enjoy, there's steak sauce on the table but I doubt if you'll want any. The spices I season with are usually enough for even the fussiest palate."

"Well, it sure smells good, what is this beef or pork?"

Vito ignored the question. "Okay, so if you need anything just yell, I have to clean up in the back. It's to close for the night." He went to the front door and turned the sign around so it now read **CLOSED**.

Tim nodded, distracted by the heady aroma of the food. There was also a baked potato as well as a side of buttered corn, though he pushed both onto a small side plate used for bread. He'd come here to eat meat, not potatoes and vegetables. The meat on his plate was quite pale, though it resembled a rump roast. It was a healthy cut and covered in peppercorn and Tim decided he had waited long enough. Cutting with his knife, he stabbed the piece he'd carved and placed it in his mouth.

It was tangy, the flavor something he'd never had before. He tried to put his finger on it. Rabbit? Venison? Ostrich? No, it wasn't one of them. He wondered if it was some endangered species, perhaps even horse or bear. Hell, it could be dog for all he knew; but as he took another bite, he decided he didn't care. It was fantastic.

As grease slid down his chin, and juice slipped out of the corners of his mouth, he devoured the meat like it was his last meal.

When he had finished on one side, he found a bone went down the middle so he turned the meat over and began working on the bottom. The juice had seeped out of the meat and the crust wasn't as hard as it should be here, the peppercorn coating falling off in some spots. This shouldn't have happened but sometimes not every recipe goes as planned.

Tim could have cared less and he dug in, slicing thick chunks off and shoving them into his mouth. It was heavenly, the best roast he'd ever eaten in his life. He knew he would be coming back here every week from now on, as he was already hooked on the flavorful meat.

It was as he was carving the end of the roast that he paused for a second, his eyes seeing something under the coating. The peppercorn had fallen off in this section, exposing the fatty tissue of the meat, and as he looked closer, Tim's mouth fell open, his eyes went wide and he began to taste bile, the entire contents of his stomach threatening to explode out of his esophagus.

There, on the corner of the roast, as plain as day, was the unmistakable tattoo of a red butterfly with a carnation in its mouth.

His mind tried to tell him he was wrong, mistaken, that this was some kind of sick joke, but he knew this wasn't the case, for he had stared at that tattoo countless times as he made love to Alice. While he had thrust deeply into her, his eyes had studied every nuance, every dot of ink on the tattoo on her back, and there was no doubt he was looking at the same one now. Even the pedals on the carnation were exact, right down to the right pedal being slightly off, as if the artist's hand had slipped at the last second.

He dropped his knife to clatter off the plate and leaned back in his seat, feeling dizzy and nauseous at the same time. His world was spinning as he tried to wrap his head around what he was experiencing. The most flavorful meat he'd ever eaten, the most juiciest cut of flesh, was in fact, his *girlfriend!*

The dining room seemed to go dark as he tried to fight off the wave of dizziness filling him and he stood up, staggering across the dining room, knowing he needed to leave, to tell someone what had happened, and as soon as possible. He felt his stomach heaving yet again and it was all he could do not to vomit over his shoes.

He stumbled to the front door, his mind reeling with the reality that he had *eaten* his girlfriend, and that it was the best thing he'd ever tasted, he found himself blocked by a shadow. He stopped and looked up to see a man he didn't know standing perfectly still and he opened his mouth to tell him what had happened, that they needed to get the police, when he saw the man held a large knife.

Tim gasped in fear and tried to take a step backward, but as he did, he backed up into another body standing there, and before he could react, an arm came up and hovered in front of his face. He saw the arm's hand held a large knife as well, and before he could so much as scream, the knife came close and slid across his throat, slicing his carotid artery and jugular in one smooth motion.

Gagging on blood, he pressed his hands to his bleeding throat but there was no staunching the flow. With each beat of his heart, he died a little more. He slipped to the floor to lie prone, now staring up at the ceiling with eyes that wouldn't see.

Vito looked down on Tim with a shaking of his head and he gestured to the new man in the dining room.

"It's about time you got here, Matt. I thought I was gonna have to take care of this guy on my own. His girlfriend saw too much and I had to kill her, then I had to stall this guy until you got back."

"How'd you do it? Keep 'im here?" Matt asked.

"I carved up his girlfriend and served her with a peppercorn coating, that's how. Now come on, help me get him into the back. From what he said, no one knows either of them came here tonight. Once they're cut up into steaks and filets, no one will ever know they were here. Get his arms, I got the feet," Vito ordered him.

Tim was falling into a darkness he would never awaken from as the two men picked him up and carried him into the kitchen. As they set him on the large stainless steel table in the middle of the kitchen, Tim's head fell to the side and when it did, he found himself staring into Alice's dead eyes, her severed head glaring at him, as if in accusation. Next to her head were her arms, now dissected and laying carelessly like large chicken drumsticks. Her legs were off to the side, just at the edge of his peripheral vision, and he saw her torso had been sliced in twain and gutted, the lower half missing—which was what he'd eaten.

He wanted to tell her he was sorry for getting her into this, and that he was sorry for her death, but before he could so much as gurgle one syllable, darkness began to fall and his heart beat for the last time.

As he let out his final breath, he could hear Vito talking to Matt.

"I want to get this guy cut up before I go home tonight. There's a dinner party for twenty coming in tomorrow and this guy'll be the perfect special. After that, we'll pack up and head to 'Frisco."

Tim's last thought as a connoisseur of meat was that he hoped he would be served in a peppercorn crust, because though it had been Alice he was eating, he had to admit, it was still the best meat ever.

SOCIAL STIGMA

DANIEL FABIANI

They pulled up to the house in a battered Volkswagen. Trees slewed about the land, reflecting thin afternoon light back into the open sky, and the roads all conferred a certain style, 'The Deep South.'

The single home rested upon the parched piece of land, its old white fences as bitter and brittle as the home itself. The paint was a lattice of old white gone gray from age, and the roof was pointed and brown, resembling a steeple of a converted church.

"This must be a church," Gerald said to his brother Harry.

"No, it isn't; just go in there and get some directions," Harry said, angry about Gerald losing his sights of the road, winding them up at the old, haunted looking place.

Gerald carried out his brother's orders, knowing he was in no mood to argue. Harry's short temper had always found ways to control Gerald, a typical older-younger sibling relationship. A secret hate boiled between them since the day Gerald slipped out from between their mother's sticky red thighs in the maternity ward. In their adult life, they came to the conclusion they were in need of a middle road; a pathway to let bygones be bygones, to let adolescent feuds not dictate the rest of their lives, and allow it all to fade away like the watery light of dawn. They planned the trip together to see if there was anything to save, aside from a shared gene pool.

Gerald stepped out of the car and strode towards the haggard-looking house. His brow was wet and sweat dripped into his eyes, then down his face, the perspiration like hot sea water in his mouth. The sun baked his colorless face, bringing a rouge tinge to his cheeks and chin. Gerald found the stairs and walked up them slowly; the front door was closed. He came up to it and knocked, immediately frightened that the force would cave in the seemingly hundred year old, hollowed wood frame. The hinges squealed like slaughtered swine and a wrinkled old woman with hair dangling like sparring silver snakes stared out from the crevice of the partially opened door; two sugar-white eyes curiously marking him.

"Hello," she muttered through odd-colored teeth, her accent so deep rooted it sounded British.

"Sorry to bother you," Gerald managed, "but I am looking to get back onto I-95, would you be..."

She cut him off with a tiny white hand, veins as rigid and red as blood clots. The lady moved to the side and opened the door fully, allowing Gerald to enter. The house was lit by daylight, lamps and light bulbs not found in any part of his eye sight. Vases of thirsty, wilted flowers took up every corner of what he could see. The only thing positive Gerald noticed was the oddly lacquered floor, iridescently sticky.

The lady showed him in, wiping her hands on her apron, the pinching smell of rot lingering thickly through the air of the house. She stood in front of him, much shorter than he, and was wiping her hands on her apron, which were wet and stained myriad colors. A viscous slime hung from her pallid collar bones like stretched out bubble gum—red bubble gum. Pink spittle dripped off her chin as she chewed on something as taut as tendon.

"Forgive my manners!" she yelled, startling Gerald, "but we make our own suppa' here."

Her pearlescent eyes marked him once again. He felt like she was seeing straight through him, like a human x-ray, down to the very calcium of his bones. He didn't blink nor breathe, and his groin throbbed along with his escalated heart rate; he wanted out. So he pulled the old map out of his sweaty back pocket to try and steer his mind away from the twisted white orbs in front of him. At the sight of the damp piece of paper, she hobbled closer to him like a peg legged pirate and stood next to him; the smell of mothballs wafted from her hair.

Then her arm stretched for it, fingernails caked with dirt, healed old scars along the tops of her palms. Her eyes lit like embers as if the old crone had once owned the old map. He pointed to the destination circled with a black Sharpie marker, and she grabbed his finger with her fever-sweat hand, and slid her lips apart to smile, showing Gerald her full set of wooden teeth. He stepped back, never so startled in his life, and she took another small step towards him.

"Look, I just need to know how to get to this spot and back to I-95, I don't want trouble."

"Oh, there's no trouble, and the way to get there is very simple. That place you're seeking is a very nice one indeed," she coughed a very dry cough, and hocked a brown wad of tobacco spit to the side of the floor. "Just know that the place is very special, I know of a family who lives there now, you know."

"Well, I'm not looking to board with any family. I'm on a little vacation with my brother..."

"Brother you say?" her eyes widening. "Excellent, how fun!"

The old woman gave Gerald concise directions, told him how to turn around and get back to the highway, and ultimately his destination so he and his brother could enjoy some alone time. He thanked the old woman for her time, but didn't accept her attempted embrace. He didn't want to smell her anymore, so he exited quickly. As his nostrils drew in the stale summer air, Gerald knew that life was damn good, until he noticed Harry's angry and sour face, his hand in love with the car horn, not letting up even when Gerald was back in the vehicle with the seat belt on.

"What the fuck is your problem man?" Gerald asked.

"Nothing, do you know how to get there now or what?"

"Yeah."

"So drive, little brother."

Harry didn't understand how Gerald could have been so inattentive, and he blamed himself for falling asleep when he should have been guiding him. But he didn't allow the vehement thump in his brain, or the short string of his patience, ridicule his brother too much. After all, they planned the trip to become friends, not remain enemies.

The road opened up before them pretty quickly, and the trees faded away, replaced by a narrow, black-topped highway and diesel trucks which blew out smog as dark as storm bloated clouds.

Before they knew it, the sky fattened with those same storm clouds, a color so inky it made the exhaust from the diesel engines seem pale. Rain ambushed them then, the clouds illuminating with webs of white lightning, cracks of thunder following. It came down in thick droplets and pounded at the windshield as if wanting to come in and warn them of danger. Kudzu lit up neon green at every snap of lightning, it was everywhere in the Deep South, wrapped around highway guard rails and the surrounding plains.

The state line of Georgia came out of nowhere, as if both of their wishes entwined and magically made the sign appear.

Welcome to Savannah it said, and the brothers smiled in unison for the first times in their entire lives. Both were worn out from the drive, eyes puffy and sleep deprived. Gerald made the decision to park the car and ride out the rest of the hurricane-mad rain; they faced eastward so the rising sun would wake them. Before the pair could even speak, their consciousness succumbed to the gentle call of sleep.

* * *

Dawn was vermillion and rich with dew and fat goblets of left-over rain which took in the sun, sparkling diamond bright. Harry still sucked in air as if he'd never slept a good night in his life, his gasps unhealthy and frankly annoying to Gerald. A fresh ray of light passed through the windshield, and Gerald swished his finger through its warmth, wishing he could just ride on it and fade away. But the vast morning azure told him that the vacation would be everything he and his brother needed to heal that open wound between them, something the city life could never do for them. Gerald nudged Harry with his finger, and he jumped as if a bee had just stung him clean on the ass.

"What the hell was that?" Harry slurred, a bit of drool sliding down his chin, eyes webbed red with exhaustion.

"Let's go," Gerald said. "It's morning!"

"You drive, man, I'm too damn tired."

Gerald knew that was coming as his brother's eye sockets were a strange dark blue that hung low like a sad animal, his face lined with sleep wrinkles as well. Harry was visibly not rested. So Gerald consulted the old map once again, started up the car, and listened to the howl of the engine. By the time the car's temperature gauge rose, the day had begun to feel as stuffy and claustrophobic as a sauna.

He turned the car onto Route 16; old railroad tracks embedded into the ground which now acted as speed bumps. The road was slim and the tarmac was broken up by thick tree roots, but Gerald drove atop them, not caring, enjoying the rocking of the car as he went along. He was in the middle of the power of nature. The trees and vines looked as if they had enough of mankind and began to envelope all non-living structures with hearty green limbs. Rusted fences, telephone poles, even the abandoned railroad stop was slowly being taken back into Mother Nature's selfish heart.

The earth beneath them suddenly grew sodden, slowing the car down. Gerald realized then he needed to urinate badly; it had just simply crept up on him, his bladder ready to explode. He'd be bound to piss in the seat if he didn't stop, so he did just that, a quick halt to the trip just to relieve himself; or so he thought. With Harry still sleeping, the deafening snores enough to wake the neighboring town, Gerald saw no harm in taking the time out to go.

He stepped out the car and felt the true soil of the south, thick like a warm tub of putty as it engulfed his feet, each step a sucking pop. A swarming wall of greenery barred him from pissing where he wanted; he felt he needed a bit more privacy. Gerald pushed passed the vines and ubiquitous shrubs and thought he heard the distant wail of police sirens whistle through the air dissonantly, but he let that go. His bladder was too tight to dwell on noises, all he needed was a clear spot to let go the pain that initiated with each step.

That is when he stumbled upon it. Hidden behind a rectangle of fresh green vines, the great and dead looking excuse for a house stood on a dead strip of land. Dunes, black and vertical, lined the hilly area, and no more shrubs were in his way, just crab grass which bit at his legs like annoying horseflies. Wind blew eastward, toward the ocean, he could smell the near odor of sun block and saltwater. Weaseling closer to the weather beaten porch, the wood bleached from the pounding sun, Gerald noticed a pile of dead insects.

They crunched beneath his feet like hollowed vegetable bulbs, paint chips following, then more piles of starved insects, all omnipresent and amazingly eerie. He tried to elude them like land mines but it was no use. He lost control of his legs; the urine was expanding quickly within his bladder and instinct made him drop his leg down hard, and the small sound of sirens cut off like a light switch. He walked some more, toward the dirty, broken window at the end of the front deck.

"Hello," he called, peering into the dark house. "Anyone home?"

Gerald had no room to flinch before heavy footsteps transformed into rage and the window exploded. A hand as gray as old metal punched through the glass, gripped his face, and sucked him into a vortex of splintering wood and shattered glass as his feet left the ground and he was picked up like he was a child. The fingers were strong and clammy, and they held Gerald's face steadfastly, not easing up at all. His shoes fell off as his feet dragged along the carpeted floor, and the hand shoved two fingers tasting of bleach into his mouth and pulled him in further.

The house smelled of wet wood and disinfectant, the air musty like that inside a sarcophagus, syrupy thick like summer in New York City. The attack ceased for a moment, the fingers slipped from Gerald's mouth, and he made a break for it, his only chance, he felt, to run and escape. He managed to get two steps before the glint of a knife swished through the air and he fell head first onto the floor, the Achilles heal on his left foot sliced. The tendon split horizontally like frowning lips and hot blood painted his ankle as he dropped, yelling out in pain.

He was dragged to another part of the house which smelled faintly metallic; the taste of metal in the air strong. His heart wanted to punch itself out of his chest, but catching his breath was futile, his eyes blurred from the angst-sweat dripping off his brow. Then the big hand came back and punched him square in the stomach, pushing the urine out of him that had gotten him into this mess in the first place. It streamed down his leg, stinging the wound on his ankle, the feeling bitter-sweet.

A new set of sounds commenced, then more hands clawed at his navel, ripping away his shirt, opening the belt buckle of his jeans. Gerald couldn't see or scream; the hands were many. Light broke into the little closet-like room as the third figure came toward him; all three looked like giant apparitions. Then the biggest of them picked Gerald up and propped him on his shoulder and dragged him out of the tiny room.

A lecherous tongue slithered across his ankle, lapping at the blood mingled with sweat, the terror within him growing. Gerald lifted his head to place the face with the tongue and saw two flailing, pale breasts, shirtless, with two unhealthy black nipples like shriveled mushrooms. The girl stared at Gerald as he was pulled deeper into the shadows of the next room, her pupils spanning black holes. The big man dropped him onto a table, bound his wrists with fishing line, cutting deep into his skin, biting into the colorful veins beneath. Seeping blood pooled warmly into his palms, and Gerald knew then that he was going to die.

Harry, Gerald thought, some odd fraternal instinct still worried for his brother's whereabouts. And before he could think anymore, the familiar voice of an old woman cackled and recoiled through the entire house. It was a feminine smoker's growl, and as if it was a command, the big man picked Gerald up and pressed him into the wall, as if he could rub Gerald into the wallpaper.

"Momma, sis, come in 'ere and get a load of this. Suppa' come to us!" The big man said in a voice like a special needs child.

Gerald was trapped. The people wanted his body, bred by the blood ties that they all craved together. The other two, momma and sis, came in, but the big man's shining bald head blocked Gerald's full view of them. He thought he smelled a very familiar smell, and he knew that voice from somewhere, but he just couldn't place it due to all the commotion and pain he felt.

The big man twisted Gerald sideways and put him in a lock between his arm and torso, his skin like sandpaper to Gerald's soft face, then walked into another room. Gerald tried to escape, but the grip was like living prison bars. They moved into the kitchen where all the windows were painted black and where everything seemed to gleam dully. The little girl came over to Gerald and bit down on his Achilles heal, and an electric shock scurried up his leg. Instantly, he moved it away and kicked the girl square in her hungry mouth. She shrieked in anger.

She whined an indecipherable word salad at him, her face twisted in rage. Anger didn't suit her well, and she didn't know how to express it. She spat a set of teeth into her hands, drool following pale red in color, long and sticky like bloody snot. It dripped down her chin in wavelets and fell off her chin, smacking onto the kitchen floor. Her teeth fell, too, and she bent to pick them up, then sat upright, rigid, and smiled at Gerald with bleeding gums.

"Bo," she slurred at the big man, "let's eat."

Bo nodded slightly and slammed Gerald down onto the table in the middle of the room, forcing the air from Gerald's lungs. Bo stretched his legs out as the young, ratty-haired girl held his wrists. They buckled him down with leather straps, spread eagled on what seemed to be an operating table. Cold metal and bright, surgical lights glared down on him like a thousand rising suns, blinding him. Gerald closed his eyes and wished for imminent death, and found some solace in the cluster of bright spots leading him away from the reality before him.

* * *

The old woman woke Gerald up, pulled his eyelids apart, and sniffed his face with wide white nostrils. Silver hair hung over her face like curling dead maggots, and the smell of mothballs engulfed the air around her and choked him. Her eyes shone under the lamplight, and the sugar-white of them was all Gerald needed to know that this was the same woman from the house he'd received directions from the previous day. Then she smiled as his eyes dizzily met hers, and she parted her lips to show him her yellowed teeth.

She opened her hand and stroked two fingers down his sweat slick sternum, the nails wiping away the blood and sweat on the way down. She stopped at the base, the point where the bone ends and soft flesh gives way to the stomach. She made two tiny circles and licked her lips, then pushed through his skin with all her strength. Her sharp fingernail cut into his flesh like a knife and as pain ripped through Gerald, tendrils of blue flame found his senses and forced a yelp from his mouth.

Breathing became a laborious task for him as the old crone's fingers played around with his insides. She stopped when the young girl entered the room, whispered something to her momma and then received a nod of approval. The girl jumped onto the table and began to rake at Gerald's chest as if it held the secrets to her survival. She ripped furrows deep into his flesh, creating shallow, scarlet motes, the surgical light above soon sprinkled with the gore.

When she was finished, she used a straw to suck up the life-blood that was so viciously offered to her. Then momma once again pushed two fingers into the hole she had made, forcing Gerald to explode with pain as dark as a bruise. She clenched her teeth and grinded them in mock of her soon to be meal. And just as she finished fingering his insides, Bo entered, drooling incessantly. His cleft lip had rendered saliva control useless, the few teeth he did have protruded from the hollow where his top lip should have been. They lay forward, showing off his permanent, soulless smile.

In one hand was a razor blade, the other held what looked like a rusted potato peeler. The old woman signaled Bo with another one of her nods and he pulled a wet rag from his pocket and stuffed it into Gerald's mouth. When that was done, Bo licked Gerald's wounds, his tongue like a ravenous desert snake slithering across the puddles of red vitality on his torso, his face becoming smeared in it.

He stopped at the nipple then, bit into it and ripped it clean from Gerald's chest, a mist of blood spraying his face. Bo chewed on the tiny piece of flesh like it was a flavor packed piece of bubblegum. Sis came back, too, declaring a vengeance for her lost teeth, and a hunger she couldn't resist.

"I know there're two of you," she whispered into Gerald's ear with hot rancid breath, "Momma told me!"

The rusted peeler was now in her hands, and it glittered under the surgical lamp like old copper. She felt for Gerald's toes and went in for the attack like a vulture, peeling away layers of skin, clogging the peeler with human flesh. Gerald yelled once again, his cries muffled by the rag, the hurt never lessening in degree, but still was enough to know he was breathing. If pain were a color he would have seen all shades by now.

The girl continued with the blade as if she had done it before, many times before. She sliced skin from Gerald's foot until it looked like a shimmering, thin red toy for a dog to chew upon; she gnawed on the exposed bone like rawhide. At the snap of his toe coming away from his foot reverberated into Gerald's ear drum, his mind was already slipping into a state of shock.

Before he could regain his breath, Bo's unforgiving blade slid into the flesh covering his groin. He carved a slick scarlet map from his navel to his scrotum, and as his fingers parted the fatty meat beneath, he pulled a flap off like fresh deli meat and ate it as such. A river of urine diluted the pool of blood at Gerald's groin.

"Why don't you just fucking kill me, you bastards!" Gerald squealed, half blinded by the powerful surgical light.

"Kill you?" the old woman asked. "If we kill you, how will we eat? My family never feasts on a meal in which the heart doesn't still beat."

"Then please let me go, you old witch."

"Tell me where your delicious brother is and we just might do that for you. I know there's two of you," she said, her face a blur of brightness.

Gerald thought of that famous saying 'desperate times call for desperate measures' and completely vouched for its truth. His mind begged him not to tell, but his mouth had caught a pleading case of explosive diarrhea and he let the words spill free. They fell in sluices of selfish intent, and with the location of his car where his brother slept given up, Bo ran out of the house as soon as Gerald finished speaking.

No sooner did Bo leave, then he returned, carrying Harry's body. The big man had pulverized Harry's face into a concavity of mince meat, his arms and legs slack over Bo's giant shoulders. He placed Harry on another table next to Gerald, his limbs laid over the table like dead weight. In the heat of the moment, Gerald became territorial over his brother, a love executed just too late to save him—it was all over. He yelled, but it was no use, the old crone stuffed his mouth with a rag soaked in warm blood.

Then the family began to attack Harry, and Gerald prayed that his unconsciousness spared him the agony of their wicked fingers and multiple blades. The old woman scanned Harry's face, then pulled out the eyes and ate them like overripe grapes. Bo hovered over Harry's body as well, the visage a mess of black bruising and split open wounds. He was drawing in a shallow breath as the trio clawed at his body, hungry for meat, for a soul.

Then another blade lifted into the air, its serrated metal teeth a smile that only evil could love, and it was inserted over the pale, washboard tight flesh that covered Harry's chest. From both shoulders, to sternum, to navel, Bo created a thin crimson Y which opened up like a river feeding into an ocean. As the skin parted wide between Bo's prodding fingers, the old woman's eyes gleamed with madness and hunger. Harry's blood splattered against the dirty tiled floor like marbles.

The old woman handed Bo a chest spreader as he sawed into the sternum, and placed it between the rib cage. He placed the two sheers onto Harry's chest and then spread the handles to crack it open with the sound of crushed twigs. Up came warm, fleeting meat; throbbing with angst, Gerald squirmed about, but was subdued by an elbow to the temple from the old woman. Throughout it all, Harry's heart was still miraculously beating, a slow steady thump after thump.

The threesome pecked at the exposed innards with vicious mouths, took jellied flesh from Harry's body as if it was theirs to begin with. They held the colorful pieces to the surgical light so Gerald could see, then squished them into dark pulp in the palm of their hands, to let it drip into their mouths like delicious honey. Then the old woman took it upon herself to dig her face into the stew of cooling intestines, drowning herself in the puddle of bodily fluids and organ seepage.

She bobbed her head as if searching for apples, like the game people play on Halloween. The faint bubbling from her exhalation was all Gerald needed to hear to know that he was next, that he was going to suffer right along with his brother. And at the sound of the fizzing like an opened bottle of soda, the others joined her. They clawed, bit, sucked, and chewed at Harry's languid intestines. When the trio came up for air, a thick ring of ectoplasm lined their lips like red lip gloss.

At first, Gerald believed he was seeing what a clown does to trick people, where the ribbon never ends as he's pulling it from his mouth, but soon realized it was Harry's colon. Long uncoiled from its resting place, it was being tugged by the family as if it was a succulent sausage. Bo grabbed the thickest, grayest piece and severed it at the base. Watery brown feces sprayed everyone in a muddy mist, including Gerald.

Then the silvery glare of the knife came up again, and the youngest of the cannibals carved out the apex-meat of Harry's heart. She scooped it out of her hands, picked up a dirty jar from the counter behind her, and put it inside, then filled the jar with rust-smelling water. With fading vision, Gerald tried to break free of his bonds once again, but felt as if they were pulling tighter, like a noose, with each passing second.

The old woman separated Harry's elbow from his arm, licking the end of the bone-joint as if it was candy, chewing on the dangling white sinews like taffy. Harry took one last gulp of air thick with rot, then swam his conscience downstream to a permanent paradise.

It was the paradise he should have been at with his brother. The calm lullaby of death came and kidnapped his mind, taking it into a vortex of ephemeral black.

His mind overloading, Gerald found himself passing out; sure he would never wake again.

* * *

Gerald awoke to his body covered in dried blood crusted on his skin like a thin layer of mud. His ankle throbbed steadily, and he dared not move it, remembering the deep cut there. From somewhere in the house, he can hear the cackling of laughter, followed by glass breaking and the faint screech of knives being sharpened. Weak from his ordeal, the cold of the house makes it worse, and the hunger tops it all off.

Looking through a crack in the painted window, he can see it's now night, a single white ray of moonshine sparkling into the space where he lays. Remembering the entire ordeal, the blood, his brother, he tried to get up, but it was no use. A pain spike impaled his ankle and forced him to stop trying to escape. He began to sob, crying deeply for the brother he sacrificed to save his own life.

His chance to make amends with Harry was gone forever. There was no point in crying, it's all over. Now he just has to wait to die. Jealousy, narcissism, it all meant nothing to him now.

So when the smell of mothballs grew so potent that he couldn't stand it, he didn't care when the old woman cackled and stepped into the room, followed by her brood. Their faces, ravenous with hunger, smiled down at him under the pale moonlight seeping into the room.

Gerald closed his eyes and waited for them to feed.

OF PRIAPSIM AND BREASTS

KELLY M. HUDSON

Gabby loved cock.

It was true, perhaps the most honest thing she'd ever admitted to in her life.

Take, for instance, the man lying in her bed, bound and gagged and completely unconscious, with a prick as thick as her wrist standing at rigid, constant attention. God bless Viagra.

In a few moments, she would bind the bottom, at the root, and then severe it, taking the engorged member and burning the cut end, trapping the blood inside, and then, depending on her mood, eat it. Sometimes she put it in a pan and fried it, sautéing it with mushrooms and onions, then she'd place it in a hot dog bun, add some mustard, and chomp down. Or, if she was of that particular mind, she would roll it in corn meal, shove a round wooden stick through it, and deep fry it. Sometimes only a Corn Dog Cock would satisfy her hunger.

There were dozens of ways to prepare a penis for consumption and she'd tried them all, but mostly she liked to stick to the methods that kept the cock in its primary shape and state. That appealed to her the most. She'd fried, baked, and grilled her favorite meat, and each method of preparation had its own advantages and drawbacks. Eating it raw, like she sometimes did, was the best method; as far as retaining the original size and dimensions. Frying it made the poor member shrivel up, which she didn't like; and this little fact led to her seeking out men with rather large proportions, to make up for the lost size. The easiest way to deal with this problem, however, was to fry the outside quickly, like a steak, and leave the inside raw and bloody.

In the end, though, as long as Gabby had a steaming piece of penis in front of her lips, ready to slurp and suck and gnaw and gobble, she was happy.

The man in her bed groaned and stirred. She needed to move quickly.

Gabby tied the stump of the cock with a shoestring and drew it tight. She fished out her favorite knife and slid the blade along the tender, soft flesh just below the string. The man's eyes popped open when she was halfway through the penis, blood spurting and pouring over her working fingers and rolling down his balls and onto the plastic sheet covering the bed. He screamed and tried to move but she'd tied him too tight and there was no give.

When he looked down and saw what was happening, his eyes rolled into the back of his head and he passed out.

She finished, tying the end off to save as much blood as possible, and ran to the bathroom where she had the blowtorch ready. She put the flame to the bleeding end, cauterizing it, then applied a touch of the fire to the tip, sealing the hole. In a moment of triumph, she held the plump sausage up to the light to study her accomplishment. She caught a glimpse of herself in the mirror and smiled like she was seeing a long-lost friend.

Gabby was twenty-five, with short blonde hair to her shoulders, straight and parted down the middle, with bangs that stopped just short of her blue eyes. She had a pert nose, high cheekbones and full lips. She was five foot three, stocky but not fat, with large breasts and wide hips. She had the kind of body that her mother told her long ago would be perfect for squirting out a few babies. Yeah, that's almost exactly how her mother had said it, too. Like kids were water in a garden hose.

Standing there, shapely as she was, with a burnt dick in her hand, she thought she might have been the sexiest woman alive.

She studied the cock, turning it over in her hand. She wished she could masturbate with it. That would be incredible, she thought. Take it and stick it inside of her, more comfortable than any dildo could be, wiggle it around and then hump her hips up against it, coming hard, coming fast, so beautiful...

Gabby shook the thought from her head. She'd tried it once, but there was only a limited time before the penis became flaccid, despite all of her experiments. And since she loved the taste so much, better than anything in her life, she decided that if she had to choose, she'd take it in the mouth.

She discovered this bizarre desire of hers back in college when she was going down on a guy and she accidentally nibbled on the tip, drawing blood. The taste, blood mixed with semen and flesh, was the most exquisite of her life. Her mouth exploded with joy, sending shock waves through the rest of her body that rivaled the best of any orgasm she'd ever had. She wanted to gobble him up right there. She didn't, of course, but over time, the thought of it became an obsession. Eventually, after much plotting and planning, she'd figured out a way to make it happen.

Gabby got her men through want-ads on the internet. It wasn't hard to do. She simply made a post, something like:

I LOVE TO SUCK COCK

```
The  bigger  the  better,  honey.  In  fact,  it
takes  at  least  eight  inches  to  make  this  gal
happy,  so  don't  bother  unless  you're  packing.
    Also,  this  isn't  a  solicitation;  this  is  the
real  thing.  If  you  want  your  little  man  taken
care  of  right,  then  email  me.
Drug  and  disease  free  a  must.
```

And then she waited for the responses. About ninety-eight percent were bullshit, either flakes or game-players, but the other two percent sometimes yielded real gold. Gabby was careful to only do this about six times a year, and she had a fool-proof system so that she never got caught.

She went to her local department store and bought a hundred dollars worth of credit card gift cards, varying each time, using Visa, MasterCard, and American Express. She used only cash to pay and always wore a hat and sunglasses and dressed in a regular white t-shirt and jeans so that the cameras they used would get no useful information. She did the same at the internet café's that she used to post her ads, dressing almost exactly the same. She wasn't too worried that any of this would ever come back to her—most places only kept their security footage for two weeks, at most—but she decided that she could never be too careful, so she always stuck to her plans. She paid for the time at the café with her gift cards and used a fake ID she had made up from when she was in college. If any cops or private eye's decided to try and track down the missing persons that she gave to the world, they wouldn't get too far.

She would lure the guy to a hotel room she'd rented with another gift card, get them there, get them excited, give them a Viagra, wait until the object of her desire got good and hard, and then drug them again, knocking them out.

From there, it was a short walk to the guy's car, him leaning on her, whacked out of his mind on the valium but still able to move—at least for a short time—and then the drive to her house out in the country. She would get the guy inside her house and into her bed, tie him up, get back in his car and drive it to the hotel, leave it after wiping it clean of her prints and any other DNA evidence she'd left behind, and then ditch it. She walked two blocks to her hidden car and then drove home.

After that, she'd dose the guy again with Viagra and valium. Then the real fun would begin.

The man moaned, his cries of pain drifting in from her bedroom. Gabby decided that she'd eat his cock in front of him, making his final moments on earth a surreal and bizarre experience.

She didn't hate men. Far from it. She loved them, especially for the tool that dangled between their legs.

Gabby quickly fried his dick, and just watching it sizzle and pop in the thin layer of olive oil she used to lubricate the pan, she felt that familiar tingle in her crotch. Her stomach growled and her heart beat faster. The moment was coming, and soon, her mouth watering with anticipation.

Plopping the penis into the bun, she dribbled some mustard on it and then carried it back into the bedroom.

The man was on her bed, fully awake again, mouth open to scream but stuffed so full of two pairs of her pink panties that hardly a peep came out. Blood gushed from between his legs. It was insane how much men bled when you cut their cocks off and it was a lesson she learned the hard way when she had to replace the carpet in her bedroom after her first kill. Now she always made sure to leave the plastic on the floor, folded so that it created a funnel that the rivulets of blood could flow down and into a bucket that she kept tipped-over onto its side at the end of the sheeting. She would fill it up, fold the ends of the plastic so that the blood pooled, go and dump the blood in the bathtub, and then put it down again. Usually, though, her victims were dead by then. That's when the real work began; the chopping and the sawing, the draining and the burying. She had a special sink set-up in the basement, big and long and dug into the ground, where she could roll and dump the body into and then cut it to pieces. After that, garbage bags and a few trips out to the acres of woods that surrounded her country home, combined with some deep holes that she had to dig, and her work was done and her tracks covered.

Sometimes she thought about eating the other parts of the men, their legs or arms or chests. She'd even tried it once, but the taste didn't take. There was something special about the penis that drew her full and undivided attention. Still, it was a shame to let the rest go to waste.

He looked at her, fear and panic in his eyes. She held her precious treasure out for him to see, a glint of delight pinging from her grin.

"Do you see what I have, baby?" she said.

The man grunted and wept. She weaved her treat and his horror through the air, flying the bun as if it were a rocket ship in space.

"Thank you so much," she said. "I bet you taste really good, don't you?"

It was this way every time. The guy would whimper and then she'd eat his manhood. By the time she finished, the guy would usually be dead or, at the very least, broken.

She always left them to bleed out, usually she would wander off to the couch in the living room, turn on the television, and fall into a deep, satisfying nap. When she got up, if the guy wasn't dead yet, she'd put a pillow over his head and lean into it until he was. Then she got to work down in the basement

She raised the cock in the bun to her mouth, running her tongue over the head, slurping it, feeling the greasy taste trickle from the meat. It was a mixture of the olive oil, the sweating flesh, the tang of the blood inside, and a hint of semen. It was the greatest taste in life.

The man screamed against her panties, the cries coming out no louder than a raised conversation, and Gabby giggled as she buried her teeth into her food. The skin split open, yielding even more delectable delight as the blood inside spurted into her mouth, more semen with this taste, and she shoved her sandwich in as far as it would go.

She chomped down as the man squirmed on the bed and watched as any hope he ever had of making babies dropped down her throat with each bite.

Gabby orgasmed then, the combination of that utter hopelessness in his eyes mixing with the juices bursting in her mouth. Her hips bucked the open air in front of her as she ground the flesh between her teeth, crunching down, feeling each gristle grind into the valleys of her molars. The meat was a little tough, but she didn't mind, even as a piece got stuck between her two front teeth. She was too busy orgasming, the fatty flesh filling her taste buds with pleasure traveling all the way down her esophagus, into her stomach, then down further, filling her loins, sending shocks of delight snaking through the rest of her.

It was all she could to not crumple to the floor and start weeping.

As for the man, he died in moments, bled out and weakened. The last sight he saw was his penis being gulped down by a pretty woman with big breasts.

Two months later, she had another fish on the hook.

It was about time, because she was getting the itch again, the need, the feel, the taste for that cock between her lips, grinding into her teeth, and sliding wet and thick down her throat. She was thankful that the desire only came on about once every three months or so; there were only so many opportunities through the internet, and if her obsession was so strong that she had to have it more often, then she'd have to rethink her plans and come up with new strategies. She hoped that day never came; she rolled her eyes at the thought of hanging out at truck stops or rest areas, a black widow on the prowl.

All of which led to that fateful day, when she went online to put up an ad and found one already there, tailored to her tastes. It happened that way sometimes; she'd come upon an ad by someone else, one that had the right words and phrases and that eventually led to a hook up. It made her work a little easier, and this ad, the one titled **Looking for BIG Tits, Giant Cock for Trade** certainly held all the possibilities to make her intrigued.

So she answered the ad, sending out a picture of her real, fabulous and full, breasts. It only took a few minutes before the man responded with a picture of his own throbbing, enormous penis. If the picture was accurate, this man was hung like John Holmes, which was something most certainly rare.

Gabby prayed that it was true. She didn't have enough body parts to count the times she'd been disappointed, when someone actually didn't flake and showed up, only to have exaggerated the size of their cock. Usually those guys were packing pickles and not sausages, and it was all she could do to keep from drugging them anyway, take them out to her home, and then cutting their cocks off with no anesthesia whatsoever. But in the end, it was too much for a light snack, and just too disappointing when what she wanted was a full meal.

They made plans via email to meet at a hotel—one Gabby had never been to before; she was very careful to cover her tracks—a county away. Tom, which is the name he gave her, was excited; he wrote that he couldn't wait to give her his throbbing manhood.

Gabby's stomach growled. She couldn't wait, either.

The next day, it all went down.

Tom showed up and he was as good as advertised, a handsome man in his late twenties, with dark hair, glasses, over six feet tall, and a gym-sculpted body that bristled with power. Gabby had him take his pants down, to prove the prowess of his penis, and she was duly impressed. He was just like in the pictures he sent. He told her he wanted to see her tits and she obliged, taking out her golden globes and letting them dance in the shoddy fluorescent lights of the cheap motel room. He seemed duly impressed, too.

Everything went like it should; she drugged him, gave him his first dose of Viagra, and got him into his car and drove him to her house. She slipped a couple more valium down his throat and left him there, tied to her bed, and went back and ditched his car, wiping it down of any evidence or DNA, and then drove back.

She sashayed into her bedroom, humming a soft rock tune from the seventies, something about a dog named Boo, when she saw her bed was empty.

Gabby only had a moment to register her shock before Tom came out from behind the door, and punched her in the face, knocking her cold.

She woke up, tied to a kitchen chair, a gag in her mouth and her shirt off. Her breasts dangled on her chest, loose and free, her nipples hard as knitting needles.

Tom was humming the same song she was humming before he socked her, shuffling his feet and dancing naked around the stove. When he saw she was awake, delight glittering in his brown eyes, he stopped and did a little jig, then sauntered over to her, like he didn't have a care in the world.

"You're so cute," he said, bending over close to her face. Gabby struggled against her bonds but it was no good; he had her tied down tight.

"Slipping me valium's like that," he laughed. "Could you just imagine my surprise when I felt them kicking in and realized what you were up to? I mean, to find out that you had me in that hotel room to do something awful to me, I just had to pretend to go along."

He stepped back and she looked down and saw his swollen cock, flopping between his legs, as long and thick and beautiful as any she'd ever seen. In fact, it was the most gorgeous penis she'd ever laid eyes on. Tom noticed her expression and grinned.

"I know, huh? Pretty impressive," he said. He turned his back to her and went to the stove. He took a skillet out and set it on one of the gas burners and then turned the heat up.

"It really gets my foot in the door, you know?" He laughed again and shook his head. "Well, I guess you do. After all, you probably use your tits the same way I use my swinging dick. I bet you really reel 'em in, don't ya?"

He poured some olive oil into the pan.

"Just a little something you should know about me, before we go any further," Tom said. He turned around, still grinning, but Gabby hardly noticed; she couldn't take her eyes off his cock, pointing straight out like a steel rod.

"I'm in therapy. And my doc, he prescribes a lot of medicines for me, anti-psychotics and the like. And one of the drugs he doses me with is valium. It's to help me sleep, he says, and it helps with the headaches." Tom's face screwed up, remembered pain straining his expression. "You wouldn't believe how bad they get sometimes. The most awful, hurtful things." He recovered and stared at her tits. "There's only one thing that really makes the pain go away."

He shimmied over to her and reached out with his right hand. He fondled her left breast, rolling the nipples between his fingers. Gabby watched as his penis twitched with each rotation, wishing she could get free and get her hands on his treasure.

He let go and turned his back on her again, going back to the stove.

"So, I've built up a real tolerance. That one you gave me just took the edge off. The other two I threw up as soon as you left. The Viagra, though, that was already running around in this old body of mine, so there was nothing I could do about that," he said. He turned around to give her a nice eyeful of the monster between his legs, grinding his hips and humping the air in front of him.

"Not that you seem to mind about that," he said.

Gabby pulled against her bonds. She had to touch it, she had to get near it and feel it in her hands and then in her mouth. She just had to. But there was no give in the ropes; she was stuck fast and hard.

Tom jammed his hand into a drawer and shoved it around, the jangle of metal ringing, filling up the room. A smile crept across his face as his hand found what he'd been looking for. He pulled out a long knife, the very same knife that Gabby used to severe cocks with. He held it up and it gleamed in the overhead light.

"Yeah, so, I hope you understand, but this isn't personal," he said. He approached her again, this time with a cautious tread, like a hunter trying to sneak up on a baby deer. His voice dropped until it was a soft whisper. "There's only one thing that makes the headaches go away, and if my doctor knew, he'd put me away forever."

Gabby screamed against the gag as the knife flashed and then slid under her left breast. Tom grunted as he plunged the tip of the blade in, piercing her flesh. He growled as he worked the blade, back and forth, back and forth, sawing open a long incision. Blood spurted and poured over his hands and into her lap. The pain was unbearable, shockwaves of agony pulsed through her entire body.

Gabby passed out.

When she woke, a sickly sweet odor filled the air. Someone was cooking something, meat, and it smelled so good. She hoped it was a treat for her, maybe a cock ready to be gobbled?

Her eyes flew open and she looked at Tom's naked backside as he stood at the stove, spatula in hand. She stared down and saw that he'd cut her breasts off, leaving two bleeding, black holes in her chest. Blood congealed and covered her body, making her sticky, hot and nauseous.

Fat popped in the skillet and Tom giggled. He reached down with his spatula and scooped something up and flipped it over. He repeated the action.

Gabby swooned, blackness filling the edges of her vision again. She was dying, bleeding out on her own kitchen linoleum. And there was nothing she could do about it.

The last smell that poured into her nose was the sizzling of her own flesh mixed with olive oil.

The last taste that tingled her tongue was the sweetness of the grease of her flesh hanging in the air.

The last sight she saw was Tom, dishing his treat out onto a dinner plate, and turning to face her.

Two steaming mounds sat on the plate. It was her breasts, the nipples still hard and pointing at the ceiling.

And as the darkness took her over for the final time, the last thing she heard was Tom speaking.

"Mmmm! Sunnyside up! Just the way I like 'em."

CANNIBAL CABAL

KEITH LUETHKE

Morrison walked into the crowded bar wearing a black trench coat and hiking boots. He breathed in the smoke filling the air and nodded to a few of the drinking patrons. He took a seat on a bar stool near a large television on the wall, and when the tired looking female bartender showed her cleavage and asked what he wanted to drink, he ordered a rum and coke. He then turned his attention to the television screen and clenched his fist in order to keep his anger in check. A clean-cut newscaster was announcing the progress on the second wave of human cattle farms.

"The President has just left the human cattle ranch named Ridgeview Farm, located in Knoxville, Tennessee. Ridgeview Farm is the twenty-second of such ranches being implemented by the President in an effort to feed the starving citizens of America. He wasn't open for comment on the ranch or the devastation of the livestock due to the unknown strain of bacteria, but he was quoted by the head manager at the ranch as saying, 'These are terrible deeds we must implement in order to survive. May our future children forgive us'."

The newscaster went on to describe the sanitation involved at the human cattle ranch and how the bacteria strain killing animals was unable to taint the new food supply.

The bartender handed the man his rum and coke. She brushed his hand in the process and gave a seductive wink.

"I guess we won't have to starve anymore," she said. "Those losers weren't doing anything with their lives anyway."

The man's hand shot out like a snake and quickly grabbed her by the wrist and squeezed. His voice was gritty and harsh. "My brother is one of those *losers* in there," he growled.

The woman tried to pull away but he was stronger than her and wouldn't let her escape.

Another bartender, a man with a bloated stomach which hung out of his black shirt, appeared from the side.

"Hey, you, let her go, now!"

The man released the woman.

She rubbed her wrist, issued a soft whimper, and went through the swinging doors behind the bar to hide her fear and shame.

The fat man leaned forward.

The man in the trench coat could smell cheap bourbon and stale cigars on the bartender's breath.

"You're one lucky jerk," he said. "If the government didn't take away all of our guns I'd fill your body full of lead."

Thomas Morrison downed the rum and coke in one gulp. He dug into his pocket, produced a one hundred dollar bill, and set it on the table.

"Keep the change," he sneered.

He slipped off the bar stool and headed for the door. Behind him, he heard the man mutter a curse at him. Before he could leave the bar, a man in a business suit walked in carrying a brief case. He noticed him immediately and approached.

"Sorry I'm late. I had to work a little overtime," he apologized.

"No problem, Sid. Let's get out of here."

"Do you mind if we grab a long-pig sandwich on the way there? I'm famished."

"You can wait," Morrison said. "I won't take long."

The men walked out of the bar, their destination a hotel two blocks away.

* * *

When Sid entered the hotel room, he laid his briefcase on the bed and fiddled with the locking mechanism.

"Can I get you something to drink?"

"No thank you," Sid said, and opened the case. Inside, were an assortment of automatic handguns, a sawed-off shotgun, four grenades, and a long barrel rifle, which was disassembled.

Morrison took a bottle of whiskey out from under a pile of dirty clothes. He drank and grinned as he looked at the weapons.

"Do you like what you see?" Sid asked.

Morrison peered inside the briefcase and ran his calloused hand over the sawed-off shotgun. "Man, I thought I'd never see one of these again."

Sid took it out of the case and displayed the firearm.

"This was a standardized double-barrel shotgun which I carefully modified. It's fast, it's easy, and if you're within range of your target you can't miss."

Morrison took the sawed-off from him and examined it. "I'll take it," he said, and placed it on the bed. He pointed at two handguns with long clips, "What's that?"

"That, my friend, is a 9mm Model 12 Beretta capable of 550 rounds per minute. It was made in Italy, weighs 3kg with a muzzle velocity of 381m/s. I highly recommend it for taking out as many targets as possible in a small enclosure. And with the purchase of both weapons, I'll throw in two extra clips for you."

"Deal," Morrison said. "I want the rifle as well, and the grenades."

"Molly was right," he laughed. "You really are my best customer in months."

Morrison ignored him and grabbed the rifle pieces. He quickly began assembling the weapon and had it completed within sixty seconds.

"I take it you've had experience with this rifle before?"

Morrison walked to the window and pointed the rifle at a man walking his dog on the sidewalk below. He sighted the man's balding scalp with the scope and counted four strains of hair on his frontal lobe.

"I was in the marines. I'm a little rusty, but I can still aim and pull a trigger."

"That's not loaded, you know."

Morrison withdrew the rifle. "I know."

"I have plenty of ammunition for it, though."

"I'll take it, all of it."

Sid smiled and ran his fingers through his dark hair. "It'll cost ya."

"How much do you want?"

He produced a calculator from his front pocket and started pressing in numbers. A few seconds later and he had a figure. "By my estimate, fifteen thousand," Sid said. "You can always buy a few items today and I'll come by whenever you have more money if the price is too steep."

Morrison put the rifle on the bed next to the other guns. He went to his knees and slid a duffel bag out from under the bed. He unzipped it and withdrew four stacks of bills.

"I'll pay you fifteen thousand for the guns, and ten thousand to keep your mouth shut."

Sid couldn't help but smile. "Mr. Morrison, you have yourself a deal."

* * *

Dr. Faustus was leaning against a brick wall, holding a chemistry book in one hand, a book on astronomy in the other, and wishing he had a cigarette between his lips. His real name was Johnny Morrison, but he went by Dr. Faustus behind the heavily secured walls of the prison complex.

Although the guards and the managers called it a human cattle ranch for the preservation of humankind, he saw all those high fences covered in razor wire and couldn't help but feel trapped. He had an A.S in English Literature from Roane State, a B.A in Technical Communications with a minor in Chemistry from the University of Tennessee, an M.A in Writing and Rhetoric from the same university, and was working on his PH.D when the police came for him. Under law 2786, all citizens between the ages of twenty-five and fifty who had never contributed to society, in that they held no job that aided others and didn't perform any suitable service to America, were deemed unfit to live and taken to the nearest human cattle ranch for processing. If they'd never contributed to society in one way then in death they would fulfill a true purpose. What other choices did America and the rest of the world have? Animals were dying; their meat uneatable, and farm crops were becoming infected as well. Without suitable food, man turned against man and Dr. Faustus, extremely educated but never contributing to anyone other than himself, was on the list. He recalled the protests around the campus as he and the other students were taken away in white vans with tinted windows. The crowds picketed and screamed, but in the end, their stomachs got the better of them and they ceased their protests. He heard rumors of an underground resistance, but guessed that was a rumor set up by the government to give the human cattle some form of hope when all hope was gone. In the end, they were stripped down, scrubbed clean, and butchered for food. There was no hope.

A skinny man called out to him, knocking the thoughts aside. The man's name was Spam and he was scheduled for processing at five o' clock tonight.

"What time is it?" he asked.

"Where's your watch, Spam?"

"It's in the same trash compactor yours is in, you prick. Now help a guy out and tell me what time it is."

Dr. Faustus looked at the angle of the sun to the earth. He found a piece of straw on the ground and knelt down to stand it up. The straw produced a thin shadow and he looked toward the sun again.

"Well, what time is it, man?"

"It's about four fifteen or four thirty. You have roughly half an hour left," Dr. Faustus said, and tossed the straw on the ground.

"I'm not going easy. They'll have to work for their meal and clean up the mess afterward once I'm through," he laughed.

"I'm sorry, Spam. But I'm sure I'll see you soon enough."

"I'll save a spot for you in Hell, I promise. But only because you were generous enough to give me your soup once a week." He walked away, smiling. "See you on the other side."

Dr. Faustus watched him drift away with the other prisoners. Spam walked casually to one of the guards blocking the watch tower. He pointed across the yard, and when the guard averted his eyes, Spam pushed him aside and ran through the door. The guard snapped to his feet and ran after him. A moment later, there was a loud siren blaring throughout the ranch and three guards running to the tower.

More guards appeared and began directing the prisoners into the adjacent building.

"Nothing to see here, move along," they said, and shook their cattle prods at anyone moving slowly.

Dr. Faustus broke away from his spot on the wall and made his way into the crowd. Everyone moved at the same pace, looking forward with vacant eyes.

Then, suddenly, someone was shouting from the top of the guard tower.

"Try to eat me after this, you fucking assholes!"

Spam spread his arms wide and launched himself off the tower. He descended quickly and wore that same satisfying smile on his face. He landed head first and his skull exploded in a mess of fragmented bone and gray matter. The rest of his body crumpled in on itself with a loud snap which sang louder than the blaring sirens.

The prisoners gasped as one, but were soon prodded into submission, forced into the prison, and then into their single cells.

Later that night, Dr. Faustus sat on a bench shaking his head, thinking. *Even if they couldn't use Spam's brains for stew, they could still cut up the rest of him. He'd be good for about twenty or thirty sandwiches, he thought. He should've jumped into the incinerator in the basement and burned into a blackened crisp, because no matter how hungry, nobody likes an overcooked piece of meat.*

* * *

Morrison drove a white van into a suburban neighborhood. The lawns were well manicured, and the doors sensibly closed. He pulled into a three-story house with a bicycle on the lawn and ran his fingers over the briefcase in the passenger seat.

The curtains from one of the upstairs windows fluttered and someone looked out. A moment later, the front door opened and a clean-cut man in a dress shirt and slacks came out to greet him.

Morrison pulled the briefcase closer and opened the passenger door. "Hey, Howard, come on in."

Howard slid into the seat and shut the door. He gave a long sigh and rubbed his eyes with his palms. "What are you doing here?"

"It's good to see you again, too."

A young boy poked his head out of the house and waved, and then a pretty blond woman came out to see what was going on.

Howard rolled down his window. "It's okay, honey, everything's fine. Go back inside."

Morrison gave a gentle wave at them and Howard made him put his hand down.

The woman and child went back inside.

"I came here to ask you a favor."

"I'm a different person now. I have a wife and a kid and a house in the fucking suburbs what..."

Morrison drew an automatic handgun and pointed it at his friend's head. Howard's hands snapped up and batted the gun away, then he coiled his arms around Morrison's, stopping any chance to fire the weapon.

Morrison laughed loud and hard. "You've still got it, you son-of-a-bitch."

Howard let him go and eyed the weapon. "Where did you get that?"

"It doesn't matter. What does matter is that you owe me big time and I'm here to collect, or did you forget how I spent fifteen years in the slammer for you already?"

Howard lowered his head. "What do you want?"

"I need you to drive this van into the Ridgeview Farms visitor parking, and go inside and ask for my brother. Tell them it's his last night there. They probably won't let you speak to him but stall them anyway."

"Your brother is in there? I thought he was a professor at college?"

"He was studying to be a teacher but since he was over twenty-five and jobless, they took him there." Morrison handed his friend the automatic, dug into his coat, and produced another one for him. "You'll need these."

Howard held both of the guns, testing their weight and shaking his head. "I thought I left this behind after the war overseas." He stared at his house. "Will I be coming back?"

Morrison put his hand on his shoulder. "I'm leaving the van here. We're going tonight. Be there at eight o' clock sharp."

Howard looked behind the seat and saw a blanket covering over what looked like twenty barrel gallon drums.

"If you keep your head on straight you'll be home before midnight," Morrison said.

"What should I tell my family?"

Morrison scratched his chin in thought and said, "Tell them we're going to that old *Night of the Living Dead* movie playing in Market Square, then out for a couple of drinks." He took the briefcase with him as he left the van. "I'll see you soon, buddy." He drifted off into the street and disappeared down the road.

Howard saw his wife and son coming out of the house and he put the guns under the seat. He got out and hugged his boy.

His wife raised an eyebrow. "Who was that, dear?"

"He's an old friend. We're going out tonight. We have some unfinished business to take care of."

* * *

Back at the hotel, Morrison snapped the grenades to a belt and slipped it around his waist. Next, he put together the rifle, loaded it, and checked the scope for its accuracy. Once he was sure it was perfect, he strapped it around his shoulder. Finally, he checked the sawed-off shotgun, wiped the barrel down, and added two rounds of buckshot. He slipped the shotgun into a special holster he had strapped to his thigh. Lastly, he donned his black trench coat and went to look in the mirror.

A man with haunted eyes and an unshaven face stared back at him. The long coat concealed all the weapons from view. Pleased, he left the hotel room and didn't bother locking it. If everything went as planned tonight, he'd never return again.

* * *

Howard kissed his wife and son goodbye and climbed into the white van. He drove away from his house, neighborhood, and onto the road, not fully knowing where it would lead him. The drive to Ridgeview Farms was uneventful. He passed rows of corn, teenagers on skateboards, and an assortment of trailer parks.

When he pulled into Ridgeview Farms, a guard blocking the gate asked him what he was doing there this late at night. He told him what Morrison had instructed him to say, that he was here to see someone because tonight was their last day here. The guard offered no condolences but allowed him entry.

Howard drove the van into visitor parking and parked as close to the building as possible. He didn't know what was in the back of the van, but he guessed it was explosives.

He saw a few guards at the main door and quickly got out, flashing them his patented friendly smile. They moved out of the way like robots would: expressing no emotion and seeming to follow the laws no matter how asinine they were. The guns tucked under his jacket bounced as he walked and he silently cursed himself for not taping them down. He approached the front desk and greeted a man sitting behind a thin sheet of glass. He had biceps sticking out of his security guard shirt. His name tag read **Earl**.

"Can I help you?" Earl asked.

"Yes, I'm here to see Johnny Morrison."

"Visitation hours are from nine to five everyday except Saturday when nobody's allowed entry. Please come back tomorrow."

"It's his last night. I need to talk to him," Howard pleaded.

"I'm sorry, sir. You'll have to leave," Earl said, and pressed a button on the desk.

Three guards appeared from a side door to escort him back outside.

"You know, I'm really sorry about this. I was never really much for talking," Howard said calmly.

Earl looked at him like he'd lost his mind.

Howard pulled out both of the automatics and shot Earl through the Plexiglass window. The bullets tore into the man's flesh and he did a little jig before toppling over in his seat. Howard then pointed at the other guards and fired. The guns jerked in his hands, the bullets smacking into the guards' heads and coloring the walls red.

Another guard came out of the door wielding a high caliber rifle, but Howard cut him down before he had a chance to use it. He stepped over the bodies littering the floor and picked up the rifle. He then ran through the door where he was greeted by an office. Desks were clustered with documents and the walls were decorated in posters depicting street bums begging on their hands and knees to be allowed entrance into Ridgeview Farms. As he continued, he found the clerical staff hiding in their cubicles.

"All right people, I'm going to make this easy for you. Tell me where the prisoners being executed tonight are held or I'll kill every last one of you."

"They're in H-Block," an elderly woman quivered.

"Fuck you," a young man said. "You can't save them all. And even if you could, you still need to eat. Where do you get off…"

Howard interrupted him by putting a handful of bullets into his chest.

The clerical staff started screaming.

"Shut the fuck up!" he yelled back, and raced down a hallway where he found a door marked, **H-Block**. He looked back and saw the clerical staff running out of the room, past the dead guards, wanting to escape from him.

A moment later, a deafening explosion shook the building.

Howard closed his eyes for a few seconds, picturing all those people running for their lives, away from him, only to realize they were headed straight for their own demise.

A siren blared above his head, shaking him out of his stupor.

He opened the door and continued, never stopping again.

* * *

When Morrison saw the men and women running out of the building, he knew it was time to ignite the nitroglycerin. He withdrew a small receiver and pressed the button. The van exploded instantly, taking with it all the people and half of the building, making a nice entrance/escape route and sending limbs and bodies into the air.

He withdrew his rifle and pointed it toward the closest towers near the prison yard. Instantly, he spotted two men with rifles pointed at the smoldering ruins of the van. They weren't trained guards, they were novices at their job, and if they'd had a lick of sense, they would have been looking somewhere else.

Morrison aimed at the guard and planted a bullet through the man's brain. He took the other one out just as easily, and smiled when the body tipped over the side of the tower and splattered behind the security fence.

He did the same to the other tower, killing the guards with ease. Once they were dead, he then focused on getting closer to the building and shooting any guards who were dumb enough to go outside.

* * *

Howard opened the door and stepped into a nightmare. H-Block wasn't a prison, it was a butcher shop. The floors were stained in blood and slanted downward, leading to drains in the floor. A conveyer belt carried arms, legs, torsos, and other choice cuts into the next room which was marked: **PROCESSING.**

He gagged on the horrible smell wafting in the air and had to cover his mouth with his shirt in order to continue. He didn't hear the sirens which had gone off in the clerical room any longer.

Strange as it seemed, he tried not to think too much about the lack of security here. He continued and spotted sudden movement from the left. It was then he saw a man wearing plastic clothing with red stains, a construction hat, and a mask covering his mouth. He didn't see the intruder yet and was busy sorting through the body parts on the conveyer belt and tossing what wasn't edible into a biohazard bin.

Howard didn't take any chances. He learned long ago to put aside any feelings for anyone caught in the crosshairs of his gun and just pulled the trigger. The only thing that was important was completing the mission, and getting home in time to kiss his wife goodnight. As he aimed the gun and pulled the trigger, the man looked up and gave a startled glare before succumbing to the bullets tearing into his flesh. Lucky for Howard, the constant roar of the machinery drowned out most of the sound.

He continued and went through the processing door. Inside, the lights were dim and there was an endless row of rooms with tiny windows flanking both sides of a long hallway. When he peered through the glass of the closest one, he gasped in revulsion.

In the room, a man was hanging by his feet from meat hooks through the Achilles' heel of both legs. His throat was slit open and his blood leaked into a drain. Howard jerked away from the window as he tried to take slow, easy breaths. He had to focus and keep his mind on the task at hand. Quickly, he looked into another room and then another, to see another man hanged from his feet, and in the next room it was a woman.

A figure appeared in the hallway. It was a bald man wearing a bloodied butcher's apron and carrying a machete with chunks of flesh hanging from the blade.

He squeezed the trigger of both guns without aiming. Some of the bullets hit the walls but the few that struck their target found their mark on the butcher's face, crashing through his skull, and making a red mist fly from the back of his head.

Another man in a butcher's apron came out of one of the rooms looking confused.

Howard ran toward him and shot out his kneecaps.

The man screamed and toppled to the ground, his machete still gripped in his shaking hand.

Howard aimed for the man's wrist, but ended up taking off the arm at the elbow.

The man screamed even more.

Howard leaned over him and shoved the barrel of his gun against the man's forehead. "Where are the live prisoners?" he demanded.

"This...this is H-Block."

"I know that, you dumb ass. Where are the live prisoners?" he repeated.

"They're dead," the man replied, shaking even more as he slipped into shock. "They're all dead. They began killing themselves after a guy jumped off one of the towers. We had to put them all down."

Howard unloaded the remainder of one of the guns into the man's chest. He tossed the weapon aside and armed himself with the rifle he'd pilfered earlier. He still had one more automatic but he wanted to wait to use it in case he ran into harder targets.

Carefully, he gazed into the room the man had exited. It was the same as all the others; a blond woman dangled from her feet, her throat slit in a wide, bloody grin. She could've been his wife. He looked into her brown eyes and shook his head. She was some-body's daughter, or future wife, but all of that was cut short be-cause of the need to feed the population. He pulled himself away from the grisly sight and continued down the hallway, checking every room he came upon, but all of them were the same. When he reached the end of H-Block, he collapsed on his knees and wept.

* * *

Morrison picked off three guards with ease when he reached the yard. They weren't even putting up a fight. These weren't soldiers. They were hired goons, and stupid ones at that.

A handful of men ran out of the building armed with rifles.

He hid in the smoke cloud from the explosion and withdrew one of his grenades. As the men approached, pointing their firearms in different directions, Morrison threw the grenade at them. They screamed just before it detonated.

He ran out of the smoke and found pieces of the men littering the yard. A few of them were still alive but missing their legs or arms. He shot them down with a steady hand. One, a heavy man, pleaded for his life. Morrison put a bullet between his eyes and continued to the main entrance.

The rifle was almost out of ammunition. He didn't count on killing so many people but it was a necessary evil if he was ever going to see his brother again. If he'd known the death toll was going to be so high, he would've asked the dealer for more ammunition. After all, nowadays, life was cheap.

As he walked out of the prison yard and toward the building, he reached for another grenade and tossed it into the building. The grenade exploded and created a hole big enough for him to crawl through. He would've preferred to use the door or the gaping entrance the nitroglycerin had created, but he didn't feel like dealing with any more guards than he had to.

Upon breeching the inside of Ridgeview Farms, he was greeted by gunfire from three men. The poor bastards were aiming right at him but could only hit the walls or the floor, as they were so dazed from the explosion.

Morrison dropped his rifle and quickly pulled his sawed-off from his shoulder. He unloaded two rounds of buckshot, shredding all three of the men. He stepped over the bodies and reloaded.

Ahead of him was a map on the wall. He quickly studied the details and discovered the prisoners were being held in H-Block.

From behind him came heavy footsteps and lots of shouting.

"Shit," he muttered, and yanked another grenade from his belt. He pulled the pin and tossed it down the hallway, then raced in the opposite direction.

As the explosion ripped through the building, he charged through a door marked H-Block. Inside, the walls were lined with doors. Small windows were set into each door and the hallway seemed to wrap around in a circle. He peered into one of the rooms and witnessed a man dangling from hooks by his feet and bleeding like a pig onto the floor.

Then, the barrel of a gun poked his backside.

Morrison lifted his hands in surrender.

"What's the matter, friend? You don't recognize me?" Howard asked jokingly.

Morrison spun around, and a wave of relief flooded over him, to be followed by worry.

"Did you find my brother?"

Howard shook his head. "I think they killed everyone after the explosion. It must be some kind of failsafe they had."

"No," Morrison sneered. "I don't believe you. He's here. He's alive."

Morrison began checking the window of every room for signs of life. He found none.

"One of the guards told me they started committing mass suicide, so they just decided to kill them all. I'm sorry," Howard said.

Morrison continued searching the cells. He jumped from one to the other, only looking long enough to decipher if the person hanging there was his brother.

Howard sighed and shouldered the rifle in favor of his automatic. He covered the door, waiting for the moment when the guards would converge on their position.

"We're finished here, Morrison. Do you have an escape plan?"

"The sewers below lead back into the city. But I'm not leaving without my brother."

"We won't be leaving at all if you don't hurry the fuck up. They're all dead, man."

Morrison suddenly flung open one of the doors. He ran to the man inside.

"Johnny..."

The bearded man's neck was split from ear to ear. He'd been slaughtered only a few hours earlier.

Morrison yanked the meat hooks out of his ankles and picked up his brother's body. Tears streaked down his cheeks but other than that his face was a hardened shell. He carried his brother out of the cell and walked down the hallway.

Howard said nothing.

What could he say?

He could only follow and look over his shoulder for approaching guards.

Morrison led them into the room with the conveyer belt. The room was devoid of guards and workers but the machine still ran. He walked toward a door that Howard hadn't seen before. It was marked: **INCINERATOR**.

Howard moved in front of his friend and opened the door.

Heat immediately slapped their faces as they entered the room. They walked down a metal staircase, which led to a large, open furnace where flames licked the sides of concrete walls, eager to be fed.

Morrison carried his brother to the burning inferno.

"I'm sorry, Johnny. I wasn't fast enough."

He dropped his brother inside and the fires burned brighter, accepting the offer of flesh. Next, Morrison walked under the staircase and began pulling at the floor.

Howard put his guns down and helped.

Together they lifted a heavy metal lid. A ladder led down into the darkness.

Howard jumped down, quickly descending into the sewers below. But he soon paused when he reached the bottom upon realizing that Morrison wasn't following him.

"Come on man. We got to get out of here."

"Take the first left you come to, then a right, after that keep going. You'll come out near 11th street," he instructed as he grabbed the sewer lid to set it back into place.

"Morrison, get down here you idiot!"

He ignored Howard's cries and dropped the sewer lid, then found a heavy box to put on top of it. He laughed to himself as he covered the lid. His research on Ridgeview Farms had paid off more than he could've hoped for. Of course they would find out about the sewer passage eventually, but by the time they did, Howard would be long gone. His friend would be free and had paid his debt to him in full.

Above him came shouting, orders, and lots of footsteps.

Morrison armed himself with his sawed-off in one hand and fingered the last of his grenades in the other.

He was on his way out of the room when he spotted Howard's automatic on the floor. The gun would come in handy when he approached the crowd of guards. He picked up the weapon and walked up the metal stairs.

To his death

To victory.

* * *

A week later, Howard sat in a smoky bar and ordered a rum and coke in memory of his friend. As he sipped the drink, he watched the television screen on the wall and grinned as the announcer spoke.

"After the devastation at Ridgeview Farm last week, authorities have added extra security to all human cattle farm facilities, but thankfully the services won't be needed much longer as the President has announced today that they have successfully found a cure for the unknown strain of bacteria destroying livestock world wide. Today marked the end of all human cattle processing plants and the first beef hamburger eaten within six months since the beginning of this travesty. The President was the first to eat the burger and said it was delicious but lacked a certain something. When questioned, he wouldn't say what ingredient it was, but that it was something everyone would probably miss."

THE NEXT BIG THING

ROB ROSEN

*T*he Next Big Thing, the headline on the newspaper shouted. *Bigger than goji berries*, read the banner just below, not so much a shout, but still loud enough to grab my attention and give it a good shake. "Oh, please, let it be cheaper than goji berries," I prayed. "And better tasting."

I continued reading, my eyes growing wider by the second, my stomach turning like so much soured milk. And then I read the article again. And again. Looking for the joke. A typo. A misquote. Anything. I mean, sure, we have to pay the Chinese a ton for those stupid little foul tasting berries, but this new thing, come on now. No friggin' way. Still, when my very own mother gave me a jingle, I had no choice but to believe.

"Got 'em at the store, Stevie," she informed me, proud as can be. "They were running a special. Lady fingers, ten for five dollars." My mother was always the first to jump on the bandwagon. Stocked up on bran in the eighties like it was no one's business. Might as well have built a silo in the backyard. Grew her own wheat grass in the nineties until she was literally shitting green. Then it was pomegranate juice all last year. Didn't even need lipstick, her mouth being so purple and all. Makes you wonder, though. Why does everything good for you taste so God-awful bad? Now this.

"But ten of them?" I asked her, wondering how she could even eat one, let alone all ten.

She sighed. "Always the naysayer, Stevie. Of course I had to buy ten. I couldn't buy just one hand's worth, now could I?"

I sighed back. "But they're lady fingers, Ma," I countered. "From a real live lady."

"Dead lady," she counter-countered. "Live fingers would be against the law. I suppose. Besides, you eat cow, don't you? Chicken? Pig?" She paused, obviously building her case, shaky as the foundation might have been. "You even ate a llama once, as I recall."

I coughed. "When, Ma? When did I ever eat a llama?"

Her cough echoed mine. "Oh, um, well, never mind. It was a long time ago. Peruvian diet. Tasted just like chicken. Mostly. The point is, meat is meat, son. And this meat, the experts say, is the best one for us yet. Seeing as, well, it is *us*. Makes it easier on the digestion. No harmful additives needed. Gets absorbed into the system faster than you can say 'pass me the Adam's apple'. Good for the environment, too."

"Because?" Now she had me curious, despite my better judgment.

Again with the sigh. It was no wonder my older brother had always been her favorite. He was probably chowing down on a tender foot right at that very moment. "Because, Stevie, no crops are needed for feeding. No pasture land, no cages, no waste disposal. In fact, this is the ultimate circle of life. You're born, you live, you die, you're someone's dinner." My mother would've made a great traveling preacher. Or Tupperware salesperson. Not that the two are that vastly different. Both, after all, bring salvation right to your doorstep.

"So, eating dead people is the ultimate circle of life?" I asked, my stomach lurching at the very thought. "Seems like, I don't know, opposing factors working here."

She shushed me, eager to be done with the conversation. Which made two of us. "Either way, Stevie, when it's my time, just shove me in the back of the Prius and drop me off at the Safeway down the street. They're offering two for one coupons in trade now. Memorial stickers on the packaging even!" And with that, she hung up. Thank goodness. I looked in the mirror and noticed that my face was as green as the wheat germ that grows in my backyard— still uneaten. *Blech.*

I folded up the newspaper and tossed it away, figuring it was all just a trend. I mean, back in the seventies, she had a pet rock that she named Stan. And yet, with a feeling of dread, I remembered that she had divorced my father about ten years later, but still had Stan, who had since assumed my mother's maiden name and had taken to wearing jaunty little felt hats. In other words, when I flicked on the television, I wasn't all that surprised at what I saw. Sickened, yes, surprised, no.

Local news. Hot trends. Human flesh. Forget those pesky crematoriums and overpriced plots of land. Besides, as they claimed, all the good eternal views were already taken. Nope, sell off your parts and let your loved ones pocket the profits. FDA approved, physician recommended. Cheaper than beef, better for the environment. Green all the way around.

"Guess that's the selling point," I said, with a grimace. "Save the planet by eating your neighbor's thigh. Odd that the circle of life should somehow dead-end at your dining table. Wouldn't Norman Rockwell have had a field-day painting that picture?"

It still didn't add up, however. Was anybody really buying dead folk besides my mother? Was anybody stocking up on it? Were new wills being drawn up all across America's amber waves of graves? Again my stomach did a series of perfect ten somersaults at the mere thought of it all. One thing I did know, however: I was staying clear of my mother's kitchen for the foreseeable future.

Only thing was, my plans were quickly hampered. As was my diet.

The Next Big Thing hung around, lingering very much like L.A. smog. Sadly, on a side note, so did those goji berries. Heck, first time I saw human flesh on a restaurant menu it was goji berry encrusted Asian lower back. Talk about your double whammies. So I stuck with a salad. Meat free. I hoped. But still, I looked around; half the tables had ordered the lower back. Yep, it looked just like chicken, though nobody was fooling me.

Nonetheless, that bandwagon of Ma's had become a veritable runaway train. Or trains, as was the case. Stations and stations full of them. Meaning, the fad quickly became the norm.

"Just try it," my brother said over lunch one day. "It's surprisingly good."

"It's death warmed over," I told him, the familiar eddying in my belly growing to cyclone force.

"The beef market is drying up, Stevie," he informed, matter of factly, mouth full of chunks of Latino and salsa. "The cow pastures are reverting back to their natural state. Chicken farms are closing right and left. Nobody's breeding pigs or sheep for food. And there's less pollution from all that animal farting. Mother Nature is delighted."

I dropped my fork of spinach and walnuts, the sound clinking all around us. "But you're eating a dead person. D-E-A-D person." I was stating the obvious, but the obvious was apparently only obvious to me. It was like that age-old question: if a tree falls in the forest and there's nobody around to hear it fall, does it make a sound? Only, it seemed that the trees were thrilled that we were slurping up our own kind and leaving them alone for the time being. Meaning, my protests were falling on deaf ears. Which was also being served on the menu, slathered in gravy.

He set his fork of flesh down and looked up at me, all older brother like, full of bullshit wisdom that didn't fool me when we were kids and certainly wasn't holding any sway now. Guess I learned my lesson with all those pies made out of mud and gravel that he was always trying to get me to eat. "But you consume dead cows, and drink their milk, and wear their hides for your belts and shoes. Seems to me, eating our own kind is way more natural than any of that."

"And environmentally sound," I added, with a derisive snort.

"Exactly." Guess he took my snort for an acquiescent sigh. Shows you how smart he is. Still, it ended the conversation. His ignorance, as usual, became my bliss, however short lived it was.

But turning off my older brother was a mere drop in the bucket in an ocean of popular opinion. Pork, like he said, was becoming less commonplace on menus from Miami to Memphis, where barbequed good old boy was all the rage. The beef market was even harder hit, McDonald's suddenly adding a whole human menu. Quarter pound neckwiches were selling like hotcakes. Which, conversely, weren't selling half as well as big toe links.

And yet I avoided it all, bucking the trend.

The months crawled by—on tender baby knees that sold for a dollar a pound. I'd reluctantly gone vegetarian during that time. What choice did I have? I even joined a dead flesh protest group, but only a dozen people showed up for the first meeting, half for the second when we realized the donuts were baked with human-infused lard. Nothing, it appeared, was going to waste. Yippy for the enemy.

Too bad for me, I was virtually alone in my revulsion. The wave spread, engulfing the planet, third world countries suddenly awash in cash. Why plant a failing crop in an arid desert when you could just wait for your citizens to die off? Survival of the fittest meant that one day you'd get to eat even leaner Indian sirloin and tastier Ethiopian chuck. Yep, old Mother Nature would've been dancing with joy on our graves. If we still had any. Which, of course, we didn't.

"Just try it," my mother pled, the Thanksgiving turkey replaced by, of all things, Cherokee pie.

"Are those Brussels sprouts coated in anything even remotely human?" I asked, glumly.

She shook her head from side to side. "No, Stevie."

"Then no thanks. I'll stick with my veggies if you please."

"Suit yourself," she replied, with a shrug. "It's even better than Navaho. I hear they're grass feeding them these days down on the reservation. The meat sells for a pretty penny, but it's worth it." She eagerly chomped down, my family quick to follow, all of them staring at me with looks of condescending pity.

Screw them, I thought, as a Brussels sprout glided mercilessly down my throat.

Though soon enough that's just exactly what they were: screwed. Royally. Well, to be fair, we all were, but who was I to point a delectable finger? *Blech*. It bears repeating.

Guess we were so busy tickling Mother Nature's fancy that we forgot to look towards the future. Go figure. How unlike us not to plan ahead. Still, you'd have thought that someone would've put two and two together and come up with something nearing four. I mean, once humans became the meat of choice, and animal farms started closing, and old Bessie got set free to wander the expanding grasslands, and geese turned into pets instead of pâté, what do you end up doing when your protein source eventually dries up? And let me tell you, the answer wasn't a pretty one. No sir, no how.

Plus, apparently, once you go human, you never go back. So, yes, Bessie and Porky and Big Bird were safe, but yours truly was now fair game. Emphasis on the word *game*.

And so it began: hunters and gatherers turned farmers turned reality stars turned hunters and gatherers again. Guess that circle of life is one of those vicious circles you hear talked about. Round and round she goes, where she stops nobody knows. Or cared to find out.

Goji berries fell by the wayside after a decade or so. The Next Big Thing: bars. Steel bars for the rich folk, wood ones for the not as lucky. The big bad wolf was huffing and puffing down our doors, and if you were one of the less fortunate ones, those with hay for window protection, well then, bon appetit. Seems we weren't dieing fast enough for some people, I guess. I mean, we all gotta eat, right? As in each other.

"What's for dinner, Ma?" I asked one day, all smug-like, braving the nasty streets to visit her.

She let me in, wearily, her head tilted to the Smith's house to our left. "That's what you get for hiring a chubby maid who can't run fast enough." The door slammed quickly behind us. "Consuela made for a better dinner than a duster, anyway." She turned and smiled. "Guess a little fat never hurt anyone."

"Except Consuela," I retorted.

My mother scowled and led me to the kitchen, the smell of Venezuelan housekeeper wafting languidly up my nostrils. *Blech*, yet again. "Still not going with the flow, Stevie?" she asked, stirring the bubbling pot.

"What flow, Ma? Haven't you heard, there's a drought now, a trickle. Bessie would be laughing her bovine ass off had she lived to see the day. Guess wild cows never stood a chance, what with their lack of any natural abilities I mean. Should've taught them how to hunt before we set them all free. First bad winter and, boom, skinny carcasses for miles. The chickens stood up a bit better, I suppose. Until the pigs ate them all. Then died from the avian flu they all came down with."

Her scowl notched up a degree. "Guess that llama is looking better all the time then, huh?"

"Nope," I said, arms akimbo. "Took off for the mountains as soon as they were released. Lots of grasslands up there now, what with all that global warming we were supposed to have halted once we switched to eating each other."

"What have the polar ice caps done for us, anyway?" Obviously, her glass, unlike her cooking pot, was still half-full.

"True, Ma. And, as an added bonus, look at all the beautiful beachfront property we've gained. Tons more shoreline. Too bad we can't go out and enjoy any of it."

She held up her pink iPhone/Taser. Yep, the next Next Big Thing had finally arrived. "No one's eating *me* for a midday snack any time soon, Stevie." With her grin returned, dinner was served, Consuela for her and my brother, the standard Brussels sprouts for yours truly. Ironically, I'd grown to like them. Better than wheat grass, at any rate. But what wasn't?

Too bad, though, pretty much everyone else felt the same way about wheat grass as I did. Meaning, no one was going vegetarian any time soon. Not when there was still meat to be had out there. Human meat, that is. Billions of people on the menu. Why stop now?

Actually, twenty years into the craze and there was no signs of it slowing down, despite the shortages at the markets. In fact, the less of it there was to go around, the more people clamored for it. Even the scientists said we'd grown reliant on it. Gee, ya think? Plus, as a people, we never were ones to be told no, even if it meant saving our own hides. Literally. In other words, those iPhone/Tasers sold real well. As did the flashlight/Taser and the miniature keyring/Taser.

As a result, human flesh became even more scarce, available only to the rich. Or anyone with the wherewithal to steal from the rich. And then promptly eat them. Not like the police cared by that point, anyway. Or the governments of the world. Besides, fewer people meant more meat to go around. Though that's when that vicious circle grew downright nasty.

I'd moved out to the country by that point, leaving my family to fend for themselves. After all, the whole damn house was Tasered, so I figured they were in good hands. And my crops were doing well enough, despite the fact that once all the cows, chickens, pigs, and sheep had died off, the vermin infestation was a trifle difficult to contend with. But still, I wasn't going hungry. Which is more than I could say for nearly everyone else that was left.

Too bad the worst was yet to come, as if eating each other out of house and home by, well, eating each other, wasn't horrible enough. But, as a people, we did have a history of learning our

lessons the hard way. Why should this little problem be any different? Though, of course, the next one was a real doozy.

My mother called me on the phone that faithful day. "So, Mister
Smartypants, have you been watching the news today?"

I laughed, gazing at the mice as they sizzled upon impact with
my electric fence. "Too depressing, Ma. I stick with the oldies
station these days. The Golden Girls never tried to eat each other.
Ditto for Friends. Happier times."

"You forget, Stevie, that many famous actors were the spokes-
men for Hormel Albino Chili."

I groaned. "I nearly forgot, Ma. That was a nice ad, as I recall.
Something about the new white meat. Pleasant stuff."

"Made for a real tender meal, too," she added, humming at the
image that had obviously formed in her addled head. Then she
regained her senses, and said, "Be that as it may, turn on the news,
quick."

Which I did, surprised for the first time in a long time. Because
really, once everyone looked to their friends as a food source, what
else could be all that surprising? Though I must say, this, in fact,
was just that.

"Well, I'll be," I said, with a low whistle.

"Huh, no I told you so?" she grumbled.

"What would be the point, Ma? I've been telling you so for the
last two decades, and all you have to show for it is a bunch of
empty houses for neighbors and twenty extra pounds of long-
forgotten friends." I paused and thought about it, then added,
"But, yeah, I told you so." And, gee, it felt good to say it.

See, eating all that human flesh really wasn't good for everyone
like the press had been reporting all this time. Not really good for
the environment either. In fact, per what was being broadcast at
that very moment, the only ones profiting from the Next Big Thing
that simply would not go away was the government. All of them
across the world, really. Every last friggin' one.

Guess back in 2009, when this mess began, all the presidents
and leaders of countries got together for a talk about global warming and other environmental issues, and what they found was that
they couldn't afford to fix the problems that mankind had brought
upon itself: not enough food or medicine, too many greenhouse

gases, the ozone hole, shrinking ice caps and glaciers, an ever-expanding population. It was enough to give any world leaders a splitting headache.

"Those bastards," my mother spat into the phone. "Convinced us to eat one other. A fast and easy solution."

"And cheap, too," I couldn't help but add.

She sighed. "And still the same problems persist."

My sigh echoed hers. "Well, at least there are far fewer people around to complain about them."

Which was true. But there were, however, just enough.

And, man, were they ever hungry.

The armies were no match for a population armed with Tasers. Capitals were overrun, government buildings set upon, politicians attacked, dismembered, and promptly eaten.

Tastefully and with the appropriate wines, of course. And then, at long last, the Next Big Thing was finally over and done with. Zoo cows, zoo pigs, zoo sheep and zoo chickens were to be bred again, free range and with no additives, preservatives, or processed with any dangerous emissions. If the past generation couldn't fix the planet's woes, the next one was sure as hell gonna try. Myself included. Oh, yes, and I planned on going back to eating meat. Because, really, how many Brussels sprouts can one man consume in a lifetime?

And I moved to the city again, near my mother and brother, all of us quite a bit older now, if none the wiser.

She had me over the first night I was back in my old stomping grounds. "Try it," she said, handing me a steaming plateful of food, a smile on her face that mimicked the one she'd since painted on Stan the rock.

I squinted into the glop. "It's not llama again, is it?"

She frowned. "Don't I wish. We should be so lucky. It'll be quite a few years before any of us gets to eat meat again."

I dipped my spoon into the mess and took a deep whiff. "*Blech*," I said. "What the hell is this stuff?"

She smiled and held up the newspaper. "Next Big Thing, Stevie. All natural. Nothing whatsoever harmed in the preparation."

I read the article and tossed my spoon into the bowl. "Goji berry stew made with wheat grass?" My stomach lurched, just like old times. "What, no bran?"

She turned around and then set the glass on the table, the thick brown liquid inside sloshing back and forth. "Drink up, son."

I groaned and took a sip. Guess Mother Nature had the last laugh, after all. Who knew she had such a sick sense of humor?

DRESSED IN BLACK

NICK MEDINA

There wasn't much money after that dreadful Tuesday in October of 1929. There wasn't much food, either. Thomas Tuttle had started a business three years earlier. It was one that wouldn't go under. His family wouldn't starve.

* * *

Nora Tuttle settled to the parlor floor. The hem of her old dressed billowed around her until it settled on the woven rug beneath her. In her hands was a doll with a porcelain face. She made it dance on the rug between the many rows of unoccupied chairs.

The bonnet covering the doll's head came lose as Nora made it bounce and spin. She could hear music in her head—a waltz performed by beautiful violins with a piano accompaniment—although the parlor was mostly silent. Every now and then a light thud or a scraping sound came from the front of the room, but Nora didn't pay the noises much mind; she was used to them by now.

Any other six-year-old girl would have run for the safety of her mother's arms upon seeing the foreboding box at the front of the room, but not Nora. She looked up from her place on the rug and smiled at the casket on the stand ahead of her.

"Good morning, Nora," Thomas said. "You're so quiet that I almost didn't see you there." He pushed his bodyweight against the casket a few more times until he had it aligned just right, and then lifted the lid.

"Who's that?" Nora asked.

Thomas strode down the center aisle between the rows of chairs. He bent to give Nora a kiss on the top of her head; the navy blue ribbon in her hair brushed against his clean-shaven cheek. "That's Mrs. Anthony," he said.

"Mrs. Anthony," Nora echoed, remembering the nice, old lady who lived near the church, the one who gave her licorice snaps every Sunday.

Thomas' lips pulled tight as he patted his daughter on the head. "She's gone to God now," he said, wiping his hands against his slacks. "I've got to drop in on Mr. Walther for a while. Why don't you run along and see if your mother needs you."

Nora nodded and Thomas patted her head once again before swinging his jacket over his shoulders and heading out on foot.

Nora waited a few minutes after he'd left before she stood up on the rug. Cradling the doll in her arms, she approached the casket. Laying there in a black dress with lace around the cuffs and collars was Mrs. Anthony. Her hands were pale and gray, but her face was made up and her hair was perfect. She must have been happy because she had a smile across her lips. Nora knew that if she touched her, Mrs. Anthony would be cold.

She danced the doll along the edge of the beautiful box and then nestled it between Mrs. Anthony's arms. It may have been Nora's imagination, but Mrs. Anthony's smile seemed to spread.

* * *

"How's Mr. Walther?" Cynthia Tuttle asked her husband in-between stirring the stew on the stovetop.

Thomas shrugged and cocked his head simultaneously. "Frank had his money in stocks. All but twenty percent of that's gone...assuming he can get it out of the bank." He sighed. "I told him I'd help him out the best I could."

"Tom," Cynthia protested, turning away from the stew.

"He's an old man," Thomas argued. He crossed the kitchen to take his wife in his arms. "He doesn't have anyone else. Besides, the Lord said to love thy neighbor and he's the closest one we've got."

Cynthia forced a smile. "What about us?"

"We're going to be just fine," Thomas assured her. "Everyone has to bury their dead. That's not going to stop."

"But, Tom... " she started.

"We're going to be fine," he said again, cutting her off.

Cynthia pulled away from her husband's arms and turned back toward the stew, which was more broth than meat and vegetables. She stirred it faster than before. "Pass the pepper, please."

Thomas reached for the pepper, but it wasn't in its usual spot. He reeled around in search of it.

"I don't see it," he said.

"We're out," Cynthia replied. "We're out of pepper and everything else."

Thomas' face turned crimson. "Don't embarrass me," he said.

"I'm scared, Tom."

Thomas' shoulders sagged. He reached for his wife, but she leaned away and his hand landed against his side.

"They're calling the day that it happened 'Black Tuesday'," she went on. "I read it in the daily. I don't understand it all...what went on in New York...but we're all going to suffer because of it."

"I have money," he said through gritted teeth. He grabbed his wife and held her tight around the wrists this time. "I have always provided for this family and I always will. We won't suffer."

Tears glistened in the corners of Cynthia's eyes. She blinked fast to wipe them away. "Dinner's ready."

* * *

Mrs. Anthony's family came to watch over her.

Her husband was there with their three sons, one daughter and fourteen grandchildren. The people from the town came, too. They crowded into the Tuttle's parlor because Mr. Anthony didn't have enough space to have his wife's wake at home.

Nora peered in on the gathering through a keyhole from the Tuttle's dining room that connected to the parlor. She'd seen countless gatherings like it before—countless seas of black suits, dresses, hats and veils. She wondered why so many people cried. She never cried.

"Nora, dear, come away from there," Cynthia said. She reached into the large pocket on the side of her housedress. "Your father said he found this in with Mrs. Anthony." She pulled the porcelain doll from her pocket. "What was it doing in there?"

Nora shrugged. She flashed her wide, innocent eyes at her mother. "I thought she might like it," she said.

"I'm sure she would have," Cynthia agreed, kneeling down on the floor to be closer to her daughter, "but you must keep it for yourself." She lowered her voice to a whisper. "Toys may be hard to come by from now on."

Nora looked perplexed. She took the doll from her mother. "But this one's from Saint Nick. I've been good. He'll bring me another."

Cynthia's eyes glistened again. "I'm afraid Saint Nick might not make it this year."

"Nora!" Thomas said from the doorway, startling Cynthia. Neither she nor her daughter had heard Thomas come in. "There's nothing to worry about," he went on, speaking to his daughter while scowling at his wife. "You'll have plenty of toys."

Nora backed away from her mother. She could feel the tension even though she didn't know what was causing it. She inched out of the room then ran for her bedroom. Thomas glared at Cynthia. He pulled a wad of rolled up bills from his breast pocket and threw it at the floor.

Cynthia's face fell. She stopped her hand just before it made contact with the money. Thomas grunted, then turned his attention back to Mrs. Anthony's wake. He couldn't help but notice that the table at the back of the parlor—the one where those paying their last respects usually left a homemade dish—was empty.

* * *

It wasn't just Mrs. Anthony's wake that went without. Over the next several weeks Thomas tended to the funerals of Mr. Jacobs, Mrs. Reed, the young Curtis Becker Jr., Mr. Kline, Mr. Yetter and Ms. Mabry. They were all meager affairs.

"The money," Thomas said to Cynthia one night after putting Nora to bed. "Where is it?"

"It's safe."

"Give it to me."

Cynthia bit her bottom lip. "Why?"

"Don't ask questions."

Cynthia hesitated, but ultimately crossed the room to a loose floorboard, which she pried up with her fingernails. She fetched the money from the darkness below and placed it in Thomas' hand. Thomas counted the bills to see how much was left. It was almost all there. He counted it again, this time placing the bills in two separate piles.

Apprehensive about questioning her husband, Cynthia stood to the side, chewing her lip more vigorously than before. Finally she asked, "What are you doing?"

Thomas rolled the two separate piles into two wads. He handed one back to his wife and slipped the other in his pocket. Cynthia questioned him again with her curious eyes.

"For Frank," he explained.

Cynthia's face paled. "Half?" she gasped. "You can't."

"He needs it."

"We need it," she argued. "We have a child."

"We'll be fine," he said again. "Besides, Frank will pay us back when he can."

"When? Years from now?"

"If that's what it takes." Thomas donned his hat and jacket and went outside to the house next door.

"We'll never see that money again," Cynthia said to no one and nothing but the empty air.

She found a new place to hide the money.

* * *

Even with the money Cynthia had stowed away, dinnertime at the Tuttles' wasn't the affair it used to be. The bread was stale. The vegetables were wilted. The meat was lean.

"It's what we can afford," Cynthia said as Thomas chewed on an unrelenting piece of gristle.

"There's more cartilage here than meat."

"It's the best I could do," she insisted.

Nora struggled to stab a rubbery carrot.

"How much money's left?" Thomas asked.

"It's almost gone."

"It can't be," he said, nearly choking on a roll more akin to a sponge than a loaf of bread.

"How long did you expect it to last?"

"There was enough money there to last us six months."

"You gave half of it away."

"Three months," he spat.

"It's been two months since the crash."

"I made money last week."

"It's still not enough."

"Where's the money now?"

Cynthia made like she didn't hear him. She helped Nora with her carrots.

"Where's the money, Cynthia?"

Her nervous eyes darted from Nora to her husband then back to Nora again. "I'm sorry, Tom, but I can't tell you."

This time Thomas' eyes darted back and forth across the table. He reached over his plate to stop Cynthia's busy hands from cutting up the scraps in front of her. He also took the knife from her hand.

"I don't like these carrots," Nora whined.

"You may be excused," Thomas said to her. He waited until Nora's chair was empty before going on. "Why can't you tell me where the money is?"

"I need it...I can't let you give anymore away."

"Mr. Walther would have lost his home without the money I gave him."

"Better him than us."

"Cynthia!"

"I'm sorry," she said quickly.

"What's come over you?"

"It's just..."

"You're not the same. Your heart's gone cold."

"Tom," she almost cried, "I'm pregnant."

* * *

The economy worsened. Thousands of banks failed. The money hidden beneath the Tuttles' mattress diminished and Cynthia's belly grew rounder while Thomas' cheekbones became more pronounced. But still, the Tuttles had it better than most.

Thomas saw it all the time; most of the families he knew in town were barely making ends meet. His weren't the only cheekbones that seemed to stick out farther than before. Everyone's clothes appeared to be hanging a little looser lately. Even the children who ran through the schoolyard looked a bit gaunt. Thomas thanked the Lord that Nora's cheeks were still full and pink.

"We need that money back," Cynthia told him one night before bed.

Thomas sighed. "Frank's doing his best."

"Has he paid you anything?"

Thomas shook his head.

"When's the last time you saw him?"

"Few days ago," he grumbled.

"He's avoiding you."

"He's not avoiding me."

"Go to him then. Tell him we need the money back."

Thomas rubbed his wife's belly and planted a kiss over her navel. "Tomorrow," he promised. "I'll talk to him tomorrow."

*   *   *

The planks of Frank Walther's front porch groaned beneath Thomas' weight. He knocked on the door for the sixth time, rapping his fist harder now than he had before. Still, no one answered.

"Frank," Thomas called, pressing his face against the front window. "Frank, it's Tom from next door."

Thomas shifted back and forth, making the planks beneath him cry out louder than before. Frank was always at home. He had nowhere to go and no one to see. He always answered the door. Standing there in the cold, a horrible thought came to Thomas' mind. What if Frank had taken the money and run?

"Frank!" Thomas hollered, fearing that his wife was right all along; fearing that they would never see the money again. And then an even worse thought crossed Thomas' mind. He pounded his fists against the door once again and then forced it open. "Frank, I'm coming in!"

The house was quiet inside. The air was cold. A stench that Thomas knew all too well invaded his nostrils.

"Damn it, Frank," Thomas muttered upon finding the old man tucked in bed where he'd been laying dead for at least three days. He kicked the bedpost and pulled the sheet up over Frank's face. Then he set out to find what was left of the money.

"It's gone. I can't find it anywhere," Thomas told Cynthia later that afternoon.

"What do you mean it's gone?" she asked, struggling to keep her voice from quavering.

"I looked everywhere...I tapped on every floorboard, overturned every mattress, searched every picture frame and opened every box and drawer in that house. There's no money anywhere. It's gone. He must have spent it."

"Spent it," she wheezed. "He's one man living alone. How could he have spent it all?"

"I don't know," Thomas said, shaking his head. "I just don't know." He collapsed into an old armchair, sending a puff of dust into the air. He rested his elbows on his knees and cradled his head in his hands.

"What have you done?"

"Cynthia..."

"We'll never see that money again. I was right. You never should have given it to him."

"Quiet, Cynthia."

"I will not be silenced," she said, throwing down a dusty leather-bound volume within reach. "Have you looked at me?" she hissed. "I can no longer be forced to choose between feeding my daughter and my unborn child."

Thomas slowly pulled his head from his hands. His eyes traveled across the room to his wife. He'd been so consumed with her expanding midsection that he hadn't paid much attention to the rest of her. Now that he looked, he was startled at what he saw. Her face was thin. Her arms looked frail. Her collarbone protruded at the base of her neck. Her body was ravaging itself to support the developing life inside it.

"My God," he gasped. "Cynthia, I'm sorry."

"Tom," she cried, "you must do something."

Thomas dropped back in the chair, his head spinning. He sat in silence, keeping the pressure of his unthinkable thoughts to himself. Mr. Walther's wake was scheduled for the following evening. It was Thomas who would have to prepare the body.

"All right, I think I know how Frank can pay us back," he said.

* * *

The townsfolk came to say goodbye to Mr. Walther. He looked almost the same in his box as he did in life. Thomas had done a good job.

Cynthia stayed in the kitchen while the guests filed past to look in on Mr. Walther. She had one eye on a boiling pot of cabbage and the other on Nora, who was playing near the doorway.

"Cabbage again?" Nora asked, sniffing the pungent air.

Cynthia nodded. It was the third time that week and it wouldn't be the last.

"I don't like cabbage," Nora said, making a face.

Cynthia sighed. She was tired of it herself, but choking down another helping of cabbage was the least of her worries. The baby inside of her hadn't kicked in days. She couldn't feel its life.

"Tom," she started when he entered the kitchen, only to be cut off by her own curiosity at what he had in his hands. "What's that?"

Thomas thumped the bundle—a nice sized package wrapped in white paper—on the counter. He pulled back one of the folds to reveal a beautiful, bright-red slab of meat marbled perfectly in all the right places.

"Where did you get that?" she asked, her voice nothing more than a shocked whisper. Her mouth salivated and her empty stomach went into a rage that made her entire malnourished body shake.

"Butcher," he grumbled.

"But how?" Cynthia asked. It was as though the cut of meat was much too fine for her feeble fingers to touch. She peeled back the paper, but refrained from picking up the meat.

"I told you we'd have nothing to worry about," Thomas said, ignoring her question. "We won't go hungry."

* * *

The fetus in Cynthia's womb kicked the instant she swallowed the first mouthful of cooked meat. Her baby was alive after all.

Nothing had ever tasted so good to Cynthia. The rich, flavorful juice that burst from the meat with each bite she took filled her with a feeling so sublime that she felt more alive than she ever had before. If it weren't for Nora, she would have eaten the entire slab of meat herself, and Thomas would have let her.

Weeks past and the meat kept coming. The Tuttles had more of it than they could consume.

"Why do you buy so much?" Cynthia asked Thomas one day. "Surely we could use the money for other things."

Thomas gritted his teeth. "You're right," he said. From that day forward he didn't bring home quite so much.

But then Cynthia got suspicious. "The extra money," she said. "What have you done with it?"

Thomas hemmed and hawed. There wasn't any extra money. There was only the truth.

"What would you like for dinner tonight?" he asked.

Cynthia looked perplexed. "That doesn't explain the money," she said.

"I know. Just answer the question. What cut would you like for dinner tonight?"

Still confused, Cynthia scrunched her face up in thought. "A rib roast," she said, knowing it wasn't exactly the cheapest cut of meat.

Thomas nodded. He turned out of the kitchen and headed for the parlor where Mr. Davison was laying in wait. He returned within minutes with a white paper-wrapped roast in his hands.

Cynthia's eyes went wide. Her lips moved, but no sound made it out of her mouth.

She understood.

Thomas put the roast down on the counter in front of her. She fell forward, clutching the edge of the counter for support. The muscles in her throat and stomach contracted.

"No," was all she could say.

"I had to."

"I don't feel very well."

Thomas slid a chair across the kitchen so that his wife could sit down. "Why should it be any different now that you know?" he asked.

Cynthia breathed heavily. "Mr. Walther..." she uttered, knowing he must have been the first.

"We saved him from losing his house. He saved us from starving."

Cynthia didn't know what to say. She stared at the hunk of fresh meat, beefy and bloody, for more than a minute.

Thomas cleared his throat and dropped a hand on his wife's shoulder. "If you don't start now," he said, pushing the meat closer to her across the counter, "it won't be ready in time for dinner."

* * *

Cynthia watched her daughter at the table that night. Nora chewed carefully, never knowing that upon her plate was her best friend's grandfather. As Cynthia watched Nora, Thomas watched Cynthia.

"Eat up," he said. "You must stay strong."

Cynthia brought a fork-full to her mouth. She thought she might be sick.

"We should be thankful," Thomas went on. "We are blessed."

Why the others had to go hungry—the ones who, in exchange for a proper casket, took to burying their dead in plain pinewood coffins to save money—he didn't know. There was more than enough to go around.

And so, instead of letting family and friends attend the wake of their loved ones on empty stomachs, Thomas Tuttle provided the meal. When Mrs. Francis died, he fed her family a roast from her backside. When Mr. Warnick passed, his loved ones dined on brisket from his chest. When widow Bishop lost her battle with whatever had caused her hair to fall out, her mourners found a hearty stew—consisting of the cuts that weren't too meager on her emaciated frame—waiting for them.

Thomas wasn't just an undertaker, he became a butcher, too. If it was tongue Cynthia wanted for dinner, then tongue she got: chuck, shoulder, rib, sirloin and round, too. He'd cut up the corpses; she'd cook them. And as long as the face and hands were untouched, the grieving family was none the wiser.

"*She looks lovely,*" or "*He looks like his old self,*" Thomas would often hear regarding the lifelike work he'd done. And then, inevitably, someone would remark on the food. "*This is delicious, Mr. Tuttle,*" and "*Mother would have loved this,*" they'd say before asking, "*What's your recipe?*"

Thomas would smile and shrug in response. "The misses," he'd explain. His job was to tend to the dead. He'd make up the pale faces and drape the bodies in black, covering up what he'd done. Thomas dressed the bodies; Cynthia dressed the meat.

* * *

Seven weeks shy of nine months, Cynthia knew something was wrong inside of her. She screamed for Thomas. He called for the doctor. When the baby came out, it wasn't crying. It wasn't even moving.

"I'm sorry," the doctor said.

Cynthia sobbed. The doctor cradled the lifeless child.

"Doctor," Thomas said, drawing the man's sympathetic attention away from Cynthia. "I'll take it from here." He held out a sheet of white paper between his hands. "I am the undertaker, after all."

The doctor placed the baby boy between Thomas' hands. Thomas took the bundle to the parlor. It had been so long since he'd had veal.

DAYS IN A BARREL

SPENCER WENDLETON

1

The popping of bubbles became Robert Allendale's world; their production, their expansion, and their inevitable breaking. This cycle kept him suspended in reality because it was easy to forget anything existed in the darkness, in a room with no parameters or shape; he could be anywhere and not know it. Maybe he was in a coma, asleep in the warm waters of the birth canal. But the birth canal was supposed to be warm and nurturing, not a snuffing deprivation into boredom and insanity.

He was edging closer to dropping off that edge of the cliff and plunging into mental nothingness. He could feel his mind grow numb in his skull, the cranium going soft, the cerebral cortex shutting down. When would he become a brain dead vegetable? Could he get bored to the point of stupidity? He'd spent days, maybe a week in this unknown place. He had no sense of time, but it crawled on with agonizing sluggishness.

That question that began to plague his mind: When will I finally be dead?

2

Robert yearned to give in to the urge to sleep forever in the heavenly blue sky, and forget his life and everything leading up to this point, when a voice banished those thoughts of solace.

"Boy, you must've thought you'se fall'en down a hole and can't get out! I got the power back on, give me a second. Generator's out. Hank's pissed I can't fix it, but here it is, fixed."

Upon saying 'fixed,' the plastic box casing the lights cast their impossibly bright beams into his eyes, blinding him; all Robert could see was purple blotches, as if he'd stared into the sun.

The man was tickled by his reaction, and jokingly said, "You should see the look on yer face, like a rabbit about to be turned into rabbit's feet. I guess you'd need one 'cuz yer one unlucky sum' bitch, now ain't ya!"

Robert's vision returned, and he studied the man dressed in a blue and black flannel shirt and tattered, whitewashed jeans, and a scraggly beard that shielded the bottom half of his face, the overall package making him resemble a backwoodsman.

Without another word, the stranger left the room, tending to an unknown errand. The reasons for his departure failed to matter to Robert; what concerned him was the netted sack slung across his shoulders heaped full of gristle-covered bones.

3

The shock of witnessing the bones faded in the aftermath of his newest observation. He was immersed, neck-down in a wooden barrel of broth the color of Guinness beer. The fluid contained pigments of green, reds and purples, a rainbow tint to the substance which was thicker than soup. A waft of chicken bouillon, horseradish, butter, and a medley of vegetables—especially onions and bell peppers—overwhelmed him, their smell so strong it was tear-inducing.

He couldn't see what bound him in place beneath the dark water; he couldn't move no matter how hard he tried.

Robert kept checking the white-walled room; the size of a child's bedroom. There was no furniture, only more wooden barrels; six in front of him and two on each side. He could only see the people in them from the neck up—bodiless. A steel panel was installed on the front of each barrel with vacuum-sized tubes jutting out that connected to a mechanical device in the center aisle—a power generator. It churned on low, propelling the bubbles swirling in the barrels.

He eyed the people in the barrels again. Only one other occupant was awake, a woman with brunette hair and a talcum-white face. Her hair, once lustrous, had demurred into a mop head of grease that stuck to her forehead in spider leg strands. He summoned the strength and saliva to call out to her but nothing came out, his lips obstructed by duct tape.

After moments of staring at her, *really* looking at the woman, he finally understood the woman's stare was a dead one.

4

Hours drifted by, and none of the barrel people woke. Perhaps they were too weak to move or talk or they had been downgraded into drooling, spaced-out vegetables; something he was working towards slowly but inevitably.

He was pulled from his thoughts by the entrance of a frail woman in a white dress. The fabric could've passed for a bed sheet stitched together by an amateur seamstress. When she entered the room, Robert could see the raised circles of fabric at her chest, shaping her marble-sized breasts, bra-less, and the bone grooves of her sternum plate. Her eyes were a size too large for her face and the nose a bit too small, lending her an inbred quality. Her teeth also stuck out over her lips, giving her mouth a rough, beak shape. She wore plastic gloves and a bored expression.

The woman smiled at him, introducing herself. "I'm Nora." She didn't follow up on the introduction.

Nora unlocked a compartment on the side of one of the barrels, a box housing a urinal bag. She dumped the refuse into a white plastic bucket, replaced the empty bag, and went to another barrel and repeated the task for each one. She stopped at the woman who had died, floating rigid and growing bluer by the hour. The eyes were still open and turning into marbles buried in gel.

"Oh, my." Her mouth tightened into an **O**, and she checked the woman's pulse, jerking in fright upon feeling the ice-cold flesh. "She's dead! I have to tell Hank. Oh, he's gonna be so mad! She ain't s'pouse to be dead yet!"

Nora rushed out the door, and then abruptly returned, lugging the plastic bucket with her this time, careful not to let the urine slosh out. Robert could overhear her hollering outside for Hank, her voice fading with each step she completed. For a brief moment, Robert caught the sunlight and sun-filled sky before the rickety door slammed closed again.

5

This time Robert had fallen asleep and was woken by the sound of fizzing water. A man, well-clad in a black Burlington suit, had his sleeves rolled up and he was dumping what looked like brown salt into Robert's barrel. The man weighed each load in a plastic cup, executing his work with serious precision. Through the bouillon stench, Robert also caught a whiff of designer cologne. The worker was a clean man with trimmed eyebrows, a freshly shaven face, and an even left part to his hair. He was handsome, though the way his eyes roamed the waters, and the way he pinched the surface with two fingers and tasted it, Robert became nauseated. But there was simply nothing in his stomach to throw up, and the jerk-spasm of his throat continued without release or the relief of a good purge.

The stirrer caught on that Robert's eyes had opened, and he stood up straight, regarding him like a trophy to behold. *I earned you*, his gaze professed. *And you're all mine to do as I wish.*

"You know, I was very angry when that dumb bitch whore came and told me that woman was dead in the barrel. She wasn't going to be finished for nine more days. It's like trying to age whiskey, right? Your buyers want it thirty years old, and instead, you give them three month old mash. It's not the same, and Nora knows better. Just because she's my brother's rag doesn't make her exempt from the rules." Under his breath he said, "That's just less they get to eat."

The man came in closer, and Robert gagged, taking in the malodorous medley of onions, garlic and raw meat on his breath. His teeth were bleached white, everything about the man a contradiction against his counterpart, Nora, and the other man he'd seen, the backwoodsman.

Then the worker smiled at him, sharing a quip. "That Nora bitch might be dumber than a box of shit, but she's a step above masturbating." The man slapped his sides, enjoying his wit. "If only she knew when to shut her fucking mouth, we'd be good. Fuckin' yokels. Oh, well, they're cheap under-the-table labor. I guess for this line of work, you have to keep it in the family.

"And it's too bad my brother's a fucking trailer trash moron. Nora's one, too, though she's an outsider to the family. And you're looking at me thinking 'then why are you here if you're smart and they're trash? You don't seem related to that Ernest-looking motherfucker,' is that what you're saying? Well, I guess I got lucky; I was born with a better brain than Davey. I go against what they always say; I'm not a product of my environment. I went to school and started my own business, thanks to the Chinese market, and I left Davey in my dust while he was banging out roads working construction and generally fucking off. Ah, but my business is catching on in America, though. It's an expanding market. Real profitable. Yeah, okay, my helpers are dipshits, but the two tend to the barrels good enough."

And that's when Nora stepped into the room, clutching onto what would normally be used as a boat oar, and walked over to Robert and stirred the broth in his barrel. The man left her to work, slapping her on the ass before making his exit. "Do what you're good at; and don't talk to him, got it? I know you, and I know you like to go on."

"I ain't talkin' to him, so fuck off, Hank," she snapped.

Hank pointed his finger at Nora, scolding her, before taking the final step out. "See you tonight. Do the job right."

She flipped him off. "I know, so get out already."

Hank kept the door open a crack, peeking in, "Now stir it good. Mix it well so it sets in right. Remember, that bitch died because you weren't paying attention. Her feeding tube had come off, and so did the Demerol drip. I swear you and my brother need me to hold your hand the whole time. Well, I can't; I've got deals to make over the phone. I've got boxes to ship."

Nora shouted, losing her calm, "Fine, just go! Git! I fucked up, so fuck off!"

She shooed him, and once he was gone for good, she delved the wooden oar back into the barrel with extra gusto, channeling her anger into her work.

Each time the oar touched Robert's lower body, he was jolted. He could feel again, his skin growing clammy and loose. He pictured his flesh coming undone with each connection of the oar and nearly passed out, but instead of going under, he lost himself, spinning and loopy, spaced out on the swirling reds and greens that frothed at the corners of his vision.

The sensation attacked him all at once and didn't relent. The colors spun as prisms in his eyes, a hypnotic cycle, and he remembered what Hank had said about Demerol and the dead woman.

He, too, had been drugged, and being drugged, he was relaxed, and all he could do was listen to what Nora had to say.

First, she talked about her collie, Baxter, and how he wasn't fixed and kept humping everything, including the dinner table leg. Then about her boyfriend, Davey, who couldn't fix a clogged toilet in the house or knew anything about how to court a girl or treat one right, though he was awesome in bed. How Hank had moved into their neighborhood and offered her and Davey lots of money for doing a little work, mostly supervision, and how if they betrayed him, he'd shoot them dead. And then she shared a secret about how Hank had snuck them special meat in their dinners and addicted them to the product. They were accessories in murder, and if they didn't want to be arrested, they'd help the business along without telling the police, Hank told them.

After she was finished speaking, she peeled off his duct tape, and he wanted to cry out, but she trained a knife to his throat and asked in a sweet voice, "Tell me about your life—and don't scream out for help. I can cut your throat and still use your body. So let's be nice. Talk to me, okay? Polite conversation."

Fearing the blade, he spoke up, obeying her instructions, though the loose banter resulted from the many doses of drugs. "I'm a medical supply salesman. I travel around the country promoting my company, MedCorp USA. I give big speeches to important people with big fat important wallets. And I'm doing this because I want to have a child. Yeah, it's strange saying that. Let me explain. My wife was in debt when I married her. She went through a bitter divorce the year before. Her good-for-nothing ex-husband didn't work, and they couldn't balance their checkbooks, and here I am, spending twenty-five days out of each month away from her just so I can pay off those debts, and then I can get a new job—any job—and then we can have a child. I love her. I really do. Money doesn't matter; it's who you wake up with in the morning, that's what matters. Money can be made, lost, replaced, but people, they're not a dime a dozen; not the good ones. So my wife and I wanted a family after making a fresh start. A clean slate. An open portfolio, you know. Then the children."

He kept repeating the same things, and Nora didn't seem to care. The sound of his voice was entertainment enough for her. She stirred and stirred with the oar, the water's surface stewing with white bubbles and black grit. Stirring and stirring, the granules of salt, bay leaves, fresh ground pepper, cumin, cinnamon and many other ingredients he couldn't place kept dissolving finer and finer until they were nothing.

The mix hurt his eyes again, stinging them, so he closed them tight.

"Sorry 'bout that. It's going to hurt more soon, mister, just so you know. It's been fun talkin' to you. Sure has. You're a nice guy. Really, you are. It's lonely out here. Nobody but Hank and Davey to talk to, and most of the time, Davey's drunk and hung over and a big cranky asshole." She lowered her tone. "And he's mad because I'm fucking his brother, but hey, it was his idea. It's the only way to get more product. We have to steal it, it's so expensive. Davey takes a bit from the crates, the prepared stuff already cooked from the grill and dehydrated and already pulled from the bones and every-thin'."

She smiled big for him, leaning down to him, and flicking a switch behind him. "I just increased your morphine drip."

I thought you'd said Demerol earlier…

"You won't feel a thing. It gets you talkin', yes it does. I love it. I love honest to God conversatin'."

Swimming up a stream of wet concrete, that's what Robert's body felt like; he struggled to convey his want of survival to her, but he only managed to spit out, "But wait, I…can't you let me free?"

She placed a new swatch of duct tape over his lips, shaking her head. "Hank can't know about none of this. I'm sure sorry. You're nice, really."

Nora said goodnight, and before the morphine put him to sleep, he swore she bent down over the man in the barrel next to him and licked his neck.

6

"You can't let it touch the ground, you idiot!"

"I…I didn't mean to; I wasn't expecting him to fall apart like he did."

"That's supposed to happen; that means the conditioning is finished. I can get ten thousand a package for this, at least. So don't let it touch the ground!"

Roused by the talk, Robert opened his eyes to see Hank and the man in the flannel shirt, Davey, working together.

Davey clutched a man's naked torso, and from the pelvis down to the feet, the corpse had sloughed off its lower half, the legs splayed on the ground like fallen bowling pins; the skin around the appendages swollen to four times their size and kicking up the bouillon stench.

Hank slapped the torso onto a gurney, and Davey scrambled to keep picking up the legs, but the flesh kept sliding off, soft as butter, the pink meat swollen and dripping with dark brown sauce.

Hank grinned at Robert, knowing he was awake. "Don't look at me like that. Once you put this meat to flame, it's," he pressed his three fingers against his mouth and kissed them, "magnificent." He winked at him. "Once you smell what I'm smellin', you'll get the hankerin', too."

After Davey slopped the legs onto the gurney with the rest of the pieces, Robert slipped back into his drug-induced slumber.

7

"The bones get good money, too, you better believe it. I don't even have to clean them. They're a bunch of dogs, buddy-boy; our clients are a bunch of drooling, floppy-eared dogs! Hey, you ever go to a pet store and see those racks of beef-flavored tibia bones and femurs on sale? Well, turns out, our customers like them too, so until they stop paying me top dollar for them, you're shipping those bones in the dog bone packaging. I call them 'Lucky Bones.' Pretty good, huh? I came up with it myself. It's the perfect cover. I'm a genius."

8

Robert woke to the startling sight of all the barrels empty except for a woman in the corner, an overweight victim who was in a special container, a double-sized barrel. She waded in the brew, eyes closed and deep in sleep, perhaps only a few short breaths away from death.

207

And there was Hank again, still dressed up in his three-piece suit, perhaps to demonstrate his importance above his co-workers, Robert thought, or for Hank to remind himself that he wasn't just a dumb, country bumpkin.

The man dipped a ladle full of broth from Robert's barrel and sipped the end, regarding Robert as an annoying formality. "Ah, not quite ready. You're a special brew. I'm trying a new recipe on you. It's supposed to prepare faster. You came on the tail end of a cycle, my friend. Lucky we found you when we did, or else I would've had to wait to try this out. It's an old Chinese recipe. They eat all kinds of crazy shit over there like tentacles and duck nuts. To them, you're the ultimate delicacy. The fat cats on Wall Street are digging it, too."

Hank's cell phone rang and he answered, "Yeah, hit me with some good news. You what? The deal went through, that's wonderful! Three-hundred thousand dollars for a down payment, well fuck, yeah, that's good news. Now I can pack this up, cut my losses, and move out of this hick dump. I've had to recruit my brother and his idiot woman, but when you get one of your boys to finally help me, then consider them finished. I'm sick of those two fuck-ups."

9

Nora visited him again that day. She sat down beside him with a bottle of beer, and without removing his duct tape from his lips, she let loose her thoughts.

"Not much happens for me—nothing good ever, is what I mean. My dad used to run moonshine. Operated his hooch still. Then he got shot by a bunch of cops who got mad he was making money under the table and not givin' them a cut. And then I had to quit school; I only made it to the fifth grade. I can't read or write. I can clean, though. I've made so many beds, mopped and scrubbed so many floors, I'm the cleanest woman in the county.

"But every second my back hurts or my wrists ache from scrubbing, I know I'm being screwed over. Fucked over by people who think I'm a dumb country whore. Dumb as shit. Dumb as rocks. Dumb as dumb. But I'm not. My father always said if someone like me was to make money and get ahead, I'd have to bloody my hands."

She tasted the bouillon in his barrel by dipping the tip of her finger into it. Nora smacked her lips, and sighing from deep within her diaphragm, she unleashed an orgasmic moan, *"Ahhhh-ahhh, but it's worth it, Dad; every red drop."*

10

"No, you can't ship the product without the special packaging. Customs will have a field day. FBI, CIA, whatever, the idiots will bury us under the fucking system if they catch us. Yes, the packaging is ridiculous, and no, the clients won't think it's beef jerky. They'll taste the difference. My clients aren't buffoons. If you're goin' to keep supply in demand, you ship that with the beef jerky packaging on it, got it, or else I cut off your balls and make you eat them! And I can make them taste good!"

11

Hank was leaning over the double-sized barrel, and gripping the woman's arm inside it. From this point, Robert wasn't sure if it was an illusion or the drugs that manipulated the scene. He watched as Hank literally unlocked the limb from the socket, the flesh ripping and breaking with the ease of a wet tissue. He then placed the dripping arm into plastic wrap, and much like that at a deli, he wrapped it up in a paper bag and taped it closed.

He grinned mischievously at Robert. "I have special needs clients. You know the kind, right? Nora told me you sell medical supplies. People give you a bit of money, they figure you owe them the world. A bunch of needy sons-of-bitches. Mr. Gullighan in New York wants an entire arm. He wants to cook it himself. Season it to his liking. I say do it, man, but you're paying me an arm and a— *hah, hah, hah,* yes, you get the joke, don't you? And I had one fucker who just wanted a female pelvis. Just the pelvis, this pervert asks me. Pubic hair and everything. He wanted to shave it himself. It's like a fisherman who catches his own fish; he wants to clean the scales, get his hands dirty, and really feel like a man, like he actually murdered someone. It's sounds like a bunch of bush league shit to me."

He suddenly whipped around, startled when the dead woman tipped over in the barrel and gurgled.

Hank smiled, relieved it was a false alarm. He spun the axe in his hand, colorful ideas festering in his mind. "Sounds like I'll need to chop the rest of her up, huh? When they float like that, they're ready to be packaged. The conditioning is finished. The skin will slide right off the bones..."

12

Nora was studying a cluster of loose leaf papers in her hands, sitting in the corner of the room by a lamp. Her long blonde hair was stuck in her mouth, chewing it like it was her cud, as she worked out a plan while nervously stamping her feet in anticipation of something.

In her peripheral vision, she noted Robert was watching her. She acknowledged him, though she didn't stop reading the papers. "You know, these recipes aren't that hard." She pressed her finger to her lips. "*Shhhh*, Hank doesn't know I have 'em. I stole 'em, but I'll put them back later. He won't know any difference. Yeah, I can follow these, easy. All I need is the bodies."

She lowered her voice when his eyes went wide in horror.

"Oh, I'm sorry. I'm bein' rude talkin' about bodies like that." She changed the subject, embarrassed. "You know, I tell people I can't really read all the time. Know why? It makes them feel sorry for me, and it makes them think I'm dumber than I really am, and I can get away with so much more, them thinking I'm a dumb trailer trash whore. Just imagine what I can do with those two idiots out of the way..."

13

"Okay, so Mr. Chambers wants twenty-five year old Hispanic meat with a quarter white mixed in. Wow, can you get anymore specific? It'll cost him, and it'll cost me time. I'll have to find these people. It's not easy kidnapping anyone, never mind when our clients are being so damn specific. Next they'll want pure breeds and quarter this, quarter that, half that, none of that! So needy, I swear to God!"

14

Davey and Nora were huddled in the corner, each of them clutching a lighter in their shaky, craving hands. Davey was in overalls without a shirt, Nora in a short, one-piece skirt. He traced his lighter up and down a human ear— and again, Robert had to double check his ability to decode reality from drugged up nonsense—with a large piece of gristle on the end much like pink crab meat, and it cooked. The man turned it over in his hand as it sizzled, oozing brown sauce.

Davey asked her, "Why does it smell so good when it's hot?"

Nora slapped him upside the head. "Cooking it makes it good. The heat brings out the flavoring, the conditioning. Once it cooks, it's *so* good."

They split the ear between them, chewing on cartilage, gnashing their teeth to suck the sauce from the flesh, and upon relishing every morsel, they finished in a hurry. Soon after the consumption, they fled the room, cautiously stepping out into the night, watching out for Hank.

15

"Yeah, one more day and that salesman asshole will be ready to eat. I'll pack it up. Then I'll put my helpers in those barrels and pickle them, too. It'll be a bonus for me. Their bodies will all be mine. Yeah, one more day, and I'm all yours again to do whatever you want, okay? I know I'm your best supplier. You can work the panties out of your ass crack and calm down. I'm as good as done. I'll hit the road the moment barrel boy is ready."

16

Nora was ogling Robert in the barrel, and for how long, he didn't know. His life had been pared down to minutes to an hour of being conscious, thanks to the morphine, or Demerol, or whatever they laced his I.V. drip with.

She swirled the broth in his barrel with one finger and ate something within a wrapping of wax paper with the other. She pulled on it with her teeth, the meat stretchy, resembling a big piece of beef jerky the size and thickness of a beef patty.

"I'm not supposed to have it, but I can't help myself," she defended herself, absorbing his mortified stare. "There's boxes and crates of it in Hank's trailer. He's shipping it out tomorrow. Says he's got another job in Nevada, and he wants me to tag along, with his brother, of course."

She dipped the meat into his barrel, then slurped the flavor off, and then ate the rest, her zest for consumption doubled by the flavoring. "*Mmm*, oh, yeah, that's much better. This stuff's all I can eat anymore. Seriously, everything else makes me want to puke. I've lost weight because of it."

The door was thrown open hard upon her last word, and Hank barreled through, ramming her down with his shoulder. Taking a swing, he struck her nose and eye with his fist. She cried out, bleeding from her nostrils. Crawling on her hands to escape him, Hank dominated her, picking her up by the face and squeezing both her cheeks with his hands, mashing her features together into bloody folds of flesh.

"I knew it; I knew you were skimming from me! That piece of meat in your mouth is two grand. *Two grand!* Your life isn't worth that much. How much have you and Davey taken from me? *Answer me, goddamn you!*"

Two more punches, swift as hammer blows and just as hard, and she was gargling on blood. Robert couldn't help but wince with each pop of mucous and crimson mushrooming out of her nostrils to roll down her face.

"If you ate this much every day, even if you only ate this much every week, you've stolen over a hundred thousand from me. You can't fuck that debt off, you bitch, you slut, you owe me, you *owe me!* I don't care if you're my brother's bitch or that you've kept my business running. I don't need you anymore!"

Hank unsheathed a boning knife from his boot, posing it to stake into her heart. And that's when the gun shot went off, blasting into Robert's eardrums.

Hank's eyes bulged, and began coughing blood out his mouth, as more spewed out of his chest, all of it spattering onto Nora.

Davey put down the shotgun, the double barrels smoking in bright white curls, and he went to Nora's side, soothing her. "It's ours now, like we talked about. I love you, Nora."

Nora's face went crooked, anything vaguely human vacating her features in that split second moment. She drove Hank's boning knife through Davey's throat and watched him choke on his blood.

17

The hammering kept Robert awake, as did the fact he was no longer being injected with drugs. He was numb and tingling everywhere, the pain limited to a horrifying sense of having no senses at all. He couldn't move, paralyzed, so weak, so hungry, that there was no energy or will left in him but to watch the world go on around him.

It was Nora doing the hammering. Her peach dress was covered in streaks of blood, sodden in the middle, and it painted her legs in red spray. She was closing up one barrel, and in the other two barrels, still open, Hank and Davey were dead.

She spoke to Robert, not breaking pace as she finished sealing the top of the barrel. "Davey really was a good-fer-nothin'. I did all the work. I fooled him, though. He believed I was fucking Hank to distract him so we could start a new life, perhaps selling this shit on our own. Well, fuck that. I'm doing it for the food. For me. I'm no one's slave. Fuck them both, the assholes! All Davey did was drive his car into other cars and force them off the road."

That's how he came to be here, Robert recalled, the memory shoved back in his mind through a haze of mind-numbing drugs and horrifying images. He was taking a shortcut suggested by his GPS navigation system to a new business meeting involving cheap catheters and their distribution. He used a road amid dense woods, and from out of nowhere, a large truck plowed into him. His car was knocked aside like it was a toy, and after rolling three times, he blanked out to awake in the barrel.

While he realized this, she had kept talking to herself. "Okay, so Davey smashes the cars left behind and puts them in the junkyard, but other than that, he's worthless. He never spread his legs for that asshole. I did!"

That's when the talking stopped.

And the guns began firing.

18

Nora was dead on the ground, a bloody pile; Robert had no way of knowing what happened to her beyond being shot to death.

Three well-clad men, near mimics of Hank, searched the premises and halted at Hank and Davey's corpses.

"Ah, the bitch did him in. When Hank didn't answer his phone, I knew something had happened. Good thing we were only a few hours drive away. We told him not to let them eat the product. They get addicted, and that's when you end up dead. Hank said he had it under control; I guess he was wrong."

Another said, "Well, the marinade is correct, though the buckshot and gunpowder will change the flavor."

They each high-fived each other, celebrating the bonus bodies.

"I guess this means he's all ours to eat."

"But what about this other guy?" the man gestured to Robert.

After discussing it, they decided what to do with Robert. They lugged him outside, still in the barrel. The sun touched his body for the first time in days, and he absorbed the rays, though it felt like it was over a hundred degrees outside. He'd been stored in a modified trailer rig—Hank's operation. Another trailer was to the right, where men now removed crate after wooden crate of what Robert guessed was the product Hank kept talking about over the phone. One of the men busted the top off with a crowbar, and he reached in and studied the packaging, reading the label out loud, "America's Best Beef Jerky. This is it, boys."

The men looked at Robert.

"Bring him with us," one of them replied, clutching the side of his barrel and staring at Robert with hankering eyes. "He's all ready. Hank was right. His conditioning is finished."

Robert couldn't see his body beneath the bouillon, but he imagined his skin was loose, like it would slide off the bones. He felt so weak, so empty, depleted and near death that he knew he was moments away from dying. Robert wanted to close his eyes and usher on death, but he was rudely interrupted by loud claps in the air.

His barrel tipped over simultaneously as each man was struck with the gunfire, each of them going down and staying down, one receiving a skull shot, the others blasted through their middles.

And there was Nora on one knee inside the threshold of the trailer door, clutching a shotgun. She eyed Robert like he was food on a plate, and before she could move an inch to reach him, she caught a gift in the cheek from one of the men she'd shot that had a second wind before he died.

Her entire face was downgraded into liquid, leaving a shattered egg shell skull, as she tipped over headfirst onto the ground. The shotgun slipped from her grip, and going off, the bullet struck the truck with the crates.

By dumb luck, the gas tank was hit and the truck went up in an aluminum crunch eruption, the bottom half of the vehicle consumed in a ball of fire that unleashed shrapnel like Roman candle balls *whooshing* into the sky.

That's when the fire began to spread.

19

Robert was sprawled on the ground, naked, in the center of the fire ring. The heavy duty truck the crew of men had arrived in was already up in flames, the fire gaining impetus with each passing second. Brush around the perimeter was also going up, the kindling dry and ripe for the burning. Hank's trailer was next, the exterior turning black and smoking until the gas tank on the semi also ignited, a quarter section imploding and then exploding out into the trees, bringing the flames even closer to him.

He watched as Nora's body was burned to a crisp, like a log on the bottommost tier of a bonfire. The other dead bodies went up the same way. A pant leg would catch a spark, then up a shirtsleeve, orange would dance, and then minutes later, the bodies burned bright as lit charcoal briquettes.

Robert was the final body left untouched by the fire. His fingertips felt the inevitable flames, fanned closer by the wind, but he was blessed to not feel a thing, everything so numb and gone. The only sense that remained keen was his sense of smell.

As the fire consumed his arm, he somehow gained the ability to move it. He attempted to spare himself of the flames, but when he raised his arm up high enough, he lost his strength, and the appendage flopped down on top of his mouth. The skin was singed, issuing smoke rings; the seasoning, the conditioning, took to the air, entering his nostrils, the odor an aromatic delicacy.

Losing himself to a fit of hunger, he ravaged his forearm, the meat coming off tender in his gnashing teeth. Consuming his body with surmounting fervor, he kept chewing until all that was left of his forearm were red, gristly bones and threads of then muscle tissue.

Swallowing what he could before he was too woozy to stay conscious, he now agreed with what Hank had told him while he lay helpless in the barrel

"Once you smell what I'm smellin', you'll get the hankerin', too."

ABOUT THE WRITERS

David Bernstein, a.k.a. MacabreZombie, is still writing horror for various anthos and magazines. The first three chapters of his novel Amongst the Dead are available online at Tales of the Zombie War with more to come. Check out davidbernsteinauthor.blogspot.com. You can reach him at dbern77@hotmail.com.

He lives in the NYC area with his girlfriend of eight years.

Daniel Fabiani is a 22 year old kid from NYC with the accent to prove it! He loves romance languages and cooking; the written word is sewed to his soul. His most favorite achievements are his inclusion various print anthologies, as well as the completion of his first novel. Credits include Lame Goat Press, House of Horror, SNM, Pagan Imagination, Living Dead Press and others. His website is http://danfabiani.webs.com

Anthony Giangregorio is the author and editor of more than 40 novels, almost all of them about zombies. His work has appeared in Dead Science by Coscomentertainment, Dead Worlds: Undead Stories Volumes 1-6, and Wolves of War by Library of the Living Dead Press. He also has stories in End of Days: An Apocalyptic Anthology Vol. 1 - 3, the Book of the Dead series Vol. 1-4 by LDP, and two anthologies with Pill Hill Press. He is also the creator of the popular action/zombie series titled Deadwater.

Check out his website at www.undeadpress.com.

Michael D. Griffiths lives in the northern mountains of Arizona with his wife, Cathi, who is also a writer and artist. Mike focuses primarily on writing Horror and Science Fiction, but has dabbled in odd Fantasy and literary works. He has won the Withersins 666 award, and several contests at Golden Visions. In the past, Mike has published two underground zines, been on over a hundred road trips, and has had his Skinjumper Series published in M-Brane magazine. He is currently a part of Abandoned Towers and Innsmouth Free Press magazines. Mike's first book, The Chronicles of Jack Primus, was recently published by Living Dead Press.

John Grover is a dark fiction author residing in Massachusetts. He completed a creative writing course at Boston's Fisher College and is a member of the New England Horror Writers, a chapter of the Horror Writers Association. Some of his more recent credits include The Northern Haunts Anthology by Shroud Publishing, The Zombology Series by Library of the Living Dead Press, Morpheus Tales, Wrong World, The Willows, Alien Skin Magazine, and more.

He is the author of several collections, including the recently released Feminine Wiles, 16 tales of wicked women as well as various chapbooks, anthologies, and more. Please visit his website www.shadowtales.com <http://www.shadowtales.com> for more information.

Kelly M. Hudson grew up in the wilds of Kentucky and currently lives in California. He has a deep and abiding love for all things horror and rock n' roll. He's had many stories published in such esteemed collections as Dead Worlds, Book of the Dead, End of Days, The Death Panel, and The Bitter End and also has a novel (Men of Perdition) on Amazon Kindle. If you wish to contact Kelly or find links to other stories he's had published, please visit www.kellymhudson.com for further details.

Mark M. Johnson is a dedicated horror and sci/fi fanatic. His short fiction and poetry has appeared in Bits of the Dead, and Vicious Verses Zombie Poetry from Coscom Entertainment, Zombology 1 and the upcoming anthology, Letters From The Dead From Library of the Living Dead Press, and the upcoming Horrorology from Library of Horror Press, Dead Worlds, Vol 2 & 3, and Book of the Dead Vol 2, Love is Dead, Dead history, and the upcoming Zombie Anthology Book of the Dead Vol 4 from Living Dead Press. Born and raised in Detroit , he currently resides in Warren MI with his wife, Cindy.

Keith Luethke enjoys writing horror fiction and lives in Knoxville, Tennessee. His zombie novel, "Dead House: A Zombie Ghost Story" is available through Living Dead Press and he has multiple short stories published with LDP as well.

Nick Medina is a young author from Chicago, Illinois. Since 2009 he has appeared in several magazines in the U.S. and the U. K . Dressed in Black is a tribute to his family's funerary ties - although his family had never gone to such extremes as Thomas Tuttle. To read more of Nick's work, visit http://sites.google.com/site/nickjmedina/.s

Matt Nord is a janitor by trade, a business owner by association, a network technician by education, and a fledgling writer of horror fiction by choice. He's currently working on several short stories for future anthologies. He lives in Central New York with his wife, Karen, and their two sons, plus one on the way.

William Todd Rose is a speculative fiction author currently residing in Parkersburg, West Virginia whose short fiction has appeared in various small press magazines and anthologies. In 2009 his experimental horror novella Shadow of the Woodpile was released as the flagship publication for Fetid Press. Early 2010 will see the publication of the apocalyptic novel Cry Havoc as well as The Dead & Dying: An Existential Zombie Novel. For more information, please visit www.williamtoddrose.com

Rob Rosen is the author of the novels "Sparkle" and "Divas Las Vegas", has had short stories featured in more than 90 anthologies, most notably: Short Attention Span Mysteries; Modern Witches, Wizards, and Magic; Southern Comfort; Hell's Hangmen: Horror in the Old West; By the Chimney With Care; Strange Stories of Sand and Sea; Damned in Dixie: Southern Horror; Sporty Spec: Games of the Fantastic; Ruins Metropolis; Don't Turn the Lights On; Speculative Realms; Bloody October; and Living Dead Press's Christmas is Dead and Love is Dead.
Please visit him at his website, www.therobrosen.com

Spencer Wendleton has published two novels under his penname 'Alan Spencer.' One is entitled, "The Body Cartel," the other, "Inside the Perimeter: The Scavenging Dead." His work has also appeared in numerous Living Dead Press anthologies, and hopes the cannibals out there will take note of how long humans should soak in "flavor barrels" before butchering them for consumption as provided in the story "Days in the Barrel." The author welcomes e-mails at alanspencer26@hotmail.com

The Zombie in the Basement
by Anthony Giangregorio
Illustrated by Andrew Dawe-Collins

The spooky house at the end of the street was the one all the kids avoided. With its overgrown shrubs and weeds, the place was a modern day haunted house. Especially at night. So when Ricky sneaks into the yard to retrieve his favorite ball, he comes across something he'd only seen in movies and bad dreams. He sees a zombie in the basement window of the old house, but when he tells his friends, no one believes him. Ricky knows what he saw, that something lurks in the old house, something that isn't supposed to exist.

With his best friend Eric by his side,   Ricky will find out the truth and prove to everyone that zombies are real. And when the night is done, everyone will know about the zombie in the basement.

Note: This book is for young adults and for those who are young at heart.

DEADFREEZE
by Anthony Giangregorio
THIS IS WHAT HELL WOULD BE LIKE IF IT FROZE OVER!

When an experimental serum for hypothermia goes horribly wrong, a small research station in the middle of Antarctica becomes overrun with an army of the frozen dead.

Now a small group of survivors must battle the arctic weather and a horde of frozen zombies as they make their way across the frozen plains of Antarctica to a neighboring research station.

What they don't realize is that they are being hunted by an entity whose sole reason for existing is vengeance; and it will find them wherever they run.

VISIONS OF THE DEAD
A ZOMBIE STORY
by Anthony & Joseph Giangregorio

Jake Roberts felt like he was the luckiest man alive.

He had a great family, a beautiful girlfriend, who was soon to be his wife, and a job, that might not have been the best, but it paid the bills.

At least until the dead began to walk.

Now Jake is fighting to survive in a dead world while searching for his lost love, Melissa, knowing she's out there somewhere.

But the past isn't dead, and as he struggles for an uncertain future, the past threatens to consume him. With the present a constant battle between the living and the dead, Jake finds himself slipping in and out of the past, the visions of how it all happened haunting him. But Jake knows Melissa is out there somewhere and he'll find her or die trying.

In a world of the living dead, you can never escape your past.

DEAD MOURNING: A ZOMBIE HORROR STORY
by Anthony Giangregorio

Carl Jenkins was having a run of bad luck. Fresh out of jail, his probation tenuous, he'd lost every job he'd taken since being released. So now was his last chance, only one more job to prevent him from going back to prison. Assigned to work in a funeral home, he accidentally loses a shipment of embalming fluid. With nothing to lose, he substitutes it with a batch of chemicals from a nearby factory.

The results don't go as planned, though. While his screw-up goes unnoticed, his machinations revive the cadavers in the funeral home, unleashing an evil on the world that it has not seen before. Not wanting to become a snack for the rampaging dead, he flees the city, joining up with other survivors. An old, dilapidated zoo becomes their haven, while the dead wait outside the walls, hungry and patient.

But Carl is optimistic, after all, he's still alive, right? Perhaps his luck has changed and help will arrive to save them all?

Unfortunately, unknown to him and the other survivors, a serial killer has fallen into their group, trapped inside the zoo with them.

With the undead army clamoring outside the walls and a murderer within, it'll be a miracle if any of them live to see the next sunrise.

On second thought, maybe Carl would've been better off if he'd just gone back to jail.

ROAD KILL: A ZOMBIE TALE
by Anthony Giangregorio

ORDER UP!

In the summer of 2008, a rogue comet entered earth's orbit for 72 hours. During this time, a strange amber glow suffused the sky.

But something else happened; something in the comet's tail had an adverse affect on dead tissue and the result was the reanimation of every dead animal carcass on the planet.

A handful of survivors hole up in a diner in the backwoods of New Hampshire while the undead creatures of the night hunt for human prey.

There's a new blue plate special at DJ's Diner and Truck Stop, and it's you!

DEAD THINGS
by Anthony Giangregorio

Beneath the veil of reality we all know as truth, there is another world, one where creatures only seen in nightmares exist.

But what if these creatures do actually exist, and it is us that are only fleeting images, mere visions conjured up by some unknown being.

Werewolves, zombies, vampires, and other lost things that go bump in the night, inhabit the world of imagination and myth, but all will be found in this collection of tales.   But in this world, fiction becomes fact, and what lurks in the shadows is real. Beware the next time you sense you are being watched or catch movement in the corner of your eye, for though it may be nothing, it might just be your doom.

INCLUDES THE DEADWATER STORY: DEAD GRAVE

THE DARK

by Anthony Giangregorio
DARKNESS FALLS

The darkness came without warning.

First New York, then the rest of United States, and then the world became enveloped in a perpetual night without end.

With no sunlight, eventually the planet will wither and die, bringing on a new Ice Age. But that isn't problem for the human race, for humanity will be dead long before that happens.

There is something in the dark, creatures only seen in nightmares, and they are on the prowl. Evolution has changed and man is no longer the dominant species. When we are children, we're told not to fear the dark, that what we believe to exist in the shadows is false.

Unfortunately, that is no longer true.

SOULEATER

by Anthony Giangregorio

Twenty years ago, Jason Lawson witnessed the brutal death of his father by something only seen in nightmares, something so horrible he'd blocked it from his mind.

Now twenty years later the creature is back, this time for his son.

Jason won't let that happen.

He'll travel to the demon's world, struggling every second to rescue his son from its clutches.

But what he doesn't know is that the portal will only be open for a finite time and if he doesn't return with his son before it closes, then he'll be trapped in the demon's dimension forever.

SEE HOW IT ALL BEGAN IN THE NEW DOUBLE-SIZED 460 PAGE SPECIAL EDITION!

DEADWATER: EXPANDED EDITION

by Anthony Giangregorio

Through a series of tragic mishaps, a small town's water supply is contaminated with a deadly bacterium that transforms the town's population into flesh eating ghouls.

Without warning, Henry Watson finds himself thrown into a living hell where the living dead walk and want nothing more than to feed on the living.

Now Henry's trying to escape the undead town before he becomes the next victim.

With the military on one side, shooting civilians on sight, and a horde of bloodthirsty zombies on the other, Henry must try to battle his way to freedom.

With a small group of survivors, including a beautiful secretary and a wise-cracking janitor to aid him, the ragtag group will do their best to stay alive and escape the city codenamed: **Deadwater**.

DEAD END: A ZOMBIE NOVEL
by Anthony Giangregorio
THE DEAD WALK!

Newspapers everywhere proclaim the dead have returned to feast on the living!

A small group of survivors hole up in a cellar, afraid to brave the masses of animated corpses, but when food runs out, they have no choice but to venture out into a world gone mad.

What they will discover, however, is that the fall of civilization has brought out the worst in their fellow man.

Cannibals, psychotic preachers and rapists are just some of the atrocities they must face.

In a world turned upside down, it is life that has hit a Dead End.

BOOK OF THE DEAD 2: NOT DEAD YET
A ZOMBIE ANTHOLOGY
Edited by Anthony Giangregorio

Out of the ashes of death and decay, comes the second volume filled with the walking dead.

In this tomb, there are only slow, shambling monstrosities that were once human.

No one knows why the dead walk; only that they do, and that they are hungry for human flesh.

But these aren't your neighbors, your co-workers, or your family.
Now they are the living dead, and they will tear your throat out at a moment's notice.

So be warned as you delve into the pages of this book; the dead will find you, no matter where you hide.

ANOTHER EXCITING ADVENTURE IN THE DEADWATER SERIES!
DEAD SALVATION
BOOK 9
by Anthony Giangregorio
HANGMAN'S NOOSE!

After one of the group is hurt, the need for transportation is solved by a roving cannie convoy. Attacking the camp, the companions save a man who invites them back to his home.

Cement City it's called and at first the group is welcomed with thanks for saving one of their own. But when a bar fight goes wrong, the companions find themselves awaiting the hangman's noose.

Their only salvation is a suicide mission into a raider camp to save captured townspeople.

Though the odds are long, it's a chance, and Henry knows in the land of the walking dead, sometimes a chance is all you can hope for.

In the world of the dead, life is a struggle, where the only victor is death.

INSIDE THE PERIMETER: SCAVENGERS OF THE DEAD
by Alan Spencer

In the middle of nowhere, the vestiges of an abandoned town are surrounded by inescapably high concrete barriers, permitting no trespass or escape. The town is dormant of human life, but rampant with the living dead, who choose not to eat flesh, but to instead continue their survival by cruder means.

Boyd Broman, a detective arrested and falsely imprisoned, has been transferred into the secret town. He is given an ultimatum: recapture Hayden Grubaugh, the cannibal serial killer, who has been banished to the town, in exchange for his freedom.

During Boyd's search, he discovers why the psychotic cannibal must really be captured and the sinister secrets the dead town holds.

With no chance of escape, Broman finds himself trapped among the ravenous, violent dead.

With the cannibal feeding on the animated cadavers and the undead searching for Boyd, he must fulfill his end of the deal before the rotting corpses turn him into an unwilling organ donor.

But Boyd wasn't told that no one gets out alive, that the town is a death sentence.

For there is no escape from *Inside the Perimeter*.

DEADFALL
by Anthony Giangregorio

It's Halloween in the small suburban town of Wakefield, Mass.

While parents take their children trick or treating and others throw costume parties, a swarm of meteorites enter the earth's atmosphere and crash to earth.

Inside are small parasitic worms, no larger than maggots.

The worms quickly infect the corpses at a local cemetery and so begins the rise of the undead.

The walking dead soon get the upper hand, with no one believing the truth. That the dead now walk.

Will a small group of survivors live through the zombie apocalypse?

Or will they, too, succumb to the Deadfall.

LOVE IS DEAD: A ZOMBIE ANTHOLOGY
Edited by Anthony Giangregorio

THE DEATH OF LOVE

Valentine's Day is a day when young love is fulfilled.

Where hopeful young men bring candy and flowers to their sweethearts, in hopes of a kiss...or perhaps more. But not in this anthology.

For you see, LOVE IS DEAD, and in this tome, the dead walk, wanting to feed on those same hearts that once pumped in chests, bursting with love.

So toss aside that heart-shaped box of candy and throw away those red roses, you won't need them any longer. Instead, strap on a handgun, or pick up a shotgun and defend yourself from the ravenous undead.

Because in a world where the dead walk, even love isn't safe.

ETERNAL NIGHT: A VAMPIRE ANTHOLOGY
Edited by Anthony Giangregorio

Blood, fangs, darkness and terror...these are the calling cards of the vampire mythos.

Inside this tome are stories that embrace vampire history but seek to introduce a new literary spin on this longstanding fictional monster. Follow a dark journey through cigarette-smoking creatures hunted by rogue angels, vampires that feed off of thoughts instead of blood, immortals presenting the fantastic in a local rock band, to a legendary monster on the far reaches of town.

Forget what you know about vampires; this anthology will destroy historical mythos and embrace incredible new twists on this celebrated, fictional character.

Welcome to a world of the undead, welcome to the world of Eternal Night.

BOOK OF THE DEAD
A ZOMBIE ANTHOLOGY VOL 1
ISBN 978-1-935458-25-8
Edited by Anthony Giangregorio

This is the most faithful, truest zombie anthology ever written, and we invite you along for the ride. Every single story in this book is filled with slack-jawed, eyes glazed, slow moving, shambling zombies set in a world where the dead have risen and only want to eat the flesh of the living. In these pages, the rules are sacrosanct. There is no deviation from what a zombie should be or how they came about. The Dead Walk.

There is no reason, though rumors and suppositions fill the radio and television stations. But the only thing that is fact is that the walking dead are here and they will not go away. So prepare yourself for the ultimate homage to the master of zombie legend. And remember... Aim for the head!

REVOLUTION OF THE DEAD
by Anthony Giangregorio
THE DEAD SHALL RISE AGAIN!

Five years ago, a deadly plague wiped out 97% of the world's population, America suffering tragically. Bodies were everywhere, far too many to bury or burn. But then, through a miracle of medical science, a way is found to reanimate the dead.

With the manpower of the United States depleted, and the remaining survivors not wanting to give up their internet and fast food restaurants, the undead are conscripted as slave labor.

Now they cut the grass, pick up the trash, and walk the dogs of the surviving humans.

But whether alive or dead, no race wants to be controlled, and sooner or later the dead will fight back, wanting the freedom they enjoyed in life.

The revolution has begun!

And when it's over, the dead will rule the land, and the remaining humans will become the slaves...or worse.

KINGDOM OF THE DEAD
by Anthony Giangregorio
THE DEAD HAVE RISEN!

In the dead city of Pittsburgh, two small enclaves struggle to survive, eking out an existence of hand to mouth.

But instead of working together, both groups battle for the last remaining fuel and supplies of a city filled with the living dead.

Six months after the initial outbreak, a lone helicopter arrives bearing two more survivors and a newborn baby. One enclave welcomes them, while the other schemes to steal their helicopter and escape the decaying city.

With no police, fire, or social services existing, the two will battle for dominance in the steel city of the walking dead. But when the dust settles, the question is: will the remaining humans be the winners, or the losers?

When the dead walk, the line between Heaven and Hell is so twisted and bent there is no line at all.

RISE OF THE DEAD
by Anthony Giangregorio
DEATH IS ONLY THE BEGINNING!

In less than forty-eight hours, more than half the globe was infected.
In another forty-eight, the rest would be enveloped.
The reason?
A science experiment gone horribly wrong which enabled the dead to walk, their flesh rotting on their bones even as they seek human prey.

Jeremy was an ordinary nineteen year old slacker. He partied too much and had done poorly in high school. After a night of drinking and drugs, he awoke to find the world a very different place from the one he'd left the night before.

The dead were walking and feeding on the living, and as Jeremy stepped out into a world gone mad, the dead spotting him alone and unarmed in the middle of the street, he had to wonder if he would live long enough to see his twentieth birthday.

THE CHRONICLES OF JACK PRIMUS
BOOK ONE
by Michael D. Griffiths

Beneath the world of normalcy we all live in lies another world, one where supernatural beings exist.

These creatures of the night hunt us; want to feed on our very souls, though only a few know of their existence.

One such man is Jack Primus, who accidentally pierces the veil between this world and the next. With no other choice if he wants to live, he finds himself on the run, hunted by beings called the Xemmoni, an ancient race that sees humans as nothing but cattle.   They want his soul, to feed on his very essence, and they will kill all who stand in their way.   But if they thought Jack would just lie down and accept his fate, they were sorely mistaken.

He didn't ask for this battle, but he knew he would fight them with everything at his disposal, for to lose is a fate worse than death.

He would win this war, and he would take down anyone who got in his way.

THE WAR AGAINST THEM: A ZOMBIE NOVEL
by Jose Alfredo Vazquez

Mankind wasn't prepared for the onslaught.

An ancient organism is reanimating the dead bodies of its victims, creating worldwide chaos and panic as the disease spreads to every corner of the globe. As governments struggle to contain the disease, courageous individuals across the planet learn what it truly means to make choices as they struggle to survive.

Geopolitics meet technology in a race to save mankind from the worst threat it has ever faced. Doctors, military and soldiers from all walks of life battle to find a cure. For the dead walk, and if not stopped, they will wipe out all life on Earth. Humanity is fighting a war they cannot win, for who can overcome Death itself? Man versus the walking dead with the winner ruling the planet. Welcome to *The War Against Them*.

DEADTOWN: A DEADWATER STORY
BOOK 8
by Anthony Giangregorio

The world is a very different place now. The dead walk the land and humans hide in small towns with walls of stone and debris for protection, constantly keeping the living dead at bay.

Social law is gone and right and wrong is defined by the size of your gun.

UNWELCOME VISITORS

Henry Watson and his band of warrior survivalists become guests in a fortified town in Michigan. But when the kidnapping of one of the companions goes bad and men die, the group finds themselves on the wrong side of the law, and a town out for blood.

Trapped in a hotel, surrounded on all sides, it will be up to Henry to save the day with a gamble that may not only take his life, but that of his friends as well.

In a dead world, when justice is not enough, there is always vengeance.

END OF DAYS: AN APOCALYPTIC ANTHOLOGY
VOLUMES 1 & 2

Our world is a fragile place.

Meteors, famine, floods, nuclear war, solar flares, and hundreds of other calamities can plunge our small blue planet into turmoil in an instant.

What would you do if tomorrow the sun went super nova or the world was swallowed by water, submerging the world into the cold darkness of the ocean? This anthology explores some of those scenarios and plunges you into total annihilation.

But remember, it's only a book, and tomorrow will come as it always does.

Or will it?

Eternal Night

A Vampire Anthology

Edited By
Anthony Giangregorio